I0838486

OLD CASTLE SPARKLE

AMANDA DAIRE

Pink Elephant Press

COPYRIGHT

Copyright © 2022 by Amanda Daire

For exclusive content and to stay up-to-date, sign up for Amanda's newsletter on her website: amandadaire.com

All rights reserved.

No part of this book may be reproduced in any form or by any electronic or mechanical means, including information storage and retrieval systems, without written permission from the author, except for the use of brief quotations in a book review.

❀ Created with Vellum

This book is dedicated to the readers who found me through the launch of Old Castle Secrets, and also to the loyal readers who have followed me from one pen name to the next. I appreciate you more than you could know. Thank you for taking a chance on reading my work and for all the wonderful feedback you've shared. <3 I hope you enjoy this next part of the journey. xoxo

ALSO BY AMANDA DAIRE

Old Castle Secrets

Old Castle Sparkle

Old Castle Road Trip

Old Castle Rumors

Old Castle Courage

1

____

KHRISTA

Khrista leaned back against the plush couch cushions and tried to let herself relax while Matt's large hands worked their magic on her achy feet. She had never imagined she'd be lucky enough to find a man who took such good care of her. Yet, there she was, sinking into a sofa she couldn't have afforded on her own in the home of a man who swore she made his world brighter.

"What's going on in your head?" Sitting on the other end of the couch, Matt lifted her foot and rested it on his chest as his strong hands squeezed their way to her ankle. "You seem tense. What's troubling you?"

Excellent question. She'd love to know the answer, too.

Khrista sighed. "How did you get so perceptive?"

Matt smiled and planted a kiss on the top of her foot.

"Raising three girls made empathy a requirement. There were a *whole lot* of emotions happening in my house when the kids were growing up." Matt shuddered. "I think I have PTSD from the teen years. I was not ready."

"They were lucky to have you for a dad. My father didn't care how I felt about anything."

Matt gave Khrista's foot a final squeeze and shifted his position so he was sitting next to her. He scooped her into his arms—solid, safe arms—and nuzzled into her neck.

"I'm here to make up for all of that."

And he had done that job well. It had been a little over two months since their spontaneous beach wedding, but her life had fulfilled her enough to never have to dream for more.

"Back to how you're feeling," Matt continued. "What's going on? No secrets, remember?"

"Never again." Khrista crossed her heart and glanced at the modernly furnished room with the tasteful art on the walls. Matt waited, as patient as ever, for her response. She thoughtlessly stroked his wrist as his arms tightened around her, searing her with the security of his touch. When would this level of security feel normal? When would she believe this lovely place was her forever home? "It's so stupid—"

"Nothing about you is stupid."

"No, it really is this time." Khrista gave a low chuckle and ran a finger over Matt's rough brown knuckles. "I just can't help but feel like... I don't know." She buried her face in his shoulder, inhaling the fresh scent of his deodorant and skin.

He hugged her for a moment and then shifted, forcing her chin upward so she'd have to face him.

"I won't have you feeling embarrassed about anything."

"Believe me, Matt, you'll think it's ridiculous if I say it out loud."

"Never."

She released a sigh and prepared herself for his laughter.

"Ok, just remember you asked for it." Khrista fiddled with the button on the front of his shirt, unable to meet his gaze.

"I just can't help but feel that things are going... Too well. That I'm too happy." She peered up at him with a tiny smirk. All Khrista saw when she looked at Matt was a fairytale of fulfilled dreams and comfort, and yet she knew he wouldn't be able to hide his thoughts about how ludicrous her statement was. Khrista counted in her head as she waited for the shock flickering across his face to erupt from his lips.

"That's ridiculous."

Four seconds. Nearly five.

"Told you!"

Matt broke into a broad grin, then pulled her close again.

Khrista snuggled into his embrace, warmth spreading over every limb.

Turning serious, she let her thoughts emerge with the certainty that he'd hold her fears as protectively as a penguin protected his egg.

"I keep waiting for the familiar pattern of disaster to come. It's hovering there on the horizon. A disaster that's waiting to wash away all my happiness and joy. It's so weird, I know. But I don't know how to get rid of this feeling. It's making me feel restless."

"I think that's a product of trauma, babe."

Khrista shivered involuntarily at the memories that washed over her. The years of abuse at her father's hands. The neglect from her mother. The turmoil and estrangements that resulted.

"You're probably right." Now that she didn't have the alcohol to numb the memories, she had to confront each one as it popped up to interfere with the life she'd created.

Matt tilted her chin upward again, forcing her to observe the love swirling in his dark brown eyes. "But listen to me, my darling. You've earned your happily-ever-after. Not just with me. With your daughter. Your mother. This entire island community. And who could forget that chubby-cheeked granddaughter of ours?"

Khrista laughed out loud. "Her cheeks are the best, aren't they?"

He kissed her, capturing her smiling lips between his own. Khrista would never tire of this. Though it had taken fifty years to get her life together, she vowed to appreciate every moment.

Against Matt's lips, Khrista mumbled, "We have to get going if we don't want the family to send out a search party. Besides, I want to make sure I get my seat so Mr. Ed's future sibling doesn't worry that my lap will be unavailable. She's just like him—she gets upset when I change the routine."

As if on cue, Mr. Ed, the cat Matt had adopted from the Kit-TEA Comfort Rescue as a wedding gift to Khrista, leaped onto the couch, waved his ginger tail in Matt's face, and rubbed his nose against Khrista's hand.

In her kitty-friendly tone, she murmured to her darling boy. "Did Mr. Ed hear Mama talking about a new sibling? You like that idea, huh?"

Matt shook his head as he got up from the couch and slipped on his shoes.

"You and that cat..."

"Don't be jealous. There's room in my heart for both of you. The two men of my life."

"Tell me again why I shouldn't be jealous of a cat. A sweet ginger one, at that. Though he's not nearly as sweet as you led me to believe."

Khrista gasped. "Take that back. Mr. Ed may come across as grumpy, but he's all heart. Aren't you, cutie pie?"

Mr. Ed hissed and stalked away when Khrista accidentally brushed a hand over the spot at the base of his tail that he didn't like touched.

"Mostly heart, with plenty of sass." Khrista shrugged and turned to tidy up the couch, fluffing up the pillows and resetting the chenille throw blanket. "Are you ready, or do you have anything you need to do before we head out?"

"I'm good to go as soon as you are. But Khrista, come here for a second."

Though not usually one to obey, she would never deny him any request.

Matt drew her into his embrace again and nuzzled his face into her neck. He held her like that for a moment or two, a fluttering of heartbeats in a melodic love song.

"You know what I'm about to say, right?"

Khrista shook her head.

"Khrista, my darling, my love. You will never go through the world or face your troubles alone again. I made you a vow and I'll keep it no matter what. So I don't want you focusing on those negative feelings. I understand you'll have them from time to time, but I want you to promise me you'll fight them. That you'll hear my voice telling you everything will be okay."

Choking up, Khrista couldn't respond. So instead she hugged him tight and thanked her lucky stars for bringing him into her life and for giving her the strength to tear down the walls that had kept his love from fully penetrating her heart.

"We'd better get going," she finally said. "Your girls will think I've infected you with my laid-back personality if their Type A dad isn't at least fifteen minutes early."

THE MANIFESTATION of all Khrista's hopes and dreams, and the culmination of her hard work to overcome her emotional hurdles, clustered around a group of tables pushed together in the Happil-TEA Ever After Tea Room. Sunday morning brunches had cemented themselves as tradition, and Clarice, sixty-something owner of the tearoom and motherly friend to all in town, had been generous in reserving the library room for the gathering each week.

"I saved you both seats over here," Khrista's mother, Daisy, declared, gesturing wildly for Khrista to come and sit.

Still holding hands, the newlyweds accepted the invitation, stopping to kiss each of their girls on the way over. They removed their coats and scarves and hung them on a coat rack nearby.

Matt's adult daughters had welcomed Khrista into their family and expressed gratitude over finally getting to meet her after three years of hearing their father gush about how wonderful she was. Nia, Aliyah, and Gabby, ages thirty-two, thirty and twenty-six, quickly nestled their way into Khrista's affections. Though they were all full-grown women, whenever their father spoke of them—which was often—his eyes lit up as any outstanding father's should. Those girls had him wrapped around their proverbial fingers, and it made

Khrista proud to have won the love of a man so devoted to his daughters.

Matt had welcomed Kaelyn, Khrista's only child, as freely as Khrista had his daughters. And now that Kaelyn had made Khrista and Matt grandparents, the amount of love in Khrista's life threatened to suffocate her. But she'd go down smiling.

Khrista bent to kiss Kaelyn on the cheek, telling her to stay seated as she nursed her newborn. She then scratched the ears of the white cat snuggled on Gabby's lap, one of the many kitties who made themselves comfortable in the tearoom while awaiting their *furever* homes.

"Sorry we were running a little late. I accept full responsibility," Khrista said.

"Don't worry, we all know Matt would never be late without your influence." Kaelyn winked to soften the blow, and they all burst into laughter at the idea of Matt willingly being tardy.

"Come and sit. Try this special blend Clarice created." Rafael, Khrista's surrogate father figure and landlord before her marriage, and now friend to Khrista's mother, Daisy, reached forward to grab the teakettle. He poured a cup for Khrista and then for Matt.

Khrista brought the steaming cup to her nose to inhale the sweet scent. "Mint? And chocolate?"

Daisy sipped hers with an exaggerated look of ecstasy on her lined face. "It's a mint chocolate chai. You won't believe how delicious it is."

"Oh, I'll believe it. Remember, Clarice's tea has spoiled me for over twenty years. Nothing compares."

Aliyah leaned forward as she joined the conversation. "I wish my new hometown wasn't so far away. I miss having Ms. Clarice's tea every day. Maybe we can talk her into moving the shop over to my area. I think she'd love starting over in Massachusetts."

In unison, her stunned tablemates turned toward her with mouths agape and shouted, "No!"

Clarice entered and raised her eyebrows at the sudden objections. Carrying a tray of pastries, she looked from face-to-face as if trying to piece together the source of the argument. Three cats gathered at her feet, meowing as if awaiting their serving of yummies.

"What on earth is going on in here?" she demanded. She retrieved several treats from her apron pocket and scattered them for the demanding felines.

Khrista struggled to suppress her urge to giggle. "Aliyah just had the crazy notion of trying to steal you from us. She wants you to open a tearoom in her town, but I think a better option would be for her to move back here to Old Castle."

"I concur," Matt interjected.

"Believe me," Aliyah replied, "if I could've stayed on the island, I would've. The housing market here is terrible."

"I've always said you were welcome to live at home for as long as you wanted to." Matt placed an arm around his daughter's shoulders.

"Daddy, I'm thirty years old. It was time for me to go out on my own. How am I ever going to find a man if I'm living with the most perfect one already?"

"Good one!" Khrista said. "But you know he had a plan to make a row of tiny cottages on his property for all of his girls to live with him forevermore."

"I don't see any problem with that plan." Matt shrugged and reached for his tea.

"There should be a rule that our favorite people aren't allowed to leave the island." Clarice lowered the tray of pastries in the center of the table for everyone to serve themselves. Though her words were lighthearted, her posture was stiff. Clarice normally embodied open-armed hospitality, but a seriousness Khrista rarely witnessed cast a fog over Clarice's typical effervescent joy. "I'll leave this right here. You all let me know if you need anything else. How's the chai?"

Nia raised her mug and grinned, her cherubic expression sparking a reluctant smile in Khrista. Khrista shoved aside the gloomy feelings that kept creeping in from the dark shadows of her mind. Given her earlier ominous feelings, she was likely casting her fears onto, of all people, Clarice.

Her stepdaughter closed her eyes and wiggled her shoulders ever-so-slightly. "Exquisite. Perhaps your best ever."

Murmurs of agreement followed Nia's declaration, and Clarice bowed her head and accepted the praise. She then left the room, and the group members conversed with those sitting near them.

"Is it me or does Clarice not seem herself today?" Khrista asked Daisy and Matt. "She's her usual friendly self, but she seems, I don't know, maybe more tired than usual? Maybe a little blue?"

Matt reached for the creamer. "Seemed fine to me."

Soon Matt and Raf were talking about the Jeep that Raf was rebuilding in his downtime. Khrista tried to stay engaged in the topic, but boredom nearly had her crawling out of her skin. She loved the family gatherings—of course she did—but her mind couldn't handle the minutiae of the rebuilding cars process. Daisy tapped Khrista on the arm and leaned closer, turning her body slightly as if about to confide a deep secret.

Would her mother finally confess that something was going on—something more than friendship—between her and Rafael? They were always together, making eyes at one another. Daisy had taken to giggling and clapping every time Raf said something even remotely humorous, and though Khrista had never seen Raf blush in all the years she had known him, his red cheeks had become a common occurrence whenever he was around Khrista's mom.

It thrilled Khrista that, after decades of abuse in a horrible marriage, Daisy would have a second chance at finding love. And though Raf was a widower who had adored his wife, he deserved another chance, too.

"I've been wanting to talk to you about Clarice."

Uh oh. Khrista didn't like the conspiratorial tone.

Alarm gathered in a spiky ball in Khrista's gut. Definitely not the secretive topic she had expected.

Her mother had been working in the tearoom to thank Clarice for letting her stay in a room upstairs, since finding an apartment on the island had become so challenging. Raf offered to set her up in the apartment Khrista had vacated, but Daisy had her pride and didn't want to rely on a man again. Because of her arrangement, Daisy had better access to anything happening in Clarice's life than Khrista did, though Clarice had been a close friend for years. Family, really. She'd been a maternal figure during all the years of Khrista's estrangement from her mother.

"I overheard something…"

Khrista held up a hand and suppressed a groan. "Wait, Mom. We don't do rumors here. Anything you heard about Clarice is her story to share. She'll tell me when she's ready."

Khrista reached for a muffin and picked up her butter knife to slice it in half so she could apply Clarice's legendary brown sugar butter.

"It's nothing like that. I'm not being a busybody."

Daisy's hushed tone told a different story. Khrista resisted the urge to roll her eyes, but it was a struggle.

"I wandered into a part of the house I shouldn't have–I was looking for where she keeps the towels. The third floor had a door that was ajar, so I opened it and noticed buckets catching water. She has a leaky roof, and it looks like it's been that way for a while."

Khrista frowned. "Did you ask her about it?"

"I did. I asked her right away, and she got embarrassed and seemed troubled that I knew. Every time I bring it up, she changes the subject. I overheard her talking on the phone to one of the rescues she works with and telling them she may have to turn away some new litters of kittens they planned to send her. I'm sure it's because she's saving to fix the roof. I know she's trying to handle things on her own, but there must be something we can do."

Khrista munched on her muffin, no longer tasting the sweetness.

Daisy sighed and twisted a napkin in her hand. "I've been racking my brain trying to think of something we could do. Do you think she'd be offended if I offered her money? She does so much for all of us, and—"

"No, don't offer her money. I guarantee she wouldn't like that."

Clarice had been there for Khrista in every way possible, and if there was trouble now, Khrista needed to help her. She'd have to tread lightly, though, as Clarice prided herself on her self-sufficiency.

The rising tone of the conversations at the table drowned out Khrista and Daisy's attempts at quiet contemplation. Oliver, Khrista's son-in-law, had the table in an uproar of hilarity with what he called "anti-jokes." Khrista didn't quite get what they were about, but the laughter at the table helped set her at ease and reminded her that this was a strong community, and Clarice was the matriarch of it all.

When Matt turned his attention back to Khrista, she told him what Daisy had confided.

Concerned, Matt folded his napkin and tucked it under his plate as he pushed his chair back and stood. "I'll take a look. I can probably patch it up temporarily, at least."

Khrista tugged on his sleeve. "No, sit back down. We can't let her know we know. That would shatter her pride. We need to think this through."

As Khrista's gaze drifted across the faces of the people she loved most in the world, an idea struck her.

Khrista could take a page from her best friend Elanna's book and throw together a fundraiser. A tea cocktail extravaganza right there in the tearoom. The beach would have been an ideal setting, but Khrista didn't dare push it off until spring or summer, and though the season had been mild so far, it was hard to trust a New England winter.

Khrista could already envision using Clarice's tea blends to make cocktails of all types—hot lemon tea with whisky, cold brewed strawberry basil tea with gin, chocolate chai with Irish cream... the ideas were endless. And it was unique enough to draw in the crowds. She was sure of it.

Unable to keep her excitement at bay, Khrista turned to Daisy. Her flash of brilliance tumbled off her tongue almost as fast as the thoughts formed.

Daisy stared blankly at Khrista for the briefest of moments before breaking eye contact.

"Oh, um, well..." Daisy hesitated, her eyes darting back and forth to nothing in particular. Her gaze ultimately settled on Matt, and she cringed a bit before biting her lip.

"That wasn't the reaction I was going for." Khrista wrinkled her brow and studied her mother. "We can pull it together quickly, if timing is what you're worried about."

Matt put a hand on Khrista's upper back between her shoulder blades and stroked. Slow, methodical petting, as if attempting to soothe her.

She hadn't been riled up until their odd reactions. Khrista had expected them to add their excitement to hers. She hadn't expected this... this...

Trepidation.

Khrista stiffened and wanted to run out of the room. But she held her ground.

"You're both being weird. You hate the idea?"

"It's a lovely idea, Khrista. It's just..."

"Just what?" Khrista glanced from her mother to Matt and back again, not liking the looks they exchanged. "Is it because of the alcohol?"

Her voice rose at the realization, and then a laugh rumbled out of her throat.

"You two are adorable." Khrista finally gave in to the eye rolling she'd been fending off. "I'm not going to *drink* it, if that's what you're worried about. I'll just be organizing the event. Coming up with recipes. That sort of thing. You know, raising money for the issue you brought up..."

Matt rubbed his eyebrow as he stared at her, and she assumed the gentle way he cupped her shoulder was meant to reassure her.

"Honey, it will be fine. I won't drink any of the alcohol, but I'm best qualified to determine what alcohol would go with what tea, am I not? I'll put together a committee for taste testing, and I'll take the notes. You know the people on the island love a good cocktail, and Clarice has talked for *years* about creating cocktail blends with her tea. We can make a big event of it. A band on the beach, a great seafood buffet, and we can charge admission. All proceeds will go to

Clarice's cat rescue—she can spend it in whatever way she deems most appropriate. It's a cause the entire island will gather around to support. I'm sure people will even come from off-island to support it if we market it correctly." Khrista lowered her voice. "And we won't mention the roof thing, but with an infusion of cash, she can shift things in her budget to take care of it."

Kaelyn tuned into the conversation and bounced in her chair at the mention of a fundraiser, bobbing Poppy's little head up and down. "I can help with the marketing. I can do the graphic design work and advertising."

"Perfect way to utilize your career skills." Khrista clapped her hands together. "See? It's already coming along perfectly."

The idea developed as word buzzed around the table. Soon enough, everyone took part in the brainstorming session.

Gabby smiled big and leaned forward to offer her input. "I'll volunteer my time to sing. Dad, you can play guitar. Some of my band members may volunteer, too, but even if it's just the two of us, I think we could pull off something pretty special."

"Wonderful, Gabby. Thank you!" Joy fueled Khrista's grateful body. How lucky was she to be surrounded by so many kind, generous souls? Though almost no one knew why Khrista suddenly started planning a fundraiser, they all dove in without question and with zero hesitation.

Her family was right to worry about Khrista as she continued to recover from her deep dive into the bottle, but she would prove there was no temptation strong enough to make her mess this up.

The ominous feelings from earlier cleared in time to allow her to see the picture of her life more clearly.

Khrista had nothing to worry about. She had earned this happiness.

Though her insecurities had tried to turn her worldview bleak, her life path had, indeed, become alight with sunshine and rainbows. And though she loved a magnificent storm, Khrista had no desire to cause one.

~

KHRISTA STOOD outside her old haunt in nearby Portsmouth, gathering her wits and settling her nerves.

She hadn't returned to the liquor store since battling that demon and winning, but she was stronger now. Married to the love of her soul, reunited with her estranged daughter, and blessed with a grandbaby, she'd gotten the redo she had so desperately craved. Khrista was also working every day to make up for lost time with her previously estranged mother. They had found common ground and a deeper understanding of what the other went through and what had influenced the decisions and actions along the way.

Though nothing would change the traumatic aspects of Khrista's crazy and dysfunctional childhood and, frankly, adulthood—repairing those damaged corners of her book helped Khrista to power on, even if she couldn't rewrite the chapters.

Alcohol had been a soldier she enlisted in her battle for survival. It had threatened to take her down when things got too real and she became too dependent on the numbing aspect of the liquor, but she wasn't dependent now.

Once an alcoholic, always an alcoholic.

She had heard the refrain over and over, and she knew it to be true. For the first time in many months, Khrista could feel herself slipping into the old character she had played as her imagination reminded her of the sensations alcohol evoked.

The sharp taste on her tongue. Harsh burning as it slid down her throat. The comforting pain as it twisted around her belly like a snake protecting her burrow. Warmth as the alcohol did its job and numbed the pain. Bubbly dizziness engulfing her brain, sheltering her from realities too painful to acknowledge.

The laughter that would cover the tears.

But now, standing on the sidewalk outside the liquor store, Khrista forced herself to remember the aftereffects. Turbulence. Shame. The threat of losing everything good—her job, her relationship with Matt, her standing in the community.

Her family.

There was nothing in the universe that would make her go back. She was stronger than the alcohol. She was the captain of the army. Khrista would make the call.

Her friends and sponsor had armed her with important skills, which Khrista employed before entering the liquor store.

She imagined herself with a barrier between her body and the bottles. She envisioned herself as a person who simply didn't drink alcohol. Who could be around it when others used it in a socially responsible way, all the while sipping on nonalcoholic beverages and enjoying a clear-eyed vision of the world.

Khrista wrapped a white light of protection around her family and held that bubble next to her chest. In her heart.

Now that Khrista wasn't hiding her habit from her community, she could have shopped at the liquor store on the island. But returning here marked an important step in her journey. An opportunity to prove to herself that she could confront the demon head-on. That she could walk into the place that had so often called to her and leave with no marks against her.

Stronger and empowered, Khrista raised her chin, straightened her shoulders, and swung open the door to the liquor store. The bells jingled, welcoming her into the familiar fold.

The same 90s grunge soundtrack played over the speakers, but nostalgia didn't fool her this time.

Khrista concentrated on the clattering of her shoes against the old wooden floor and tried to keep her stomach from emptying its contents. The putrid smell of alcohol reminded her of the aftereffects of taking things too far.

"Khrista!" The young woman working the counter had been the person Khrista probably spent the most time with without really knowing her. She had been the gatekeeper, the one Khrista had to face every time she stocked up. The one whose eyes Khrista could never meet.

Today, Khrista met her eyes.

"Lynn, so good to see you. I'm not here for myself—I'm still on the wagon where I intend to remain."

Lynn threw her hands up in a teasing surrender.

"This is a no-judgment zone. I'm just here to take the money of anyone who wants to hand it across the counter."

Khrista smiled, yet she ached for the people who hadn't been able to conquer their pain yet.

Empathy could be a burden, so she pushed it aside and instead thought of all the people who purchased alcohol to celebrate big wins in their lives. People who used it to complement already fun times and who never had to face the shame of relying on it too much.

Khrista removed the folded reusable grocery bag from her purse and shook it open.

"Time to fill this baby up. I'm playing around with some combinations of tea and liquor for a cocktail fundraiser we're holding to support Clarice's rescue. I won't be sampling the creations, but I'll play bartender. Just need a few nips of each of these old favorites, and then I'll be back when I've committed to whichever ones I'm going to use so I can get the bigger bottles."

"Aww, is this for the Kit-TEA Comfort Rescue where I got my kitten?"

"Sure is."

"Well, let me know when the fundraiser will be, so I can get a ticket. That kitten has made me and my daughter so happy."

Lynn helped her select the nips she wanted and rang them up before handing them to Khrista to put in her bright pink tote bag. Lynn chatted about her third-grader who was begging to be home-schooled because of some kids who weren't being nice to her. "You're a teacher, right?"

Khrista couldn't recall sharing so much personal information with Lynn. Had she been in that much of a fog all those years?

She cleared her throat and nodded, and then shifted into teacher mode. "I teach preschool, but third grade is tough. I've never taught it, but I remember my daughter going through some of that stuff. You tell your daughter that whatever they're picking on her about is probably what makes her the most special. For my daughter, it was her beautiful red hair and freckles. Tell your little love their mean words don't matter, and the best way to get them to back off is to speak up and defend herself confidently, and to find someone else to play with. Mean kids don't learn to not be mean if they're able to derive power from the people they pick on."

Khrista chose a few more nips from the fishbowl container on the counter and handed them to Lynn, who held them while she continued to listen attentively. Khrista was never sure how much advice to dish out, but with Lynn hanging on every word, she figured the young mom needed more.

"The kids who are picking on her are hurting too, but they're too young and self-centered to understand the damage they could do to someone," Khrista continued. "If using her words doesn't help, tell her to always speak up and get an adult to help her. This will pass, and she'll find good friends who will help her feel better about being where she needs to be and who will stick up for her even when she's not there to do it herself."

Khrista handed her credit card across the counter as a grateful Lynn smiled. Khrista marveled at the kindness in Lynn's features and the sincerity as she expressed her gratitude for the advice and the pep talk.

"It's so hard when your kid is going through something."

Khrista nodded, slipping into the past to all the times when Kaelyn would come home crying about something cruel another child had said. Had Khrista ever handled it well? She thought she had. But when had things started shifting? When had she started pulling away? Hiding from her own daughter and her life? When had she started leaving her daughter to fend for herself?

Khrista inhaled deeply and tuned back in to the present moment and the mom who needed a listening ear. She knew to only dip a little toe into those tarnished memories and to yank herself out to look at the future instead. But she wanted Lynn to realize she wasn't alone and she would get through this.

"There's nothing as painful as watching our children suffer.

Knowing there's not much we can do about it and wanting to make things all better for them. You stay strong, Mama, and she will too."

Khrista took her bag of bottles and left the store, attempting to shake the feeling of hypocrisy from shoulders that struggled to remain proud. If only she had known so much when Kaelyn was small...

Why had she waited to educate herself?

In a therapy session they had gone to together since their reunification, Kaelyn had confided that she had felt betrayed and saddened when Khrista went to school to study early childhood development when Kaelyn had already suffered through a childhood of having a mother who hadn't understood.

Khrista rubbed her chest as she plopped into the driver's seat. Hearing that from Kaelyn had hurt. Bad. She had offered an apology and a smile to her daughter, and thanked her for giving a glimpse of that pain. But moments like this, when the weakness tried to sully all that was good and clean, fighting off the toxic memories proved more challenging than anything else.

One breath in. Hold. Release. *Slowly.*

Using her pain to help others eased something inside her. Khrista needed to grasp on to that feeling.

As soon as Khrista drove over the bridge into the small island town of Old Castle, she remembered the single main street leading from the bridge to her home would be blocked off for the annual post-holiday snowman festival setup. Community members would have free rein to cross back and forth with no danger to the many children who took part in the event. Khrista detoured into the lot near the community beach park. She could walk home and pick up the car later, once things in town settled.

Since the winter weather was strangely pleasant, despite the downpours predicted, Khrista took the long beach route home. Going the street way would be quicker and easier, but the beach route with its rocky areas to climb provided mental health care she couldn't deny needing. Besides, she could avoid the chaos of the snowless snowman festival this way. She looked forward to seeing the scarecrow-style snowmen once everything was set up, but for now, the beach beckoned to her.

The clink of the bottles as they bumped against each other in the bag mesmerized Khrista as they blended into harmony with the gentle lapping of the waves on the shore. The cove on this part of the island rarely summoned big, rolling waves, but the gentle caresses of the water against the sand soothed her as little else could.

And though the nostalgia of the bottles' song brought Khrista back to her time of weakness, her hands no longer itched to uncap and consume one.

She'd call that a win. She'd let her sponsor know she had tested her strength for the first time.

Khrista was passing the test. She had to congratulate herself on every victory.

A seagull called out and Khrista watched the bird play atop the small waves, diving for something to eat. A small cry that sounded human redirected Khrista's attention to the land, and the cry grew more urgent as Khrista walked further.

Khrista ventured toward a pile of rocks and noticed her daughter's bright red hair shining in the setting sunlight.

"Kaelyn, what a lovely surprise."

Kaelyn brought the baby to her breast and Khrista smiled as the wailing ceased, followed only by a couple of little grumbles as the baby expressed her displeasure at the endless wait she had endured while her mother had prepared herself for the feeding.

"I'm especially surprised to see you over here. Why not on that lovely beach in your backyard?"

"Poppy's been struggling with sleeping, so I thought maybe the salt air would help. You always said the fresh air could wear out a child." Kaelyn dodged the question of her location.

"It's true. You always slept the best after time on the beach."

Khrista lowered her tote bag onto a flat boulder, about to sit beside Kaelyn, and then paused. She and her daughter were just getting to know each other again and Khrista shouldn't make assumptions. "Okay if I join you? Or do you prefer to be alone?"

Kaelyn shrugged and gestured for Khrista to sit. "I've been doing a lot of the alone thing lately. I'm good with some company."

"Oliver working a lot?"

"Yeah, he had to fly back out to LA this morning."

"Oh no. Why didn't you tell me? What can I do to help?" Khrista thought back to their brunch days ago, trying to remember if Oliver had mentioned anything about his job on the West Coast. Last Khrista had heard, he was caught up in contract negotiations and trying to work out a deal with his company where he could work remotely full-time.

"It's okay. It's only supposed to be for a couple of days. I guess it's good for me to not rely on him so much. Besides, his mother is here to dote on me and the baby."

"Let me guess." Khrista smirked, imagining Ruby bustling about, trying to be helpful while Kaelyn lived for her independence. "That's part of what brings you out here?"

Khrista had met Ruby, but so far Oliver's mother had kept her distance. She'd been friendly enough, but had declined joining their weekly brunches. Kaelyn had told Khrista that Ruby wanted to give them the time and space they needed to reunite without her interference.

Kaelyn tipped her head and grinned. "I love her so much, but yeah. It can be a bit much having to entertain her and feeling like I'm not doing things right."

Kaelyn pulled the cuff of the baby's snuggly fleece bunting over her tiny fist.

"Oh, honey. You couldn't do things wrong if you tried. Is she making you feel that way?"

"It's not her. I guess it's just new mother syndrome."

Khrista reached out and gently squeezed the baby's tiny foot. "You're so self-aware. I envy that in you."

"I don't know about that," Kaelyn said. "But thank you?"

"Is everything else okay? You seem a little blue. You were in such good spirits when I last saw you..."

"I'm okay. Great, really. Of course."

Why did it sound like Kaelyn was trying to convince them both?

Khrista sat with her daughter in silence as the sun continued its descent. She'd sit as long as Kaelyn would have her, but was she mothering too much?

After five years of not communicating with Kaelyn, Khrista remained unsure of where the boundaries belonged. She only knew she never wanted to mess up again.

And though Matt had worked hard to assure her that her happily-ever-after was written in ink in the story of her life, that familiar sense of impending doom drummed inside her.

2

KAELYN

After a sleepless night and another long day of trying to soothe her daughter, Kaelyn slipped Poppy into the sling-style baby carrier and attached the baby to her chest. The close contact didn't settle her cries. If anything, Poppy sounded more distressed. Ruby twisted her hands as she watched Kaelyn prepare to go out. Kaelyn and Poppy had developed a routine of walking the beach and sitting on the rocks before bedtime, and Kaelyn had to believe it would work. The baby had to sleep. Kaelyn needed peace.

Ruby moved closer and rested a hand on the baby's back, looking like Poppy's cries were shredding her to pieces. "I honestly don't mind looking after her if you want to take a break. It's getting dark out, and it's so cold out there, especially by the water."

Ruby's English accent was stronger than Oliver's and showed no signs of diminishing, even after years of living in the States. Kaelyn hoped neither of them would ever lose those lovely lilts.

"She's got a bunch of layers and is probably going to be too warm. I appreciate the offer, but you deserve a break too. You've done so much to help. I hope you can enjoy a little quiet with a cup of tea while we're out."

Her mother-in-law smiled wanly, barely showing her charmingly crooked teeth, but didn't seem convinced. Ruby brought a blanket to wrap around the already bundled-up baby.

As Poppy fussed, Kaelyn tapped her bottom through the sling and bounced up and down. "Shush, it'll be all right, little sweetiekins."

Kaelyn hummed a lullaby that had become her favorite to sing, though she wasn't convinced Poppy actually liked it. She wasn't sure Poppy even liked *her*. But the baby did like the fresh air and the beach, so she was willing to gamble on spending a couple of hours out on the sand if it meant a few more consecutive hours of sleep tonight.

Ruby helped Kaelyn tuck the fleece Winnie the Pooh blanket around the carrier. "If you change your mind, I'll be right here not doing anything."

"Please take a break to relax. You've been cleaning this place non-stop. I know it's cluttered with all this baby stuff, but Oliver and I are going to get things straightened out when he gets home. For now, we all need to maintain our strength."

Kaelyn kissed her mother-in-law on her weathered cheek, grateful for her kindness and fighting off frustration over her well-intentioned interference. Did Kaelyn want to leave the baby with her? Undoubtedly. Would it make her the world's worst mother if she handed over her daughter when she had convinced Oliver she should leave her job to be a stay-at-home mother and it had only been a little over three months? No question.

"Are you quite certain you'll be all right?"

"I've got this. In New England, we like to go out during all kinds of weather."

"Oh, her little hat is popping off. Let me slip it back on."

Kaelyn shook off the suspicion she was being judged for not noticing the hat had slipped. She would have noticed soon. Most likely.

Then again, this morning she had put the butter away in the oven instead of the refrigerator and had stashed part of her breast pump in the freezer with the bagged milk. Then, in dramatic tears, she had searched the house for it, convinced fairies hid it to make her question her sanity.

Newsflash. There were no fairies. But the sanity was still in question.

Poppy continued to fuss as they walked the tiny distance to the beach. Though there was a housing crisis on the island, Kaelyn and Oliver had lucked out in finding this gem, thanks to Clarice hearing about the listing before it hit the open market. The house was a worn Cape-style home with landscaping that had seen better days—nothing like the modern, well-kept home they had left in California—and it needed work that neither she nor Oliver could do, but it had a small in-law suite that Ruby insisted was just right and the cutest screened-in porch overlooking the ocean. Most importantly, they had direct access to a beach.

Although the house wasn't perfect in the "move-in and never make any changes" sense, it was perfect for them. They could YouTube as much as possible to figure out how to do stuff to make it more their style, but in the meantime, they were happy to be on the island. It would be a beautiful place to raise a child, especially since Old Castle had always been where Kaelyn felt most at home.

Kaelyn hadn't known returning to the island was what she needed, but she'd never forget the thrill when Oliver recognized it and helped her to see where she belonged.

But what had she been thinking, quitting her job to raise a baby when she had no clue how to keep a young human happy? Heck, there had been years when she hadn't been sure how to keep *herself* happy.

Kaelyn settled into her new favorite spot on an outcropping of rocks, appreciating the crunch of old, battered seashells mixed with the sand filling in every crevice. She lifted Poppy out of the carrier, whispering sweet nothings to her, convinced that if she only kept talking, the baby would feel reassured and eventually calm down. Poppy hadn't been an exceptionally cranky baby since birth, but the last couple of days had been doozies.

Kaelyn lifted her sweatshirt and brought her daughter to her breast, shivering slightly as a chilly breeze hit her bare flesh. Poppy wasn't interested. She shoved her tiny, wrinkled fist in her mouth and wailed, and the trail of tears running down her chubby cheeks made Kaelyn's tear ducts kick into gear.

She'd known motherhood wouldn't be easy, but Kaelyn never dreamed her baby would hate her.

How stupid that sounded. Poppy was a baby. She didn't love, and she didn't hate. But what was logic when Kaelyn barely remembered the last time she slept more than an hour at a time?

"I want to help you, lovey buggy, but you've got to help me here. I promise I ate nothing spicy or garlicky today. Just latch on and you'll feel so much better."

Poppy ignored her and released a shriek that would have impressed an opera singer. The sharp sound sent several seagulls flying, squawking in response to the outcry.

"Yeah, I wish I could escape it, too," Kaelyn mumbled, imagining what it would be like to grow wings and fly away from anything unpleasant.

Oblivious to anything but the baby and her intense emotional outburst, Kaelyn startled at the sudden, anxious barking of a dog. Heart pounding, she jumped up with the baby and prepared to flee if the dog were to attack.

Kaelyn clutched Poppy close to her chest and scanned the beach, her eyes struggling to adjust to the darkness.

"Kaelyn, is that you over there? I thought I heard my favorite granddaughter."

Not a coyote. Not a rogue dog hunting for a baby to eat.

No danger.

Relief rushed out in a stream of released air as Kaelyn's hammering heart settled. Adrenaline had kicked in and had her ready to fend off a pack of wild dogs to keep her Poppy safe. Even though she could now see the leashed Labrador retriever, her reptilian brain still worried she was being circled by a pack of coyotes. Were there coyotes on the island? She couldn't remember. But stranger things had happened.

Kaelyn's mom approached, standing with the dog right near Kaelyn and Poppy.

Kaelyn sank back onto the rocks, shifting until she was nestled comfortably between two medium-sized boulders that made a perfect seat.

"Baby can't sleep again?" Khrista asked. "I was wondering if you'd be out here again tonight. Figured we'd pass this way just in case."

"Yeah. She's having a tougher time today. Won't even latch on. Just wants to chew on her fist, but then cries."

Khrista studied the fussy baby.

Now that her fear had dissipated, Kaelyn had questions. "Did you and Matt get a dog?"

The mystery dog pulled at the leash as he attempted to sniff the baby's feet. Kaelyn shifted to guard Poppy with her body. She loved dogs, but she didn't know this one, and her brain wasn't yet operating from a level place.

Khrista laughed and gestured for the dog to sit. The pup obeyed immediately.

"This is Moby, my neighbor's dog—I had their son Willie in my class a few years ago. They're visiting a sick relative off-island and wanted to stay late, but if Moby doesn't get his evening walks, he tears apart their couches. I love having the company while I'm out walking the beach, so I offered to bring him with me. I think I finally wore them down. I've offered dozens of times but this is the first time they've taken me up on it."

"That's so nice of you. I'm sure they appreciate it."

"It's beneficial for both of us. Sorry if his bark scared you, though. He's gentle as a lamb, but his bark could scare off a burglar, that's for sure." Khrista leaned down to peck Kaelyn on the top of her head, then kissed her own hand and pressed it on Poppy's cheek to transfer the kiss. "I don't think I will ever be able to look at the two of you and not have my heart swell so big that I worry it will explode."

Kaelyn sat back on the rock and stared down at her infant daughter, chewing away on that wrinkled little fist of hers and occasionally letting out a cry. Fate had worked in funny ways. A year ago, Kaelyn never would have envisioned herself reuniting with her mother, whom she hadn't even spoken to for five years at that point. Destiny had smiled on them, allowing them to heal the damage done.

Healing the past benefited Poppy more than anyone, and thankfully, she would never know the pain of fractured family roots that Khrista and Kaelyn and Daisy, Kaelyn's grandma, had known. Kaelyn would be open with Poppy and any future children about her own history, but the lessons would be about forgiveness, therapy, and the seeking of common ground. She'd learned how important it was to understand what motivated people's behavior and to not take everything personally. She also wanted her children to realize that even with this understanding, they shouldn't let people treat them badly. Despite Kaelyn's love for her mom, if Khrista hadn't committed to repairing herself, Kaelyn would have needed to maintain the boundaries she sought when she ran away.

Poppy's cries turned piercing as Kaelyn remained lost in dreamland. Kaelyn tried all the techniques her mother-in-law had taught her for enticing Poppy to nurse, but Poppy still wouldn't latch on.

Kaelyn groaned. "If you're hungry, latch on, Poppy."

"Is everything okay?" Khrista asked.

Kaelyn didn't want to answer, because irritation and frustration and self-loathing fueled her every thought, and it wouldn't do any good to share that with her mother. She didn't want anyone pitying her, or thinking she was stupid for the choices she made.

"I'm good. We're good. Just exhausted."

Khrista extended her hands and looked pointedly at the baby in Kaelyn's arms. "May I?"

Kaelyn held Poppy up in offering, grabbing the dog's leash in exchange. A leashed dog she could handle. Her arms immediately relaxed when freed of the burden of constantly holding an entire human, but then felt empty for not having her.

Kaelyn could barely summon the energy to raise her arms to pet the dog's ears, but she did. It was amazing what a person could make themselves do to save face.

Khrista paced the sand, cradling the baby on her shoulder and tapping her diapered bottom while bouncing. Poppy's cries diminished and eventually stopped altogether. Kaelyn held her breath. Her baby daughter was probably working up the energy to let out an ear-piercing wail.

And yet, no wail came.

"How did you do that? I can never get her to settle like that." Kaelyn jumped up to check her daughter's breathing. She touched the side of Poppy's face. Nice and warm. Her eyes had closed and her mouth hung open. As Kaelyn watched, her tiny little mouth made sucking movements, but her fist remained tucked between her body and her grandmother's body. "She's sleeping. Do you think she's okay? She didn't eat."

"She's absolutely fine. What a caring mommy you are, looking so worried. I guess it's the magic grandmotherly touch knocking her out cold."

"She never seems to want me to hold her unless we're nursing, which is pretty much always. But then she doesn't want me to put her down, either. But sometimes she seems so hungry and won't take it. I don't get it."

Khrista's voice was jovial, and she didn't even try to whisper. "You're just too delicious. When you're holding her, she's probably so drawn to your milk that she insists on nursing. Besides, and I mean this in the most loving way, I always tell parents their children pick up on their own energy. So when she's restless, you get tense, and she gets anxious in return. It's not a bad thing—it's natural. But you, my lovely girl, are probably utterly exhausted. And I'm happy to bounce her around anytime you want me to. Delighted, actually."

Kaelyn dropped back onto the rocks. The coldness of the stone seeped through her jeans, the chill slicing through her haze.

Why did Kaelyn fantasize about curling up on the hard, jagged rocks and falling fast asleep? She'd sleep under the light of the moon for a week, and perhaps then she'd have the energy to keep chugging along.

Of course, she wouldn't give voice to those crazy thoughts. What kind of mother of a newborn expected to sleep? Everyone knew that didn't happen. And who was she to complain? She had an entire support system around her. It was dumb to feel like this was so hard.

Kaelyn stared out at the water, admiring the shimmering of the moonlight on the gentle, rolling waves. The dog settled at her feet, licking his paw and then resting his head on it.

Khrista's chattering jolted Kaelyn back to the moment. Had Kaelyn fallen asleep with her eyes open? Was that a thing?

"She could be teething."

Had Kaelyn heard her mother correctly? "Already? She's only three months."

Khrista shrugged and continued bouncing and swaying at the same time. "You got your first tooth when you were only three months."

"Really? I didn't know."

Kaelyn hadn't given her mother enough credit. She never thought Khrista would remember details of Kaelyn's infancy and childhood. They had rarely spoken about those times, and most of Kaelyn's memories involved her mother being drunk or hiding in her room. Maybe things had been different when Kaelyn was a newborn.

Or maybe Kaelyn had always misunderstood. She'd been working with her therapist on how she perceived her mother and the childhood she had. Speaking of which, Kaelyn had to remember to make an appointment with her therapist—she hadn't seen her since the baby was born. She kept waiting for a good time.

Maybe next week when Oliver returned home.

"Can I walk you back to your house? I can carry the baby and help you put her in her bassinet."

Kaelyn hated the tremulous squeak in her voice. "No, thank you. We're good. I think I'd like to sit out here for a little while longer. Make sure she's fully out. Maybe even get a feeding in before we head back. The fresh air feels nice, actually."

"Totally get that. I spend a lot of time out here on the beach, and always did when you were young. I always wished we had a beach when you were an infant, but when we moved here, you took right to the water like you were born for the waves." Khrista moved to hand the baby off to Kaelyn. "I hate giving her up. I have to get Moby back home, and I'm meeting Matt and his girls for dinner. You want to come?"

"Thanks, but no. I don't want to get her too off-schedule. Not that we really have a schedule, but I'm trying."

Khrista laughed, sounding every bit like a grandmother who understood the irony of trying to fit a baby into your lifestyle.

"If you change your mind, we'll be at Raf's place. I can also order you something to go if you prefer. I'd be happy to drop it off so you can have it later."

"It's okay. Ruby has made enough casseroles to last us months."

"She's a blessing, that one."

Kaelyn nodded. Sometimes it was strange letting Khrista hear about how close Kaelyn had grown to Oliver's mother during the years of their estrangement, but despite the awkwardness, Kaelyn wouldn't change a thing about her relationship with Ruby. That woman had been her family from day one, and now there was room enough in Kaelyn's life for two mothers. Kaelyn wouldn't diminish her mother-in-law's role because she had reunited with her mother. She just needed to remind herself how lucky she was.

"It doesn't weird you out that I'm so close to Oliver's mom, does it?"

Khrista rubbed Kaelyn's upper arm. "Not at all. Did I have moments of envy that she had you when I didn't? Absolutely. But I'll be forever grateful she was there to mother you when I couldn't. How could I resent a woman who took care of my daughter and made sure she knew she was loved and wanted? Besides, she raised a son who reveres my daughter. Ruby gets points all around."

Khrista kissed Kaelyn and gently touched Poppy's elbow before departing with Moby. Khrista paused as the dog found something interesting in the sand to dig up, but after some gentle persuasion, he followed her as she led him away.

As soon as Khrista disappeared from view, Kaelyn rested her chin on the top of her sleeping infant's head and burst into tears, keeping the outpouring of emotion as quiet as she could.

This nightmare of inadequacy was too much. She loved her baby more than anything. *Anything.* She was so lucky she got to have this time with her baby. Kaelyn had a supportive husband and family, and the resources to stay home and raise Poppy on an island with the community that had been her chosen family since Kaelyn was five years old.

So why did putting on a cheerful face feel so fake? Why did she have to wake up every morning and paint on a new mask? Why did nothing feel like she pictured it would? Would anyone understand if she were anything but overjoyed every minute of every day?

Kaelyn adored her baby.

Her love wasn't the question.

And Poppy was simply doing what babies did.

But everyone was always telling her to enjoy every minute. Kaelyn had once thought that was obvious, but now she spent hours every day wondering if she'd ever feel like herself again. If Kaelyn could ever bond properly with the baby while she was elbow-deep in dirty diapers and laundry and the constant responsibility of nursing.

And boredom. *Oh,* the boredom.

But she could never speak of that. Who got *bored* with their own baby?

The fluctuation between being worn out and bored out of her ever-loving mind had her feeling like a crazy person. Would anything ever make sense again?

Tears spent and a raging headache starting as a thank you for the release, Kaelyn wiggled Poppy back into the baby carrier and started for home.

She entered the house quietly, hoping Ruby wouldn't hear her and come out to say hi. Normally Kaelyn loved having an evening cup of tea with her mother-in-law, but she didn't relish answering questions about her splotchy red face. No, she needed alone time, so when she didn't hear movement, Kaelyn closed her eyes in relief. Ruby must have retreated to her suite.

Kaelyn slipped out of her shoes and tiptoed up to her room with Poppy. She shut the door softly and settled in for some quiet time with her babe, who squirmed and wiggled in the carrier and let out tiny squawking noises that let Kaelyn know she was finally hungry enough to latch on. Maybe.

Three hours later, after a vigorous nursing session, three explosive diaper changes, some playful tummy time where Poppy rocked back and forth as if she wanted to flip over, and making it through two baby storybooks without a peep from little Poppy as she eagerly drank in the black-and-white images on the board book pages, Kaelyn performed a miracle.

She got Poppy settled into her bassinet.

Kaelyn watched in disbelief as the baby remained sleeping in her bed, her angelic face more relaxed than Kaelyn had seen it. Poppy sucked on her knuckle while sleeping, and love rushed through Kaelyn's chest. Quite literally, it seemed, as her milk let down and leaked into her nursing bra.

She made a mental note to research how long that party trick would keep happening, then laughed at the direction her thoughts continued to venture. Kaelyn also made a mental note to research when babies could start doing more interactive things. Kaelyn didn't want to miss a single developmental beat. She'd be a Pinterest mom who did really cool art projects with her infant. And even cooler things when Poppy grew into toddlerhood. Were flashcards a thing? She certainly didn't want to miss out on stimulating her baby's intellectual curiosity whenever she could.

How did women work full-time and raise babies? This was a full-time job. She had to educate herself.

The bubble of hope and excitement burst before it could carry her far.

How could she have thought she'd be equipped for this? Kaelyn was a graphic designer. A marketer. She knew nothing about infants and raising them into people. Not that Poppy wasn't a people already, but Kaelyn was responsible for making sure she became *good* people. Strong people. Smart people. Kind, compassionate, contributing-member-of-society people. It was overwhelming just thinking of it.

Poppy was a person. Not a people. And yet the more Kaelyn said the words in her head, the stranger they all sounded. People? Person? Poppy?

She made a mental note to add calming down techniques and ways to assuage postpartum anxiety to her research list.

Then she scoffed at herself, knowing full well she wouldn't remember any of these thoughts. Dozens, hundreds even, of similar thoughts had cluttered her mind every night since she found out she was pregnant, and most fluttered away before she had a chance to follow up or act on them.

How would she ever become a good mother if she couldn't remember the things to research?

Kaelyn repeated her to-do lists in her head over and over, hoping the repetition would cement the thoughts there until the morning. A field trip to the bookstore was in order. She would stock up on child development books—real, paper books with pages she could turn with her fingers and not flick on the screen—and stack them on every surface of her house so she wouldn't forget to read them.

Yes. That's what she'd do. And she'd buy more books for Poppy because Poppy seemed to like the ones they'd read earlier.

Kaelyn didn't remember flopping on the bed and drifting off to sleep, but when Oliver's ringtone interrupted a dream about the washing machine overflowing, she startled awake. She wiped a pool of drool off her cheek and fumbled to quiet the phone before the overly cheerful tune woke the baby. There was no light other than a tiny sliver of moonlight and a distant street light streaming in her window. Why would he call in the middle of the night? What was wrong?

"Oliver." Kaelyn waited for him to drop the bomb. A car accident? An incident at work? What was wrong?

"Hello, love. You sound breathless. Did I catch you at a bad time?"

She flopped over on her back and placed a hand on her forehead. Kaelyn closed her eyes and took a breath, counting to three before responding.

"I was sleeping. What time is it?"

"It's ten p.m. your time. I thought you'd still be up. So sorry. I'll let you go. I've been in meetings all day and haven't had a chance to check in with my beautiful bride. But we can catch up tomorrow. Get some sleep."

"No, no, wait. I want to talk to you. How are things going there?"

Oliver practically lulled her back to sleep with his talk of work. Had Kaelyn ever understood what Oliver did for a living? She seemed to remember being an active part of conversations. Once upon a time. Now all she could do was press on one of her breasts and think about getting up to pump to relieve the pressure.

"But I don't need to bore you with all that," Oliver said. "Tell me what's going on in the fabulous world of your life. What spectacular things did my beautiful offspring do today?"

Kaelyn almost unleashed her litany of complaints about the baby's refusal to nurse, crankiness, and the betrayal of falling asleep on Khrista but not on Kaelyn. But those were stupid and boring things to say, and she didn't want him to feel bad. And he would. Oliver wanted to be there with them. Kaelyn had no right to feel annoyed he was away when it had been her decision to uproot their entire world and move to the opposite coast. Not to mention her last-minute decision to quit her job, effectively cutting their income nearly in half. Oliver had smiled through all the changes, and it wouldn't be fair for her to express frustration at him having to be away for work while they struggled to get through contract negotiations. He couldn't abandon his job on a whim like she had.

"Everything here is great. Your little girl misses her daddy, but my mom thinks she might get a tooth soon."

"A tooth! Already?"

"I guess it can happen. My mother said I got my first tooth at three months."

"That is a treasured piece of information I will hold dear." Though Oliver's sigh was dramatic, she had, over time, learned to believe his enthusiasm was sincere. "I'm so glad you made up with your mother. I love learning these nuggets of information about you. And of course, our daughter will be as brilliant as you and get a tooth early."

Kaelyn laughed, flushing at the flirtation in his voice. He believed the earth revolved around her. Or the sun. Or whatever. Kaelyn was incapable of having a rational or well-informed thought, but Oliver loved her regardless, and that was what mattered. Even if sleep deprivation had her feeling like she had early-onset dementia.

"I'm not so sure getting an early tooth is indicative of high IQ, but I'll add that to my list of things to research," Kaelyn teased. "Besides, I have no doubt she'll be madly intelligent, just like her daddy. She sure as heck won't be getting that from me."

"I strongly disagree. The only intelligent thing I've ever done is convince you to spend your life with me. You're the brilliant one. Now tell me more about this research list. That sounds hot."

Kaelyn cuddled up in her blanket and wished he were there to hold her.

They chatted for a few more moments before Oliver convinced her she should rest while the baby rested.

"I'll be home soon, love. Take good care of my girls."

Kaelyn pressed a hand to her chest. "Oh, hey, has your boss said anything about when you can work fully remote? This traveling back and forth is insane."

Oliver's pause stretched on far too long. "Love, I need to go. My team is sending a deluge of texts and I need to see what I can do to help. I'll see you soon. I love you."

Kaelyn hid her annoyance and said her goodbyes and *I love yous*, fervently praying that things would get better.

Before they got worse.

3

DAISY

Daisy wiped down the last of the tables after the morning rush. She found the tasks at Happil-TEA Ever After Tea Room rather exhilarating, and though she had never done this kind of work for pay before, she had spent her life in service to others, so it came naturally. Only in this role, people's faces lit up when she placed tea in front of them, and there were never disparaging remarks made. Daisy enjoyed the bustle of conversation, merry faces, and the sense of community as people gathered in this mini utopia Clarice had created.

Clarice had been quieter and quieter lately, not as chatty or upbeat, though still a calming presence. Daisy wished she could get her friend to open up, but she had to maintain boundaries and honor Clarice's desire for privacy. As it was, Clarice had gone beyond kindness to offer a room upstairs for Daisy to stay in when she joined her daughter and granddaughter and great-granddaughter on the island. Clarice had insisted she stay as long as she needed to, and Daisy insisted on repaying her by helping around the tearoom, especially since Clarice had been so short-staffed.

The arrangement seemed to work for both of them. Daisy refused to make herself a nuisance and respected Clarice's space. For the most part.

Daisy sighed as self-realization hit harder than an acorn on the head.

She shouldn't have wandered into the area of the house where she found the leak... She shouldn't have mentioned it to Clarice, either. Maybe that was why Clarice had been more distant.

She straightened her stiffened body and rubbed her lower back. The pain had kept her up last night, and though she'd taken the pain medication the doctor had prescribed, it only seemed to take the edge off. She made a mental note to mention it at her next appointment... if she went to her next appointment.

Daisy watched as Clarice busied herself behind the counter. The woman was always on the go. Her whole life seemed to revolve around the island and its inhabitants, and Daisy admired her dedication so much. For not the first time, Daisy wondered what life would have been like for her if she had possessed a drop of the courage Khrista had. If Daisy had found the strength to leave Harold with her daughter in tow...

The past couldn't be undone. She had married him when she was too young and foolish to see the signs of what he'd turn her and her life into. She hadn't understood then how he cultivated fear in her. How he put her down so she'd never want to better herself. How he withheld things from her—money, food, knowledge of how to drive herself or do anything other than cook and clean for him. His calculated efforts to isolate her from her family and friends.

And, eventually, her daughter.

Daisy lifted her cleaning rag and wiped down more chairs.

She understood well what drew Khrista to Old Castle all those years ago. The island gave her a family Daisy couldn't provide. And now, despite Daisy's sins and mistakes, they accepted her, too.

Daisy smiled as she thought of Khrista's plan for the fundraiser. Clarice was always helping others. Everyone on the island talked about it. And now they'd give back in some tangible fashion. To ease Clarice's burden the way she so often eased everyone else's. The maternal figure of the island would be rewarded, and it wasn't even Mother's Day.

Clarice approached Daisy and paused.

"Are you okay, Daisy? You look tired, and I've noticed you rubbing your lower back. I have Mary coming in soon if you want to go upstairs and take a break."

Daisy waved her rag in the air. "I'm perfectly fine. A little backache, that's all. Nothing an Aleve won't take care of."

Clarice regarded her skeptically, as if attempting to see through her. There was nothing Daisy wanted to tell her. Daisy was there to do her work and make up for all the times she had messed up in her life. She wasn't there to make anyone pity her. And she intended to keep her secrets close to her chest.

Daisy abhorred the thought of being treated like an invalid or worrying anyone. Though her recent doctor visit had ended with bad news, she didn't need to focus on it, and she had no intention of letting anyone know about the potential diagnosis. They had all helped her through her heart surgeries months ago. She wasn't about to put them through anything else.

Besides, if the diagnosis remained merely a potential, what was there to tell? And if she didn't follow through on the biopsy, she didn't need to know.

Problem solved.

Daisy had too much living to do with whatever time the good Lord was willing to grant her. She only prayed she'd have the ability to live her full life right up to the last day. That way, no one would have to feel responsible for her.

"Anything you want to tell me?" Daisy pointed the question back at Clarice, the gun of inquisition loaded.

"Honey, I've been tired since 1970. But it has nothing to do with the work. This energizes me." Clarice grinned at Daisy and sashayed over to her tea blend area where she pulled tins of bulk tea off the shelves and assembled them on the counter. "Oh, if Amanda Martin stops in later for her usual afternoon scone and tea, and you end up ringing her up, please make sure you don't charge her. She's going through a rough time. Rambo, one of the elderly kitties she adopted, died last night."

"I don't know how she does that. I couldn't handle it."

"Amanda's a godsend for adopting elderly cats to give them wonderful final months, but her heart breaks every single time one of them crosses the rainbow bridge. I dropped off a care package to her last night, but she usually likes to come here to pick a new senior kitty the day after losing one."

"What a heart on her." Daisy meant every word of the praise. It took a special soul to look past their own grief to bring light to another creature.

"Agreed. But she always says, and I fully believe it, too–we all get to the end of our stories, eventually. So she gives the cats as much pampering as they can tolerate, and they expand and break her heart, and she begins the process again. She's a hospice nurse for humans, too, so I believe she's a special angel put on Earth for this very purpose."

Daisy agreed with the logic, but she couldn't understand Amanda Martin's commitment to the cause. Daisy had lost the one cat back when Harold punished Daisy by taking the cat's life, and she'd never been able to bond with another. Losing something she loved hurt so much she could barely breathe, so why would she willingly put herself through that torment? Animals had such short life spans as it was.

Thank goodness for people like Ms. Martin, though. "Does she like fudge? Maybe I'll make her up a batch of my special peanut butter fudge—it won awards at a county fair, you know. If you wouldn't mind me using the kitchen, that is."

"I think that would be lovely. You're welcome to use the kitchen anytime. Especially if you're making fudge."

Daisy straightened chairs around tables while Clarice organized her tins on her workspace.

Daisy loved watching the woman create her blends. Clarice always slipped into a sort of haze. A flow. A creative moment where she could simply toss things together and produce the most exquisite tea anyone had ever tasted.

She had a gift, and it was no wonder her talents resonated so deeply with everyone on the island. Daisy wished she would share more of her history, but so far Clarice spent more time looking outward than reflecting on whatever her past held. And Daisy wasn't one to probe.

Something started beeping from across the room, and Daisy and Clarice searched for the source of the sound.

"I think it's your phone." Clarice retrieved the phone in question and extended it to Daisy. Apparently, Daisy had set it on one of the vacant tables and forgot to pick it up again when she moved on to clean another table. Daisy took it and brought the screen closer to her face, wishing she had worn her glasses.

"Excuse me, it's my friend from back home." Daisy thought it okay to answer a call in the middle of her shift since the only customers remaining had tucked themselves into side rooms to work on their computers and would be there all morning.

"You go right ahead," Clarice mouthed as Daisy answered Edith's call. She then left the room.

"Daisy, so good to hear your voice."

Edith had been a childhood friend of Daisy's, but Daisy had lost touch with her when she ran off with Harold. They had reunited once Daisy had become a free woman following the death of her husband.

"Wonderful to hear you as well, my friend. How are you, Edith?"

"I've been better. But things are looking up. Sadly, Peter passed a month ago."

Daisy clapped a hand to her gaping mouth. She'd known Peter wasn't well, but she thought he had years. Had more than a month really passed since she had last checked in with her friends? Daisy had been so consumed with her own life and work, relationships, and rebuilding that she hadn't been a good friend. Not that it was unusual, considering that until her own husband's death, it had been fifty years since Daisy had spoken to Edith. But still. She should have done better.

"I'm so sorry. I didn't know."

"It's okay. I wasn't telling anyone. I didn't want a big fuss made. Peter and I cocooned for the last several weeks before his passing. Even if you tried to reach out, you wouldn't have gotten me. It was beautiful, really. And now I want to honor his life by celebrating what's left of mine."

"I should have at least been at the service."

"We didn't have one. Just a small goodbye ceremony with close family. It's what Peter wanted—he was such an introvert. And now he wants me to enjoy the freedom he felt I was missing out on by taking care of him."

Tears gathered in Daisy's eyes at the thought of all the loving years Edith shared with Peter and how intense the loss must be. The evidence of the pain rang true in Edith's voice, and the way her brisk tone crested on a wave of grief she couldn't quite hide.

"Are you okay? It can't be easy losing the love of your life."

"You know how it is," Edith said, but Daisy didn't. All she had felt when her husband passed was relief. Harold's death had been the best thing that ever happened to her.

"If there's anything I can do…"

"Actually, that's why I'm calling. I was hoping you wouldn't mind if I came to visit you on your island. It's been forever since I've put my feet in the sea. I could use the nurturing of sand between my toes and the sun rising on the horizon. A restorative retreat is exactly what I need. But if it's too much for me to come there, I can go elsewhere."

Daisy rushed to respond. "I would love for you to come here. Absolutely."

"Great! You're sure it's no trouble?"

Daisy shook her head and then remembered her friend couldn't see her do that over the phone. "No trouble at all. It will be a delight. But I have to warn you, it may be too cold for putting your feet in the ocean. The locals tell me it's been mild, but a New Hampshire winter is nothing like a Kentucky one."

"I don't care if there's snow on the ground when I get there. These old feet are going to bury themselves in salty water and New England sand."

"Well, you know I won't let you do it alone."

Daisy's mind shifted to all the preparations she'd need to make. She'd, of course, have to check with Clarice about taking time off to host her friend. Daisy briefly considered asking if she could help open another room upstairs—the home had long ago been an established bed-and-breakfast, but Clarice closed off the rooms over the years to focus on the tearoom—but quickly nixed that idea. Clarice didn't need anything more on her plate, and Daisy already felt as though she were taking advantage of Clarice's kindness.

Edith interrupted Daisy's wandering thoughts. "Excellent. I'm not sure if I'll drive or fly, but I'll let you know the details as the time approaches. I'll send you an email and we can coordinate dates that way."

Giddiness bubbled in Daisy's chest. How exciting to imagine having what equated to a sleepover party with her friend. She had barely done that as a teenager, and now as a woman in her seventies, it sounded both peculiar and blissful. With the burden of health worries on her mind, this would give her the distraction she needed.

Daisy's mind spun. She should have mentioned that she hadn't yet settled into a place of her own, but with the shock of Peter's passing and her eagerness to see her friend, the thought hadn't occurred to her.

As she swept the floor in the library room, a lovely side room in the Victorian-home-turned-tearoom, inspiration struck. Daisy remembered talking to a group of tourists at the tearoom about the rental cottages on the other side of the island that they favored when they came for beach vacations. The rental cottages were available for short-term rentals year-round and would be perfect for hosting her friend.

Problem solved. She'd rent herself a nice place to vacation with Edith.

For the rest of the day, Daisy floated.

Later that week, once she and Edith finalized the dates, Daisy called the cottage rental management office and put a deposit down. The cottage she reserved was too big for her and Edith, but it was the only one available for those dates. Daisy kept her plan hush-hush until the rental contract was signed. She knew if she told Clarice her plans, Clarice would insist on hosting her friend at the tearoom.

As soon as she had the dates secured, Daisy requested the week off, which Clarice granted with no objections. Daisy planned to spend one night alone at the cottage so she could figure out what other preparations would make this girl's week as perfect as possible.

The next morning, Clarice invited Daisy downstairs for an early breakfast before they opened. Clarice served a raspberry scone with lemon icing and a freshly brewed cup of peppermint ginger tea, which Daisy always appreciated as it helped her stomach to settle. Clarice sat across from her, sipping her tea, and Daisy squirmed under her scrutiny. Why did it look like Clarice had something she wanted to say?

Clarice broke the ice at last. "Daisy, my friend. You know your help here is appreciated but never expected. You don't have to do work here at all. You especially don't need to ask for time off or worry that I won't have coverage. "

Oh, just that. Tension drained from Daisy's shoulders, and she hadn't even realized she was tense.

"Oh, *skattledats.* Of course, I need to help. You putting me up here is such a blessing, especially since you don't open these rooms to the public, though heaven knows why you sit on that cash cow. If you would at least take my money..."

"Never! We're family."

Clarice would never know how much that sentiment warmed Daisy's heart. A heart that had withered from lack of love and now nearly burst from tenderness day after day since her arrival in Old Castle.

Clarice took a bite of her scone. "You should have talked to me before renting the cottage. We could have made it work to have your friend here."

"Which is exactly why I waited to tell you. You've done enough for me. This is actually perfect. I'll be out of your hair, and we won't have to worry about us being too rowdy for your guests." Daisy watched the tea swirl in her cup as she placed it back on the saucer. She then glanced back up to meet Clarice's eyes, hoping Clarice could see how genuine her words were. "I'd never want to take advantage of your generosity. But I hope you'll join us for a campfire at some point. I know Edith will adore you as much as everyone else does. You'll love her, too."

"Well, isn't that the nicest invitation? I'd love to join you if I can get away for a bit."

"Wonderful!" Daisy peeked over Clarice's shoulder to check the time on the teapot-shaped clock hanging behind the serving counter. "If you'll excuse me, Rafael will be here to pick me up shortly."

Clarice stood and collected the cups and the teapot while Daisy slung her purse over her shoulder and gathered the plates and utensils. As they set the items on the side counter, a loud bang from the kitchen startled Daisy. A clatter of metal followed. Daisy rubbed her ears, sure she was losing her mind when she heard a loud bleating noise that sounded very much like a...

"What in heavens was that?" Daisy asked.

Clarice ushered Daisy toward the exit, and if she was concerned about whatever mayhem occurred in her kitchen, she didn't show it. She seemed to want Daisy out.

"I need to get things started before the morning rush."

"But..." Daisy tried to maneuver around Clarice, certain they should check the kitchen.

Clarice practically herded Daisy out the door. "Thanks for the chat, my dear friend."

Though Clarice's behavior was odd, Daisy figured she must honor her friend's wishes and leave her alone.

She wasn't waiting outside long, as Rafael arrived right on time. They would spend the morning at his restaurant—prior to opening —planning the fundraiser menu, since they both volunteered to cover the catering. It made sense—he owned a restaurant, and she loved to cook.

Didn't bother her one bit to have all that extra time with him...

Rafael held the truck door open and lent her a steady hand as she climbed in. Daisy loved the way he hummed along with the soft rock songs on the radio and the way he glanced over at her every so often. She almost wished the restaurant was further away so she could continue to feel like the young person she morphed into as they rode side by side, with the smallest distance between them.

Raf had become a great friend since that first day Daisy wound up on his doorstep searching for her long-estranged daughter, and he probably would never understand how much his comforting presence had meant to her. Rafael had invited her to wait inside his apartment, reassuring her that he had looked out for Daisy's daughter ever since Khrista found her way to Old Castle all those years ago.

Daisy had never believed healing was possible, but the people of Old Castle proved her wrong with every salty-aired breath she drew on that island. Though her body kept pummeling her with dodge balls, her spirit had never been lighter and her soul never more pure. And though she'd promised herself not to think about whatever illness grew in her body, peaceful moments like this magnified her belief that living life to the fullest was more important than living longer.

Once he parked in the spot with the "Boss Man" sign one of his employees had given him, Rafael hurried to her side of the truck and helped her down. This had become a treasured part of their routine; she would take her time unbuckling and gathering her purse so he could open her door.

"I jotted down some notes with a few ideas, but I'm open to any suggestions," Daisy said as they ambled into his large, rustic kitchen. All the appliances and counters were modern and stainless steel, but the exposed wooden beamed ceiling and the giant stone pizza oven contrasted nicely.

"I had a feeling you'd say that," Raf said, grinning. "And I didn't want to look like a slacker, so I jotted down some notes as well."

With a dramatic flair, he reached into the back pocket of his navy blue slacks and withdrew a crumpled-up, folded piece of paper. He opened it slowly, eyebrows wiggling, and turned the paper to show her, but then folded it playfully before she could peek.

"Show me yours first."

Daisy blushed, sure he hadn't meant to sound so flirtatious. She needed to rein in her thoughts to the task at hand, and she especially needed to tell Khrista and Kaelyn to stop giving her their cast-off romance novels.

His keen attentiveness made her hyperaware of how alone they were in the vacant restaurant.

She pulled her notebook out of her purse and dropped it on the food prep center island, still unable to make eye contact and praying he didn't notice her speechlessness or her wild blushing. So far he hadn't teased her, but...

Raf leaned against the other side of the counter and peered over as if to glimpse her homework.

Daisy flipped the notebook open and studied her list. Would he find her ideas stupid? Some of these dishes she had never made before, but she had wanted to try.

She exhaled a deep breath and told herself to be brave. Rafael had never belittled her or chastised her for having ideas of her own. Why should he start now?

"Should I read you my list?" Daisy asked, attempting to moisten her lips with her suddenly dry tongue. Her stomach twisted and heat rushed over her body. Had he left the ovens on? "Or do you want to read it for yourself?"

"I want you to read it to me." Raf cleared his throat and stood upright. "We can compare ideas and pick the ones we think go together the best."

"If you hate these ideas, I can—"

"I won't hate them."

Daisy squeezed her eyes shut. She needed to rid herself of the blatant self-doubt. He wasn't Harold.

He was Rafael. And he was waiting. Patiently.

"Okay, I thought we could start with appetizers that could be served with the first round of cocktails. If we're sticking with the seafood theme, I thought maybe—tell me if these sound good— small, bite-sized chive crab cakes, crab dip, which could be spicy or mild, blue cheese stuffed shrimp, and maybe deviled eggs with smoked salmon. I have a few other things written down for appetizers, but do you think I'm on the right track so far?"

"By all means. You've got my stomach growling, and I had a hearty bowl of oatmeal already this morning. I like your idea about coordinating the courses with the rounds of cocktails served. If you agree, I'd be interested in adding a shrimp skewer or two in addition to your other ideas."

"That sounds delightful!"

He liked her ideas. He seemed impressed she had planned so thoroughly. And when Raf encouraged her to read off her thoughts about the other courses, Daisy's confidence grew with every suggestion, from seafood quiche to salmon roll-ups to the tried-and-true traditional pasta salad with tuna.

Raf slid his paper across the counter. "Looks like our thoughts were aligned. We shared several of the same ideas."

"Truly?" Daisy lifted the paper and tried to read his chicken-scratch. Once she deciphered his handwriting, she could see he wasn't teasing—they did indeed have several matching items on the list, with variations in what they called the dishes.

"That was easier than expected," Rafael said, turning to a music player on the wall. He pressed some buttons, and the room livened up with a slow song and his bright smile. "A dance to celebrate?"

A dance? He wanted to... dance? In the kitchen? With her?

Daisy hesitated, tugging on the hem of her sweater and trying to remember how to speak.

When had Daisy last danced? She couldn't recall. And with a man?

Rafael held his hand out, bowing slightly. "Come on. Don't be shy. Friend to friend. I've always said a ceremonial dance can help secure good fortune. In the early days of the restaurant, it was a rule that everyone had to participate in the kitchen dance before we turned on the ovens for the day."

Okay, so it wasn't something special he intended for her alone. Not because of an attraction. Dancing was a tradition. A rule. She'd be rude to turn him down.

She could allow herself this one thing. This one moment of security and comfort and touch.

Daisy reached deep inside herself to find the courage she needed to give him this moment. To give herself this moment.

Though her adrenaline spiked as if she were walking herself off the plank and into deep waters with unknown creatures waiting to feast on her fear, Daisy stepped forward and inserted her trembling hand in his.

The man could dance! She fumbled about as Raf clasped the palm she had offered, and his other hand held her with gentle pressure on her lower back. Their bodies didn't touch, but a spark jumped between them, nonetheless.

Daisy didn't have to fake her smile. She allowed herself to rejoice in the warmth of his embrace and the thrill of his surprising skill while he twirled her around the kitchen. Daisy savored the spicy scent of his cologne as she struggled to catch her breath, grateful she hadn't yet stomped on his feet.

When the song ended, she smiled up at him, loving the glint in his eye and the sweat that gathered on his forehead. Raf stood at least a foot taller than her, and yet she detected no threat. Even so, she should pull away. Step out of his magnetic field.

But all Daisy could do was watch the way his eyelashes lowered as he studied her face.

As if someone had flipped the lights on, Daisy became acutely aware of how their hips had drifted closer. How his fingers splayed against her back. When had she rested her hands on his arms?

Her heart raced, and her limbs trembled. Every nerve-ending in her body warned her to step back. To get out of the situation.

Every neural pathway in her brain lit up a flashing fluorescent exit sign, directing her to evacuate.

Danger. Leave. Stop the madness.

Daisy dropped her hands from Raf's body as if he was poison. Ever the gentleman, he allowed her to escape.

She couldn't say a word. Her throat had closed and she could barely gulp enough air to propel her forward. Somehow, Daisy grabbed her purse and her notebook and bolted out of the restaurant. She waited by his truck, kicking herself for fleeing without a word when she still relied on him for a ride back into town.

He approached slowly, maintaining a polite distance.

"Daisy?"

She clutched her purse tightly to her chest. What could she say? How could she make this less awkward? Daisy didn't want him to think he had done something wrong. She didn't want to lose his friendship. Or his companionship.

"My apologies, Rafael. I remembered I need to get home quickly to make arrangements to rent a cottage." She squeezed her eyes shut to clear the fog. "My friend called, and she asked to come to the island."

"Anything I can do to help?" Rafael extended the courtesy of allowing the change of topic. He helped her into the truck the same way he always did and then listened to her gush about Edith.

Rafael was an empathetic listener. A compassionate friend. And she probably read way more into that dance than he intended.

Before he dropped her off in front of the tearoom, they chatted about the menu and planned to meet again in a day or two. He'd shop for ingredients and they'd prepare some samples in his kitchen.

Daisy vowed to get her act together before then. And she did. At their cooking session, she carefully avoided touching him and he didn't ask her to dance. But they brainstormed new recipes and whipped up batches of the tastiest seafood dishes she'd ever had. Daisy considered herself a decent cook, but Rafael possessed a magic ability.

The days passed quickly, and Daisy woke up extra early the morning before Edith would arrive. Daisy had already packed, but she had lost sleep wondering what she may have forgotten.

Rafael picked up Daisy to drive her to the cottage. He carried her bag to his truck like her own personal hero.

During the drive across the island, Rafael shared stories about the young man he had been training to take over some management duties at the restaurant, and Daisy marveled at his work ethic. He was older than her by a few years, yet he still spent a great deal of time at the restaurant he had opened with his wife decades ago.

"Here we are," Rafael announced as he turned into the sandy gravel driveway.

Daisy hadn't seen the cottages before booking, and gratification warmed her. The cottages were far enough apart so the neighbors wouldn't crowd one another, yet close enough to not feel isolated, and each one had unique external decor. Daisy adored the teal door with the matching shutters on the cottage she had rented. Though the driveway was on the street side, when she stepped out of the vehicle, the rushing whoosh of the ocean waves greeted her ears as they soared to the shoreline. From the driveway, she could see the expansive beach with the smooth sand.

As Rafael retrieved her suitcase, he asked in his breezy way, "Excited for your gal time?"

Raf's smile engulfed his face, and his tone was teasing and flirtatious. She looked at the ground and then forced herself to look back up. His eyes mesmerized her, and Daisy had no reason to avoid them.

"I've never done something like this. Do I sound silly if I say I'm really excited?"

He carried her bag to the front door, speaking over his shoulder as she followed. "You'd sound silly if you said you weren't excited."

He waited, whistling melodically, while she searched on her phone for the code the manager had sent to unlock the door. After a few attempts, Daisy finally got the door opened. Rafael set down her bag inside the entrance. Together, they toured the cabin. Though she'd been packing as many adventures into her life as possible since Harold made her a merry widow, this ranked high on the list of things that excited her the most.

She couldn't wait to show off the island to Edith.

Rafael leaned against a doorframe and watched her open and close cabinet doors in the kitchen. The cottage was stocked with nearly everything they might need for their short stay.

"Daisy, I'm awful sorry you missed out on this kind of thing. My wife used to take a week off every year to go on a retreat with her girl-friends. She always came back happier. It's good for the spirit."

His face lit up whenever he spoke of his wife, who had passed away years ago but remained alive in the flicker of his eyes and the tender smile he couldn't keep from his lips whenever he spoke of her. Daisy would have killed for something like that, but seeing it through the lens of other people made her almost as happy as if she had experienced it herself.

"She was a lucky woman to have such an understanding husband."

"I wasn't always so understanding, but she stood her ground. I could either support what she needed or cause friction in our marriage because I was selfish. At first, I went with the latter, but eventually, I got smarter and switched to the former."

Rafael's laughter was deep and rumbled through the room, and Daisy swore she could feel it tickling her insides.

"Still, she was a lucky woman to have a man who appreciated her value."

"I think the trick wasn't so much that I was such a smart guy, but that she appreciated her own value and wouldn't accept anyone else treating her less."

Daisy couldn't respond. A knot of tension gathered in her throat and pressed on her chest. How she wished she could have had the strength and self-worth his wife had possessed. How she wished she could have taught that to her daughter.

Wishes, wishes, wishes.

Her phone buzzed, reeling Daisy back to the present and providing a welcome distraction from the pain of a past she couldn't undo.

"Oh, excuse me. Edith is calling."

Rafael slipped out to the car to carry in the rest of her belongings, mainly grocery bags with food and wine for the week. She had messaged with Edith to figure out her favorite snacks and her dietary restrictions and shopped accordingly. Daisy loved playing hostess and would have enjoyed doing it more in her life. If only she hadn't been so isolated.

But enough about that. Those thoughts didn't serve her.

Edith's tone was positively gleeful as she burst out her greeting. "Daisy, I've been keeping a secret, but I wanted to let you know before we get there."

"We?"

"Yes! The whole Quad will be there! I didn't want to let you know until they made the arrangements in case it fell through, but I'm so excited we'll have this time together. I checked out the link you sent me to the cottage and it looks like there are plenty of beds, so I thought, why not go with it? Surprise!"

Daisy couldn't identify the roiling storm that gathered in her belly. Was it excitement? Dread? Fear? Or the most genuine happiness she had ever known?

"Even Florence?"

"Of course Florence. What Quad did you think I meant? Alice too, in case that's your next question."

Edith didn't mention Daisy's conflict with Florence, so neither did Daisy. She wasn't sure how much Edith and Alice knew, and shame still made it difficult for her to disclose the story.

Daisy could hardly believe Florence had agreed to visit the island. Did that mean she forgave Daisy? Maybe she had realized that Daisy had been working hard on changing? Daisy had reached out to Florence many times, but her calls always went straight to voicemail. Daisy's granddaughter, Kaelyn, told Daisy that usually when voicemail picked up right away, it meant the person on the other end declined the call.

So what did it mean that Florence was coming when she hadn't returned any of Daisy's calls or texts?

The fight they'd had when they stayed together in California had been explosive. Florence had advised Daisy against inviting

Khrista to Kaelyn's baby shower, since Kaelyn hadn't spoken to her mother in over five years. Daisy had been determined to fix their broken link, and knew that if she could just get the women into the same room, they'd remember the love they had for one another. Naturally, the whole thing had blown up in Daisy's face, and Florence was less than sympathetic. Instead of empathy, she had unleashed fury about Daisy and their history that Daisy hadn't been ready to absorb.

Daisy hesitated before bringing it up to Edith but ultimately she had to know. "Florence realizes she's coming to see me?"

"Of course she does. Why are you being odd about this?"

Raf re-entered the house, and Daisy used his presence as a reason to shift the direction of the conversation.

"Excellent. I'll have everything set up and ready for your arrival. There's plenty of parking right next to the cottage, but let me know if you need anything on your way. When you get into town, if you need a caffeine boost, stop at Happil-TEA Ever After Tea Room. It's right over the bridge by the first beach you'll see. Can't miss it. Of course, if you want to just get here, I stocked up on a variety of her tea, so you don't have to stop there if you don't want to."

Daisy was babbling, she knew, but her nerves challenged her. She had mentally prepared herself for Edith's visit, but with two extra guests, would she be able to hide her symptoms from everyone?

And would it be awkward between her and Florence?

When she disconnected the call, Raf stepped closer. "Everything okay?"

"Oh, yes. She's bringing our other girlfriends. I'm a touch surprised, that's all."

"I can't read what you're feeling. You seem kind of happy, but also a little anxious." Raf lifted Daisy's bottle of water from the counter she had dropped it on and handed it to her. Kaelyn had been hounding Daisy about carrying around a reusable water bottle and drinking as much as possible in a day. Daisy had never consumed so much water in her life, but she had to admit her limbs felt better when she drank up, and drinking more frequently helped to dilute the blood in her urine and ease some of her discomfort. She accepted the bottle and chugged.

After several sips, she recapped the bottle and considered how to answer Rafael, who awaited her response. "I don't know what to say. You've summed up my feelings perfectly."

Raf continued to hold the silence, probably knowing she wouldn't be able to keep the story to herself.

He was right. Daisy couldn't hold it in any longer. "One of my friends who's coming hasn't spoken to me since we were in California together. She thought I made a big mistake by inviting Khrista to Kaelyn's baby shower. At the time, it seemed as if she was correct. But things turned out well, eventually, so I like to think my interference helped. But Florence said some things, and I said some things, and I don't know if the damage done to our relationship fifty years ago has ever actually healed, as much as we tried to believe so."

Daisy took a deep breath and forced herself to explore the mingling of sadness and annoyance that gathered in her gut whenever she thought of Florence.

At Raf's questioning expression, Daisy waved the shaking hand that held her water bottle in the air. "The damage had to do with the man I married. She liked him, too, and, well, that's a story for another day."

She took another sip of water to lubricate the desert in her mouth.

"I've tried reaching out to her, and she has repeatedly ignored my attempts. I can't imagine why she'd want to come here to see me. And to be honest, I'm pretty angry over the whole thing, too. But I'm trying to let go of the past and move forward. I've spent enough of my life in a state of anger. I don't want to live that way anymore."

Rafael didn't ask questions, for which she was grateful. He did, however, reach out and hold her hand. Her hand seemed small in his, and as she stared at their connected fingers, she hated the aging so evident in her skin—the wrinkles and the sunspots and the bulging veins.

But then he stroked his thumb over her hand, and she morphed into a young lady again. A spark of something was there, and it wasn't the first time that spark tingled during one of these small displays of affection. She and Raf had been having dinner together several times a week since her move to the island. Daisy had assumed it was because he was lonely and they had both lost spouses. She had no intention of falling for a man again—once was enough, thank you very much—and her overactive imagination probably fueled whatever she thought she felt. It probably stemmed from a lifetime of mistreatment and difficulty accepting kindness without becoming attached. And being surrounded by happy, loving couples in her reunited family.

Her growing feelings were an extension of her gratitude for the new life she had the honor of living, no matter how short that time may be cut.

Even as Daisy accepted his kindness and reassurance, and even as she warred with herself over whether to feel happy about the Quad being reunited for a week, she knew she had to go with it. They'd arrive tomorrow, and though she could stop it if she chose to, she didn't want to live with regret.

Her new doctor hinted at a diagnosis she hadn't shared yet with anyone, and she preferred to hold the secret in a hidden vault inside. She hadn't asked questions, but the doctor wanted her to go for more testing to be sure that if it was indeed the bladder cancer he suspected, it hadn't yet spread. He had tossed out all kinds of potential scenarios she hadn't been prepared to hear—she had thought she had a urinary tract infection, not a life-threatening cancer, for goodness sake! Hearing things like chemotherapy and surgery and potential bladder removal... nope. Not ready to deal with it.

She'd already lost too much time with her loved ones. After years of a marriage miserable enough to make her wish she'd develop a terminal illness, she wasn't about to succumb to the realities of one.

The past year had been the happiest of her life, and she considered every day a gift. Her health hadn't been great, but she hadn't allowed any of it to stop her from doing the things she wanted to do and appreciating every moment.

As soon as the doctor had delivered the news, Daisy had promised herself she wouldn't tell anyone about it. Sure, she'd had to modify some things. She'd had to cancel the trip to Italy she had planned with her friend Margaret.

But Daisy had also spent more time snuggling her great-grand-daughter, going for walks along the beach with her daughter, dropping off treats to her granddaughter, and listening to people discussing their passions at the tearoom.

And soaking up the joy of spending time with a good man.

Daisy would make the rest of her life—no matter how long she had to live it—as glorious as possible. She would take nothing for granted.

And that meant accepting every new challenge as it came.

4

KHRISTA

Khrista worked like a chemist, spending the week jotting down ideas for combinations of teas and liquors that would create the most tempting cocktails for the fundraiser. She tried to imagine how they would taste without actually sampling them herself, and had even mixed the drinks in cups and performed the smell test.

She had a spreadsheet where she tracked the level of alcohol smell compared to tea smell. Khrista's goal was to create drinks that would accentuate the flavors of the tea while giving a mild, relaxing buzz. Her first batches had been far too strong. Khrista would have loved them, but then again, when she was at the height of her dysfunction, she had preferred the alcohol straight from the bottle. Most people would rather have a small bite on their tongue and the fruity taste of a punch.

But she also didn't want to disappoint the party guests, so it was important they feel the alcohol in their veins.

Excited to share her creations, she invited Kaelyn and Daisy to join her for a taste test. They both agreed, although, in reality, Daisy would be the only one able to taste the drinks since Khrista was on the wagon and Kaelyn was nursing and didn't want to take any chances.

Gathering with Kaelyn and Daisy, and sweet Poppy, of course, at the tearoom for an early afternoon caffeine fix and a quick planning chat, Khrista tried to convince her daughter to loosen up a bit. Just for one night.

"You could always pump and dump," Khrista offered. "You deserve a fun night, baby girl."

"Mom, that sounds disgusting. Besides, I don't need a break from my newborn. What kind of mother do you think I am?"

Khrista wrapped her arm around her daughter, enjoying the precious *ga-ga-goos* of her granddaughter as Poppy waved her rattle between the table and Kaelyn's chest. "The very best mom."

Daisy clinked her teacup back on her saucer and she sat up straighter. "Come to the cottage I rented. My friends don't arrive until tomorrow, and I have everything situated for their arrival. Can you both come later this afternoon?"

Khrista appreciated the offer. "I sure can. Matt's going to a game with his daughter's new boyfriend. The girls plan to head into the city with them and go to a movie while the guys are bonding, and I would love to get together with both of you and get at least the first round of drinks squared away. I have other ideas, but the ones we serve first are the most important to figure out."

Daisy clapped her hands. "It's a date, then."

Kaelyn peered down at her phone and made a face. "I've gotta run. I'm starting sleep training with my little muffin here and need to get her back to the house for the pre-nap routine before she gets overtired. We're switching to the crib."

Khrista took the baby from Kaelyn's arms and dropped a kiss on her pert little nose. The baby smiled, officially making the morning the best ever. Poppy had been smiling for weeks now, but Khrista had been so busy with work and planning the fundraiser that she hadn't had a lot of opportunities to hang out for these leisurely moments.

She needed to make more time. Khrista never wanted to miss a single smile. Unrealistic? Absolutely. But if she aimed for Jupiter, at least she could grab a smile from the moon if she missed her mark.

Khrista handed the baby back and collected her purse from the back of her chair. "I'll catch you both later. Mom, is Raf driving you back to the cottage, or do you need a ride?"

Daisy's cheeks pinkened, and she refused to make eye contact with Khrista. Khrista bit the inside of her cheek to keep from smiling and taunting her mother.

"He had to run to the hardware store to pick up some new door-knobs for one of his apartments, but he said it was no trouble to swing by when he's done to pick me up."

"Sounds good. Then I will catch you later."

LATER THAT DAY, Khrista gathered her supplies and stopped at Kaelyn's house to pick her up. Kaelyn and Oliver had bought the cutest house on the street, one Khrista had always dreamed of being able to live in with her daughter when Kaelyn was young. She had never given her daughter the life she had wanted to give, so watching Kaelyn live out her dreams now fulfilled Khrista in ways she couldn't describe. Her daughter was living the fairytale. And despite Khrista's mistakes, she now got to have a front-row seat to witness it all.

Kaelyn rushed out of the house without the baby. As she got into the car, she released what seemed to be a pent-up breath. Anxious energy rolled off Kaelyn and filled the car.

"I hope you don't mind, but Ruby offered to keep the baby for a few hours, and I thought I should let them have their bonding time. I've been sort of stingy with keeping her to myself lately, and I figured maybe it would be more fun if we didn't have a crying baby to contend with tonight."

"I think it's a great idea. Not that I would ever mind a crying baby, especially my little Poppy flower, but I think a grown-up night on the beach sounds exactly like what we all need." *Especially you.* But she kept that last part to herself. No way would she utter a single word that Kaelyn could misinterpret as criticism. Not when Kaelyn was already so vulnerable. "I'm so sorry—we should have invited Ruby."

"Nah, it's all good. I've invited her out several times, but she's working on a big ancestry project and has preferred to spend all her time doing that. When's she's trying not to win the Clutter Wars, anyway."

Over the years, Khrista had seen preschool parents burning themselves out, desperate to be everything to their young children. Khrista struggled with watching Kaelyn's attempts at being super-mom. Little did Kaelyn know she already was—without even trying. Kaelyn didn't need to do everything herself to be an amazing mother, but Khrista wouldn't butt in. She was just glad to see her daughter deciding to leave the baby behind for a few hours.

"I'm really excited to see what you came up with. And I think I might actually have a sip or two. I wouldn't even have to dump my milk for that, according to my online sources."

"Aww, that's great, honey. So glad you decided to let your guard down for a minute."

To cover the sudden silence, Khrista switched the music over to Bluetooth so she could surprise Kaelyn with a custom playlist of songs she remembered her daughter loving as a child and high schooler. They sang along for the first one, and when the next came on, Kaelyn gaped at her mother.

"These were some of my favorite songs. So weird they came on back to back."

Khrista couldn't hide her smile, though exposing her vulnerability had her feeling sheepish. "I made a playlist to help me feel closer to you when you went away. You had great taste in music. I wish I had taken the time to realize that back when it was important to you."

"Mama..."

The anguish in Kaelyn's voice squeezed on Khrista's heart, threatening her oxygen flow. Khrista hadn't meant to cause pain. Only bonding and maybe happy nostalgia to replace the sour memories stored in their minds.

"Hold on, I want to skip ahead and see what else you have." Khrista switched to an upbeat dance song. "Car dance time!"

Kaelyn obliged, joining Khrista as they scream-sang the lyrics and danced in their seats like the world was one big concert and they had a spot on the stage.

After they pulled into the driveway, Kaelyn jumped out and grabbed their overnight bags while Khrista carried the box and tote bag of supplies. Khrista hadn't been on this part of the island for some time, so it amazed her to see the improvements the owners of the cottages had made. All the cottages seemed to have had a facelift, and it looked like they were fully rented out, based on the number of cars parked and lights on.

They stood together in the driveway, taking in the scene from their vantage point. Though the sun was setting, families gathered on the beach, couples strolled hand-in-hand, and a small group of middle schoolers tossed a football near the shore, laughing hysterically when one friend dove to catch it and fell flat on his face into the salty water.

Khrista shivered. Sure, the winter had been mild. But that water was icy even during the summer, so she could only guess how frigid it would be now, even though the temps had been hanging in the low fifties all week–more like spring than winter.

Apparently, the cold didn't faze the kids. Khrista and Kaelyn watched them wrestle in the ankle-deep water.

"Is this what I have to look forward to?" Kaelyn asked. "Kids are crazy."

Khrista laughed and soaked up the day's liveliness. She would have to make it more of a habit to drive down this way and walk this beach. Clearly, she was missing out on a slice of life by sticking to her favorite spots on the island. Khrista didn't recognize any of the people, so most likely they were from off-island. Vacationers soaking up the unseasonably warm winter sun.

Daisy welcomed them at the door with cookie-scented hugs. She invited them in, showed them where they could put their bags, encouraged them to help themselves to the freshly baked chocolate chip cookies, and gave them a tour of the small two-bedroom cottage. When they returned to the kitchen, Daisy showed off the charcuterie boards she had created for her friends.

"Only thing left to do is slice the cheese tomorrow. I don't like when it gets crispy when you do it too far in advance," Daisy said, smoothing the saran wrap along the edges of the tray.

"You're quite the hostess," Khrista said. Khrista had grown up in a house that never felt like a home. Where dark energy lurked around every corner and hung in the toxic air she breathed. She had vivid memories of her mother engaged in chores and meal preparations, but never with joy. Never with the lighthearted spirit she showed now.

"There are Adirondack chairs outside, and I dragged them to the edge of the patio so we could put our feet in the sand if you'd like. Or if you prefer, I can move them back and we can stay clean and warm. Whatever you want."

"Toes in the sand." Kaelyn and Khrista spoke in unison, then glanced at each other and laughed.

"Two peas in a pod," Daisy said.

Kaelyn circled one arm around Daisy and one arm around Khrista and pulled them close. "*Three* peas in a pod. That's us. The peas. And this town is the pod that keeps us huddled safely together."

"That's beautiful, Kaelyn." Khrista clamped a hand over her heart as if she could stop the swelling that pushed against her chest. Never did she imagine this closeness. This love.

"I'd say it was more on the corny side and definitely not worthy of weepiness." Kaelyn pulled away and delivered a stern look to Khrista. "Don't be getting all sappy. We haven't even had a drink yet."

"Speaking of drinks," Daisy said, reaching up to grab the fancy glasses from a cabinet near the stove.

"Don't dirty those–I brought plastic." Khrista rushed over to the tote bag with the supplies she had brought.

Daisy wrinkled her nose. "Nonsense. This is a special night, and we shall celebrate properly."

The idea of clinking glasses together with her mother and

daughter appealed to Khrista, and so when she poured their cocktails, carefully following the recipes she had narrowed down, she served herself some of the virgin iced tea in a fancy glass.

They carried their glasses out to the patio, each selecting a chair. The sun had started its descent, and although they were on the east coast and enjoyed daily sunrises, from this part of the island, the sun appeared to set into the water of the cove.

Khrista raised a glass dramatically in the air. "First, a toast. To the O'Donnell ladies."

Daisy interrupted, "How about for just a second we pretend our name isn't linked to that man's? Let's pretend we are Simmons ladies instead. If you wouldn't mind obliging an old woman."

Khrista nodded solemnly. "I wouldn't mind at all. In fact, if I hadn't already married Matt and changed my name, I would happily change it to your maiden name and rid myself of anything to do with Harold."

"It's crazy, isn't it?" Kaelyn asked. "We don't even have matriarchal lines of names anymore. For so many generations, society has forced us to take the name of fathers that may not have even been involved in our lives. I mean, I took Oliver's name, and I don't regret it, but now I'm feeling a little guilty that I never gave my daughter the chance to have her matrilineal option."

Kaelyn had been lucky enough—or smart enough—to find a man who actively worked to build a life with her rather than to push his on her. She shouldn't feel anything but pride in her decision. Khrista rushed to reassure her daughter. "A name is just a name. What matters is that we all embody the strength of our ancestors. Women who endured so much to get where they are. Where *we* are."

"I'll drink to that!" Daisy's shout had them all raising their glasses.

Daisy and Khrista, on each side of Kaelyn, leaned forward so they could all clink their glasses together as they shouted, "Cheers!"

Then Khrista observed their faces while they sipped the strawberry tea with gin.

"What do you think?"

"I think I'm going to need another," her mother said.

"Oh, I have another thing we can drink to. My new baby kitty is coming home tomorrow. She's finally cleared all her vet checks, and she's ready to give Mr. Ed a run for his money."

"That's so exciting!" Kaelyn raised a glass. "Congratulations. I can't wait to see my furry siblings getting to know each other."

Daisy clinked her glass against theirs again. "I'll miss her in the tearoom. She's always rubbing against my legs when I'm trying to clean. She has the loudest purr of any cat in the place."

Three drinks later, Daisy couldn't pull herself to a standing position for a bathroom break. Khrista tried to help her mother out of the chair, nearly dropping her because her arms lost strength thanks to the extreme, full belly laughter. Kaelyn was no help either, doubled over and complaining about her cheeks hurting. They were all snorting messes, and Khrista had never known until that moment that snorting was one of their family traits.

Khrista had never heard her mother laugh. Her thought at first was that she had never heard her mother laugh this much, but to be honest, she couldn't remember a time of laughter in their household at all. Ever. That thought sobered her up—figuratively, not literally, since she was only drinking plain tea.

Daisy demanded her attention. "If you don't hurry and help me out of this chair, you're going to have quite the mess to clean up."

That comment, delivered with a slight slur, had Khrista doubling over again and locking the old pain behind a door in her mind. That pain no longer served her. She needed to live for the moment now.

"Stop being so hilarious and I might hold on to you."

Eventually, the laughter stopped enough for Khrista to drag her mother out of the chair and walk her to the bathroom. Once Khrista delivered Daisy safely back to her Adirondack chair, Daisy said she wasn't sure she wanted to get back into it since the chair sat so low and getting up had been such a challenge.

"Should we move the party into the cottage?" Kaelyn asked.

As if forgetting her earlier words, Daisy plopped back into the low chair and gripped the arms. Her expression turned serious as she gazed out at the purple-blue sky.

"I want to stay on the beach forever. How did I go my whole life without spending all my time on the beach?" Daisy stared off into the dark, seemingly mesmerized by the gentle roar of the rising waves and the boisterous shouts of kids playing nearby.

Khrista needed to get her mother's mind off the past. The past was too dark a place to visit while intoxicated. "You're quite the lightweight, Mom."

"She's a lightweight?" Kaelyn raised her half-full glass, still on the second serving. "I'm afraid to get up. Don't really want to test my post-partum bladder, but my head is already spinning while sitting here so I don't dare take the chance."

Daisy tried to lean forward, but she quickly gave up the struggle and sat back, closing her eyes. "I stocked the bathroom with disposable adult undergarments—don't laugh! I don't need them yet, but thought some of my friends might and didn't want to risk not having them. Help yourself, sweet love. They're in the cupboard under the sink."

"Grandma! I'm twenty-six! I don't need those!"

The trio burst into snorting laughter once again, and Khrista was fairly certain if this kept up, she would need to borrow the disposable underwear.

A memory darted into Khrista's head and demanded to be shared. "Kaelyn, I must have told you about the time after I had you when I was lifting your carrier out of the shopping cart and my bladder let go right there in the store? Oh my goodness—I never returned to that store!"

Daisy pointed a finger in the air. "I remember that! I was with you. That old biddy who used to run her mouth off about everyone asked me for months why you hadn't been back. I finally had to tell her to buzz off and mind her own beeswax."

More raucous laughter, and a horrified daughter, only served to amp up the hilarity.

As Khrista offered her mother another round, Daisy waved her off, telling her she didn't mean to lose her wits.

Khrista waved the small pitcher in front of her mother. "Why not?

It's fun to lose your wits sometimes."

Slurring, Daisy said, "Did I say not to pour me another cup? I meant, 'Yes, please.'"

Khrista obliged, thrilled to see her mother letting down her guard and relaxing a bit. "Okay, but this is the last one. I want you able to function when your friends get here tomorrow."

Daisy didn't respond. She grasped the glass with both hands and stared into the abyss.

"I think I have feelings..." Daisy clamped a hand over her mouth, causing the cocktail in her glass to slosh over the sides, and her eyes practically crossed.

Khrista and Kaelyn exchanged meaningful looks. They had talked about Daisy and her companionship with her fellow widower, but they had agreed they would wait until she was ready to talk to them about it before mentioning the growing relationship.

Apparently, the alcohol had loosened her tongue.

"Everyone has feelings, Mom."

Kaelyn sat up in her seat and leaned forward with her arms on her knees. She looked like she was about to embark on an intensely deep conversation.

"Careful what you say, Grandma. You've been drinking and you aren't really thinking."

"I've been wanting to talk to you both. This is all so confusing to me. And I didn't mean to start feeling things."

Khrista rushed to reassure her. "Mom, trust me when I tell you it's no secret you've got a little crush on Raf."

"How did you know it was Raf?" The shock on her face made Khrista burst into laughter again, joined by Kaelyn. Daisy remained silent.

"Does everyone know?" She buried her face in her hands and her shoulders trembled. Khrista knelt in front of her and pulled her hands away.

"Mom, there's nothing to be embarrassed about. You're a single woman. He's a single man. He's very handsome and a wonderful guy. It's natural you'd develop affection for one another."

"Oh, I don't think he has affection for me. Not like that."

Khrista shrugged. "I'm not sure. I don't want you to get your hopes up, but I don't know many men who spend as much time with a woman as he's been spending with you if he's not interested in some sort of way."

"So everyone already knows? I thought I was hiding it so well. That's it. I have to move. Good thing I didn't find an apartment yet. I'll stay somewhat nearby, but far enough that no one in this town will ever see my face again. You'll visit me there, won't you?" Daisy took a long swig of her cocktail, her eyes wide and her thinning eyebrows high.

Kaelyn reached out a loving hand to touch her grandmother's shoulder, and Khrista chuckled at her mother's dramatics.

Seeing the pained look on her mother's face, Khrista searched for words of reassurance.

"Of course, we'd go anywhere you are, right, Kaelyn? But that's not necessary. Nobody else knows. I promise I haven't heard any rumors, and believe me, it would get back to me if anybody wanted to talk about it."

Khrista crossed her fingers behind her back to cover for the lie. There was a time when she would have been privy to all the rumors, but since her own mess-ups, she had been somewhat on the outs with the community. The people who knew Khrista and loved her had welcomed her back into their loving embrace, but the ones who lived for gossip and enjoyed the drama of watching somebody fall from grace still gave her looks and whispered behind her back. But she wouldn't trouble her mother—or worse, her daughter—with that information. She was happy enough to ignore those people.

Daisy sighed and swirled her glass, watching the liquid slosh back and forth. "He really is such a nice man. Your father never treated me as nicely as Raf treats me."

"I say go for it," Kaelyn interjected. "Life's too short to not be as happy as you can be."

Daisy waved one shaking hand in front of her as if swatting a fly.

"I wouldn't even know how to let him know I have these feelings.

In my day and where I lived, the woman waited for the man to declare his intentions. Unless she was brash. And I've never been brash."

Kaelyn giggled. "Good thing that wasn't the case with me and Oliver. He pursued me first, but I had to make all the moves. He was too nervous. If I waited for him to get the courage to move things forward with me, there wouldn't be a Poppy." Kaelyn pressed her hands to her milk-swollen breasts. "Aww, I miss my little pumpkin."

Khrista needed to change the subject quickly before Kaelyn dissolved in a puddle of maternal tears. Alcohol would amplify that effect, and the last thing they needed was a sad new mom with a cocktail-induced buzz.

Khrista went back to teasing Daisy. "We just have to get you a good push-up bra. Then he'll get the hint."

"You stop that, young lady. A push-up bra won't do anything for these girls. They're too far past their prime. I need a crane to get them where they belong."

The women dissolved into laughter again. Daisy's humor shocked Khrista. This was not a discussion they'd ever had, and Khrista never knew her mother could be funny. It was strange and wonderful, and Khrista wondered how much more there was to her mother that she hadn't yet seen.

Kaelyn came to the rescue. "Okay, well, let's work on your flirtatious gaze. You've got to make eye contact with him, hold it for a few seconds, and then look away with a smile on your face. Let's practice."

Daisy batted her eyelashes, barely there and hard to see because they were nearly translucent and the patio light cast shadows, but she looked like she was having a seizure in her attempts to blink flirtatiously. Kaelyn guffawed and snorted, causing Khrista and Daisy to follow suit.

"Please, not like that. I think batting eyelashes is a thing of the past. Men today like you to be a little more direct," Kaelyn assured her.

"But Rafael isn't a man from today. He's from your grandmother's generation. He might enjoy a little eyelash batting."

Kaelyn held her ground. "Or it might lead to him calling 911."

Laughter again, and then Daisy started singing. Loudly and terribly off-key.

Khrista jumped when a high-pitched voice behind her interrupted their joyful play.

"Excuse me, would you mind keeping it down? I have a son who's trying to get to sleep."

Khrista turned around to face the familiar voice.

She recognized the intruder as a mother from her current class of preschoolers. Khrista rarely saw her because the nanny dropped off and picked up the child, but the woman was forever sending emails to the director complaining about clothing getting stained from the paint or mud or playdough or any other number of things. Khrista had sent notices home to explain what it meant if a child came home with messy clothing and how that was actually a positive thing, but this mother always responded by going straight back to the director to escalate the director's involvement. She seemed to have a particular vendetta against Khrista.

"Oh hi, Leann. I didn't know you and Will would be here. What a small world."

"A small island, anyway. We're having a staycation, and we wanted to get out of the house. You, as an educator—" Leann made air quotes around the word, "—should know how important it is to keep a child on their schedule. And we certainly didn't expect that in this family-friendly area, we'd have to contend with a bunch of drunks."

Khrista let the cannon Leann had lodged at her bounce right off the shield of armor she had forged since the whole town had found out about her drinking problem. She could handle criticism, and though she didn't like this woman's tone or her insinuation, Khrista was already walking on thin ice with the preschool director. She had been lucky to get her job back and didn't want to risk losing it over someone like this. Someone who didn't really know Khrista. Khrista needed to get through this moment, and she would hopefully never have to see this woman again.

"I'm sorry we disturbed you. We were just getting ready to go in for the night. Tell Will I said hello and that I look forward to seeing him in class soon."

Without a word, the snotty-faced woman stomped away.

Kaelyn didn't hide her annoyance at the interruption. "What does she have up her—"

"Come on. Let's just go in."

"It's like nine p.m. I feel like it's okay if we sit out here on the beach at the rental cottage Grandma is paying good money for. She can get her kid a white noise machine or something."

"It's all good. I should get you home to Poppy, anyway."

Khrista encouraged Daisy to drink a big glass of water and use the bathroom again while Kaelyn cleaned and packed up the cocktail-making station. Khrista then helped Daisy get ready for bed. Daisy's movements were stiffer than normal, and she doubled over, gripping her belly, before lifting her legs with Khrista's assistance.

"You okay? Is something hurting?"

"No, no. I'm not sick. There's nothing wrong with me. I'm happy!"

Khrista eyed her mother, suspicion darkening an otherwise bright night.

"You did a fine job with those drinks, Khrista. I'm proud of you." Her slurring voice trailed off as she snuggled into the pillow.

Tears prickled, and her sinuses ached. Her mother had never— not once—said she was proud of Khrista for anything.

Khrista brushed silver hair off Daisy's face. "Thank you, Mom. I'm proud of you, too."

Daisy nodded and closed her eyes.

Khrista wasn't sure about leaving her alone. She covered her mother with the blankets, kissed her on the cheek, and told her she'd drop off Kaelyn at home and come right back to spend the night with her. Daisy's face brightened in a way Kaelyn had never seen before.

The drive back to Kaelyn's house was quiet, but not in a bad or awkward way. They listened to the music on the playlist Khrista had put together, but neither of them had enough energy to bop in their seats.

Before getting out of the car, Kaelyn paused with her hand on the door handle. "Thanks so much, Mom. This was a lot of fun. I think you were right—I needed this."

"I think we all did, baby girl. Now get on in to your baby girl. I'm sure she missed her mama something awful."

Something passed over Kaelyn's face before she retreated. Doubt? No, that couldn't be. Of course Kaelyn knew her baby would be glad to see her mommy. There was no reason to think otherwise.

Khrista waited until her daughter had safely crossed her threshold and then headed back to Daisy's place. Once parked, she messaged Matt to let him know she'd be staying with her mother for the night. He filled her in on the great time he was having in Boston and said he'd see her in the morning.

After tiptoeing through a nighttime bathroom routine, Khrista climbed into bed with her mom. Though Khrista had assumed her mother was sound asleep, Daisy's raspy voice startled her.

"I'm scared of what it might mean if I open up to Raf or let him know. Maybe it's not worth the risk of losing him."

Something about her voice sounding so vulnerable caused an ache in Khrista's chest. As hard as Khrista's life had been, she had escaped Harold when she reached adulthood and Kaelyn's father once he turned abusive. It had taken time for Khrista to heal those old wounds, but her mother had been trapped and at the mercy of a cruel man for decade after decade.

Khrista desperately yearned for her mother to fall in love. With a good guy, this time. Like Raf. To have the second chance that Khrista had been lucky enough to get with Matt. To know the love of a good man.

"Mom, on the off chance that he's not interested, he won't turn away your friendship. He's a good guy. If he's not looking for a partner, he'll be really nice and let you know. But he'd still be your friend. Don't worry about things being awkward."

Khrista thought Daisy fell asleep because she was silent for so long.

"Even worse, though."

Khrista leaned forward, unsure if her mother had continued the thought. Her voice had grown so faint—almost eerie.

"Even worse will be if he does like me the way I like him. Because liking a man and giving him your loyalty leads to him hurting you. I know it's not good to give a man that kind of power. I loved your father once. And he killed my spirit. I don't think I can go through that again."

"Mom. Rafael isn't Harold. He had a wonderful marriage. He cherished his wife, and she never had a major complaint about him for as long as I knew them. I know you had an unhappy marriage, but it's never too late for a second chance. If you want to move forward with Rafael and if he feels the same, which I suspect he does, it will be amazing. You deserve a second chance, and so does he."

The idea of her mom and her surrogate father-figure making a go of a relationship gave Khrista the same feeling that slipping into fuzzy socks in front of a fireplace invoked. Warm, toasty, comforting, and as if the combination was predestined.

"Rafael suffered watching his wife get so sick and losing her so young. It would be awesome for him to have someone to grow old with. It would be nice for you, too, Mom. You deserve a shot at happiness."

The only sign that Daisy had heard the advice was a slight sniffle.

"Mom, don't cry. It's the alcohol making you feel this way. This is a good thing. Something to be excited about."

"I've never imagined myself being cherished."

"Imagine how wonderful it'll feel."

"But what if..."

"What if what, Mom?"

"What if it was me all along?"

"What do you mean?" Khrista suspected she knew—she herself had found ways to absorb the blame for things she hadn't caused— but now was not the time for assumptions.

"What if I'm the one who caused your father to turn into the monster he became? And what if, heaven forbid, I do the same to Rafael?"

KAELYN

The thing Kaelyn loved most about Sunday mornings when she was a kid was waking up early to watch cartoons and eating cereal straight out of the box before her mother dragged herself out of bed—if she dragged herself out of bed.

The thing she loved most about *this* Sunday morning was Oliver kissing her softly on the cheek and leaving a fresh pot of tea on the nightstand beside her bed.

She laid there for a while, a smile engulfing her face as she listened to her husband singing softly to their daughter down the hall. The jingle of a rattle shaking had never brought so much joy. The ability to stretch out in the bed, knowing she could fall back to sleep if she wanted to, was sheer ecstasy.

Better even than Cap'n Crunch.

The sweet sound of Poppy cooing up a storm to her daddy brought a warm sensation to Kaelyn's chest and belly. Kaelyn didn't blame Poppy for wanting to impress him. Hadn't Kaelyn always been that way, too? Oliver was the kind of man who could make any girl go gaga.

Kaelyn sat up in her bed and poured herself tea from the pot. It smelled like a tropical chai blend she loved, but that had been out of stock at the tearoom for ages. He must've stopped on the way home to pick up some of the new batch.

Oliver always thought of everything.

Kaelyn held the teacup between her two hands and continued to listen as he made silly noises, eliciting the most melodic of laughter from their baby.

She couldn't take it anymore. She needed to be a part of their play.

Kaelyn kicked off the covers and slipped her feet into the slippers she left beside her bed. The slipper habit had come from Oliver and his mother, who were never without their own raggedy pairs of slippers. After years of making fun of him, she now found the act rather endearing. Her mother-in-law had given her a pair of slippers that matched Oliver's for Christmas one year, and though she and Oliver had the private joke between them, eventually the coziness of slipping into said slippers overrode her pride at having been wrong.

She shuffled down the hallway and found Oliver leaning over Poppy on the floor, preparing to blow raspberries on her belly once again. Poppy kicked her legs and waved her arms joyously on her giraffe quilt, anticipation vibrating through her entire body. Kaelyn had heard her laugh several times, but not like this. This was the full-bodied kind of laughter Kaelyn always imagined when she thought of babies.

Of course Oliver could elicit it. He was the better parent.

She sank to her knees beside Oliver and wrapped an arm around him while he played with the baby. He glanced at Kaelyn with a grin and blew a kiss to her before delivering another raspberry to the baby's belly.

"Excuse me, my precious Poppy Princess, but Queen Kaelyn, also known as your marvelous Mummy, needs some attention, too."

"Don't stop. I came in because you two are irresistible. Though I do appreciate your alliteration."

He brought his warm, smiling lips to hers, and she closed her eyes and allowed herself to be swept away in the familiar and intoxicating scent of him. Of the comfort he delivered so effortlessly.

"You don't know how much I've missed you," he said, then got up on his knees and turned to face her fully, pulling her closer.

Her breasts ached from the milk that gathered there. She must have missed the morning feeding—she assumed Oliver got home and gave the baby a bottle. Kaelyn needed to either nurse or pump, and since Poppy was staring at her father with her little face scrunched up because she so desperately wanted his attention, Kaelyn chose the latter. The baby wanted her father, and he didn't have a single bit of anxiety in his body the way Kaelyn always did. It was probably her fault Poppy was so cranky when they were alone together.

Kaelyn had always suspected she might fail as a mother.

Having her instincts validated gave her a strange sense of solace. It was okay. Really.

Poppy had Oliver. The best man on the planet, and the kind of father every child should have.

Kaelyn may not be doing as well at the new mom thing as she had hoped, but the one thing she excelled at was producing vast quantities of milk. She had often heard about women struggling to establish their milk supply, but she had the opposite problem. Even when she was home full-time with Poppy and Oliver was away, Kaelyn had stockpiled a freezer full of labeled baggies of milk. They would never run out. So much so that she had considered donating to a milk bank, but she held off just in case Poppy needed them.

"She wants you to keep playing. I'm going to go—" Kaelyn's throat closed around her words and she gestured toward the door, quickly turning away so he wouldn't see the tears.

Why was she always crying so much? Why did everything have to be so hard?

Kaelyn heard Oliver coming after her, but she locked herself in their bedroom and tried to compose herself enough to tell him she preferred her privacy while pumping.

"Okay, love," he said from the other side of the door. "That's new, but I'll respect it. I'll give Poppy a bottle and then we'll make you a scrumptious breakfast."

Kaelyn bit her lip to keep the sobs inside.

Being a new mom was supposed to fulfill her every fantasy. Though Poppy's conception had been unplanned, she and Oliver had celebrated throughout the entire pregnancy. She had wanted kids relatively young, and they had been in a financial position to do it. Everything was supposed to be perfect.

And everything was perfect.

Except her. Except her mothering skills.

Kaelyn wiped the tears away and concentrated on the ho-hum motor on the pump and the rapidly filling bottles.

Everything would be okay. Not everyone had to be close to both parents, right? She could be a loving mom and accept that Poppy would always love her father more. And her grandparents, of course. And Kaelyn would watch from a distance and be grateful her daughter had this beautiful, glorious life to live.

Kaelyn could do "good mom" things in the background. Regardless of anything else that may happen, Kaelyn would love her daughter unconditionally. She would cheer her on in everything she did, even if her cheers came from the sidelines.

Kaelyn had once thought self-pity would consume her if she birthed a child who didn't like her, but that's not what happened. She could accept what she couldn't change.

Just as the bottles filled to the brim, and the flow slowed, Kaelyn received an incoming text.

She finished putting herself away, capped the bottles so she could bring them downstairs to pour them into the storage bags, which she would carefully label with the dates before setting them in the freezer, and then checked her phone.

Kaelyn hadn't kept in touch with her best friend from her Old Castle school days, Sienna, other than through social media, so receiving a text from her was a welcome surprise. They had never had a falling out or anything. They simply went in different directions and fell out of touch over the years. Kaelyn had noticed her friend had dropped off social media lately, and she'd wondered how Sienna was doing.

Kaelyn responded right away. They chit-chatted back and forth for a few moments, with Sienna asking how life with the new baby was going.

Kaelyn typed out the first response that came to her.

"Exhausting. Exhilarating. Euphoric. The most beautiful thing in the world. The most frustrating thing in the world. I love her with every fiber of my being, but is it wrong that I also kind of miss the life I had before? And sleep? My goodness, what I wouldn't give for a full night of sleep."

The words swam in front of her, and shame poured hot oil over her entire body.

She deleted her text. All except the one word.

"Euphoric."

She sent it without considering another change and squeezed her eyes shut at the horror of the words that had so easily fallen out of her.

Almost immediately, a photo text came in from Sienna. A photo of Sienna holding a newborn, cheek to cheek.

"Oh my goodness, is she yours?!"

"Yes! Surprise!"

"I had no idea you were pregnant. I'm so excited for you! Tell me everything."

While awaiting her response, Kaelyn zoomed in on her friend's picture. No exhausted shadows under her eyes. No sign of a fake smile. Her baby's smile was big and wide, and they looked very much bonded to one another.

Kaelyn hadn't been able to get a decent selfie of her and the baby. She hated the way she looked in every single picture, and no filter could erase the frustration and fatigue from Kaelyn's face. Not to mention, Poppy wasn't crazy about being photographed, especially if Kaelyn tried to hold her cheek to cheek.

The next message was a long paragraph gushing about how glorious it was to be a new mom. Sienna went on and on about the joys of spending every moment watching her baby's little toes grow, which Kaelyn found weird. It wasn't as if you could see toes grow. Luckily, Sienna finished the text with a call to action Kaelyn could accept without having to respond to the rest of it.

She asked if she could visit.

Kaelyn responded right away. "I'd love to see you! You're welcome anytime!"

Sienna replied immediately, asking if this week was good.

Kaelyn hesitated. The idea of having company drained her. But hadn't she just said her friend was welcome anytime? It would be rude to tell her no, so she made an invitation for dinner and told her she was pretty open and Sienna could take her pick of nights. Just her luck... Sienna chose the earlier part of the week.

Great. Kaelyn just got her husband back, and now she'd have to share him.

Oliver would make her feel better about it. He'd probably offer to cook them up something delicious, and Kaelyn could impress Sienna with the amazing husband she had landed. She forgot to ask if Sienna would bring her husband or boyfriend and hadn't even asked about the father of her baby at all. She had grown so disconnected— from everyone, really, but especially from her friends.

Memories assaulted her of all the times they had shared through their school years—bonding over their red hair and the way their classmates had picked on both of them for this trait. The bullying they'd endured had driven them closer, and at one point, Sienna had been the most important person in Kaelyn's life.

Oliver had always found it weird that people tormented her for the feature he loved the most, but Kaelyn had grown to understand that everyone had something they got picked on about. Still, having a twin soul in middle school had been life-saving. In high school, Sienna and Kaelyn had been inseparable, until Kaelyn's mother tore them apart by moving away. But even then, they had kept in close contact and shared every little secret with one another. Sienna was the one who knew everything about Kaelyn's life, her past, her secrets.

In some ways, Sienna knew her better than Oliver did. He only got a glimpse of Kaelyn's past filtered through the lens of a grown woman talking about her childhood, and didn't live through it alongside her.

Sienna had been there.

Kaelyn could muster up the strength to make a darn dinner for her friend after all they had been through together.

Besides, wouldn't it be nice for Poppy to have a little friend? Maybe seeing the smiling face of Sienna's little cutie would inspire Poppy to feel better, too.

Oliver would be thrilled at the prospect of company. He definitely wore the extrovert pants in their relationship.

When Kaelyn rejoined her family, the baby was fast asleep in his arms, milk-drunk and more relaxed than she had seen her.

Oliver's face drained of all color when he looked up at Kaelyn, and a pit in her stomach warned her something was wrong.

"Did someone die?"

She wanted to smack herself on the head for that question, but it was the first thing that came to mind with the grave look he wore.

"No, no, love. Not that dire."

Kaelyn's legs trembled as Oliver got up to place the baby in her vibrating bouncy seat. He carefully tucked a beanbag caterpillar beside Poppy so she could feel as if she was still being held. He switched the seat on to vibrate, and the rush of the motor traveled through the floor and tickled Kaelyn's feet, grounding her to the room and the moment and keeping her mind from splitting in a kaleidoscope of crazy assumptions about what could be wrong.

He was too calm for anything truly terrible. But would he spit it out already?

She'd never considered herself an anxious person, but everything had her on edge these days. She despised the sensation of falling off the edge of the world.

Oliver crossed over to her and took her into his arms, but Kaelyn remained stiff.

His lips pressed against the top of her head, and his breath warmed her scalp. Holding her like this normally calmed and soothed all her jagged edges, but right now, Kaelyn's scalp stung like a million pins were poking into her to see how much more she could take before popping. Before tarnished confetti would fall out of her and land in another mess she'd have to clean off the floor.

"Oliver, you're making me anxious. What's wrong? Is it your mom?"

"No, no. Of course not. She went into town to give us time alone." He pulled away enough to look her in the eye, but kept his arms wrapped around her. "I'm sorry, love."

"Tell me."

"I have to go back to LA."

Dread morphed into a lead ball, anchoring her to the spot. Part of her wanted to run. Part of her wanted to demand he take the baby with him since Poppy liked him better anyway and he seemed to love this whole parenting thing. A bigger part of her wanted to scream and stomp her foot and throw an epic tantrum that only two-year-olds could get away with.

But she didn't do any of that. Kaelyn closed her eyes, gulped, counted to three, and opened her eyes again.

Normally, she would make herself smile.

Today there was no smile to be found.

"When?"

"First thing tomorrow morning."

Kaelyn wriggled away from his touch, and her quick action elicited a sharp intake of breath from him.

She spun toward Oliver, letting him see the anguish and anger and agitation on her face. "I just got you back! Why are they taking you again? Don't they know you have a baby? And a wife?"

"I know. Kaelyn, I tried to explain that to them, but things aren't good at the company right now and we all need to do our part. I'm so sorry, love. Mum will be here with you, and when I get back, I swear I'll spoil you rotten."

"I don't need to be spoiled rotten. I need my husband. Poppy needs her father."

Kaelyn had never burned with such anger.

She had especially never directed such fury at him.

But rage threatened to drive flames from her fingers, and if she didn't calm herself, her hair would spontaneously combust.

Hurt etched lines in his face she had never seen before. Oliver didn't deserve her wrath, but she couldn't bring herself to stop.

Oliver was strong enough to handle her, but he still winced as she lashed out. She wanted to stop. She didn't want to take this out on him. And yet, Kaelyn no longer felt in control of her mind or her mouth as she laid into him. "I can't believe you're doing this. We agreed we would move here. I kind of thought that meant we were both moving here."

"Love, you're not being fair."

"I'm not being fair? You think it's fair for me to be here alone with Poppy while you're..."

He quirked a brow and smiled.

"While I'm three thousand miles away from the ones I love the most, working in a cramped cubicle instead of from the beach view office in my new home?"

Kaelyn both loved and hated how easy it was for him to tame her. Her shoulders slumped as he drew her into his arms again, the scent of his freshly washed sweater engulfing her nostrils and soothing her rage away.

Deflated, she mumbled into his shoulder, "I'm sorry I'm such a beast. I know it's not your fault."

"You're the most beautiful beast I've ever seen." Oliver kissed the top of her head all over, making a trail over her temple and then to her cheek before finally capturing her mouth. "You know I want to be here, right?"

"I know. I'm just so frustrated. And tired."

"I don't have to leave until the morning. Why don't you take the rest of the day off? Spend the entire time in bed. I'll bring meals to you so you don't have to lift a finger."

Kaelyn accepted Oliver's offer, excited about the idea of living so luxuriously like a sloth.

"Is there an end in sight to this in-between work thing? Are they gonna demand you come there every single week forever and ever?"

"I'm hoping we're at the tail end of things. They agreed to my terms when I agreed to stay on with them, and if I can't transition to a full remote position soon, I'll find a job in Boston. I don't like this any more than you do, love. You know how hard it is to be away from these ears?" Oliver kissed the tops of each of her ears and then nibbled gently on her lobes. "And this face." Butterfly kisses across each of her cheeks before rubbing his nose against hers. "And this nose."

"I miss you so much when you're gone."

"I miss you more. And our angelic baby girl. But I promise this is temporary. I promise I'm doing everything I can to make this work. If I never see the inside of another airplane again..."

"Don't say that. We still need to plan our European tour for our fifth anniversary."

Oliver's smile consumed his cheeks as much as he consumed her heart.

"I'll be ready to climb aboard for that. Counting down the days, actually."

Kaelyn nuzzled into his neck and breathed him in deeply. She wanted to memorize the smell of him so that each night he was away she could call it up in her memory banks to feel him close to her again.

"You're going to miss out on meeting my friend Sienna."

"What? When will she be here?"

"Day after tomorrow. She's coming for dinner." Kaelyn left out how she had fantasized about him volunteering to make the meal. "I don't know if I should make something or just order pizza."

"Pizza. For sure. Everyone likes pizza. Simple crowd-pleaser."

Oliver swept her up into his arms and carried her upstairs to their room.

"We can't leave Poppy down there." Kaelyn squealed as he tossed her on the bed. "By herself?"

"Poppy will need to understand that Mummy and Daddy need alone time sometimes."

Kaelyn accepted his offer of a massage and promptly fell asleep, and when she awakened, she found that Oliver had kept his promise and left lunch on the table next to her bed.

6

DAISY

aisy had to admit that having her friends at the house made her feel fresher than the broccoli and kale she had picked up from the local market—and those veggies came from the owner's greenhouse, so they were particularly fresh. Everything had gone so smoothly since her friends' arrival half an hour before. They had all been free with joyful greetings and reassuring words as they offered gentle comfort to Edith after the loss of her beloved husband.

During a lull in the conversation, while her friends filled their snack plates from the vegetable and dip platter Daisy had placed on the coffee table, she grew more aware of the tension between her and Florence. Though they had greeted one another like nothing had happened, Daisy couldn't deny that the things left unspoken shouted through the silence.

Unable to bear it, Daisy jumped up from the sofa. "I'll make us tea."

She didn't wait for anyone to approve or object.

The chatter in the living room resumed and provided background noise as she worked in the kitchen, but Daisy needed a few minutes alone to quell the urgent pattering in her chest. She had to find the strength to address the fight she and Florence had back in California. She had to find a way to fix things. Only then would she fully relax into this adventure.

As Daisy removed the tea infuser from the kettle, Florence popped in, saying, "Knock, knock" as she entered. Alice and Edith remained in the living room.

Sweat gathered under Daisy's arms, and yet an icy chill cascaded over her skin. Her hands shook as she put the cover back on the teakettle.

"Need some help in here?" Florence, tall, thin, and graceful, asked, her hands buried deep in her pockets and her shoulders up near her ears. Daisy had rarely seen her friend looking uncertain, but she looked sheepish and uncomfortable, mirroring the way Daisy herself felt.

"I think I have everything all set. If you want to put out some crackers, I'll slice the cheese."

Florence washed her hands and then opened the box of crackers and laid them out neatly on a tray she found in a cabinet, her hands trembling slightly.

"Sounds like things turned out well with your family." Florence stole a glance at Daisy before looking back at the tray.

"I'm so happy with how things are going."

Clearing her throat, Daisy tossed down the cheese slicer and turned to her friend. She focused on the kindness around Florence's eyes and the nervous way her friend chewed on her lower lip. Fixing things would be good for both of them.

Daisy took a deep breath to steady her rising blood pressure.

"But Florence, you were right. I shouldn't have done what I did. After you left, I realized you were right about everything. I'd always been so lost in my own troubles that I didn't think about how my actions and choices impacted everybody else. You set me straight."

Florence dropped the crackers and pivoted to face Daisy. Tears gathered at the corners of her eyes and her face reddened. She rested a hand over her stomach and sucked in already hollowed cheeks.

As if steadying herself, Florence released a long breath and said,

"I shouldn't have freaked out on you the way I did. It wasn't right. You were only doing what you thought you needed to do to help your family get back together. I had too much of my own ego and my own unresolved past tied up in that situation. As much as I thought we had put things behind us, there was still too much left unsaid. I don't want these unresolved issues hanging between us anymore. Life is too danged short."

Though Daisy had never been much of a hugger, the urge to open her arms to Florence was strong. But Florence had never been touchy-feely either, so Daisy hesitated.

"Florence, I treasure your friendship. I can't tell you how wonderful it feels to have our group of friends together again. Let's not let anything get between us."

"Agreed." Florence extended her arms. "We probably should hug it out."

Daisy smiled and hugged her friend, surprised at how much lighter she felt.

When they drew apart, Florence brushed a tear away with the back of her hand, staring at the ceiling as if embarrassed by the show of emotion. "Enough of this mushy stuff. Let's get the refreshments out to the girls before they wonder what's going on in here."

"I'm surprised they haven't come looking for us yet. You know how Alice can't cope without her tea."

Florence delivered the cheese and crackers while Daisy carried the teapot on a tray with the creamer, sweetener packets, and a tiny jar of honey. She had brought a tea set she loved for this occasion— one she had stumbled upon at the local thrift store—in case the cottage didn't have something adequate to present Clarice's tea in. Daisy had grown rather addicted to Clarice's special blends and wouldn't want to settle for a lesser option while her friends visited, and yet it was strange thinking about putting Clarice's sophisticated tea in anything other than a beautiful vessel.

And while perhaps it had been silly to purchase a tea set when Daisy didn't have a home of her own, Clarice had agreed it was a wise decision. Daisy had her priorities lined up, that was for certain, and the part of her that hadn't been able to entertain anyone dear to her for too many years thrilled at the idea of impressing her friends.

How many times in the early days of her marriage had she dreamed of hosting a tea party? Smiling, she set the tray on the coffee table, adjusting the veggie tray to make room.

"Ooh, fancy tea time, I see," Alice remarked. "Lovely. You didn't need to go to all this trouble for us."

"Nonsense," Daisy said. "I'm thrilled to host my first tea party. I guess what they say is true—you're never too old to have your dreams come true."

The ladies spent the next hour chatting and catching up, shedding tears as Edith filled them in on the details of Peter's last days and how they had made them the most special times they could.

"I know we always talk about death as though it's the worst thing, but having experienced the final days with Peter... It was actually... quite nice." Edith dabbed at her tears with a napkin. "I never thought I'd be able to let go, but he looked more relaxed than he had in ages. He smiled at me and reached for my hand and told me how much he had loved our time together, but that he looked forward to spending eternity on the other side. He'd wait for me there, and he expected me to continue living the life I deserved."

"Oh, honey." Alice brushed a reassuring hand over Edith's bicep.

Edith shook her head and then nodded, her freshly dyed hair bobbing around her face. "It really was a beautiful thing. I guarded those last days greedily, and the kids all came over for a last goodbye the morning before he passed. But he knew it was his time, and he asked for it to be just him and me for the rest of the time."

Tears traveled over her cheeks, but she didn't seem to notice.

"I was devastated—naturally I was sad to lose the love of my life. But I also experienced a joyful lightness in some odd way. I never felt burdened by him—not ever. I can't explain it, but there was this magical warmth that ran through me when he took his final breath. And it was eerie, too, because it had been raining all week, but right when he passed, a stream of sunlight fell into the room."

"Sounds beautiful," Alice said in awe.

Daisy sat in silence. Her experience hadn't been so beautiful or relatable when her husband had passed. She had felt lighter, she supposed, but more from being freed of the shackles than relief that he wouldn't suffer anymore.

She had, in fact, *wished* he had suffered.

But that was the past, and life was too short to focus on the bad.

Harold's passing had led her to much better things. Reunification with her daughter and granddaughter. The opportunity to know her beautiful great-granddaughter.

And this.

Friendships.

Laughter.

Love.

Florence bounced out of her chair with an energy that continuously surprised Daisy, who relied on regular doses of anti-inflammatories to get herself out of bed in the morning, but Florence bandied about like a teenager high on caffeine.

"Another pot of tea?" Florence asked, already heading into the kitchen.

The ladies nodded their agreement, and Daisy followed Florence into the kitchen to help, reassuring Alice that they didn't need help and with her recent double hip replacement, she should accept their desire to bring things to her.Once they had settled back into their spots, fresh tea in hand, they all laughed as Florence regaled them with tales of her impromptu trip to Greece and the flings she had while over there.

"A fling? At our age?" Alice didn't hide her shock, which made the rest of them dissolve into fits of giggles.

Really. Giggles. At their age. And yet, Daisy couldn't seem to stop.

"Flings, Alice. Plural," Daisy pointed out, adoring the shock on her friend's naïve face. After living with Florence in Los Angeles, she had learned to overcome some of the shock.

Florence shrugged and stirred honey into her tea.

"You know what they say. You're only as old as you feel. And there are plenty of men eager to have an experienced woman."

"I gave up on wanting any of that about thirty years ago," Alice said. She'd had a relatively happy marriage for twenty-five years until her husband decided he wasn't in love with her anymore and left her and everything they'd built together behind. Neither she nor their two grown children had heard from him since.

"Wait," Florence said. "You've had... relations... since your husband, right?"

Alice sipped her tea and told Florence she had a dirty mind. "I don't need... that. I have hobbies."

Daisy nearly choked on the bite of cookie in her mouth, not wanting to tell them exactly how long it had been since she had wanted anything to do with the physical acts of marriage. But then she thought of Rafael and wondered if her mind had changed.

Nonsense. All schoolgirl nonsense. Daisy had never been treated well by a man, and spending time with a man who went out of his way to show kindness sowed clouds of confusion. That was all.

"Tell us about the museums you went to. What was the architecture like there? And did you spend a lot of time at the beach?" Daisy tried to get the conversation off the one that made her so uncomfortable.

Florence knew she was skirting the issues that no one other than Florence enjoyed talking about. Daisy could see it in the jovial tilt of Florence's head as she studied Daisy with a smirk. But Florence took pity on her friend and changed the subject, which helped Daisy's palms stop sweating and her shoulders to relax.

Truthfully, Daisy wanted to hear more about Florence's adventures, especially since she'd had to call off her own international plans. If her dream of traveling abroad couldn't come true, Daisy would happily live vicariously through her friends and their stories.

Florence danced in her seat, wiggling her shoulders and shifting her knees from side to side. "I brought us special mud masks I bought in Greece. Made from the hidden clay on the island of Corfu. The locals raved about it. It's considered powerful. And you can only buy these particular masks from a tiny local market, hidden from the masses."

"Woo, facials!" Edith exclaimed, clapping her hands together. "I've been meaning to do something about this skin. I haven't had a facial in too many years to count."

Daisy and Alice cleared the tea and the trays of snack foods from the coffee table while Florence gathered everything they'd need for their spa treatment.

Once they'd all slathered the thick, muddy substance onto their tired skin, age slipped out of Daisy's body and she jolted right back to her youth.

Daisy vocalized the time jump. "Remember when we used to do things like this when we were girls? Isn't it funny how we revert to those days when we get together?"

Alice's head bobbed. "Almost makes me think if we didn't lose touch, we would've just stayed young."

Florence snapped her fingers in the air. "Speak for yourself, honey. I haven't aged a day."

They dissolved into laughter once again, and Florence reached into her bag and extracted a bottle of Moscato and plastic champagne glasses.

"I brought these along because I wasn't sure a little cabin would have the right supplies."

"Your preparedness is admirable." Daisy decided not to offer the real glasses since Florence had already set the plastic flutes in a line on the table.

Florence popped the cork open like an expert and poured the bubbly wine into each of their flutes. They raised the cups and clinked them together, and Daisy felt compelled to make a toast.

"To the Quad. The fabulous four for whom time cannot separate or diminish. Though we've gone our separate ways over the years, fate has led us back together when we needed each other the most. May neither time nor distance separate us again."

"Cheers!"

As they sipped their bubbly, a gentle knock on the front door had them all turning in that direction just as the door swung open. Daisy's heart skipped as Raf entered, carrying a small stack of pizza boxes. The aroma of the pizza quickly filled the small room, and the sight of that man filled her soul and her imagination.

"Rafael, I didn't know you were coming!" Daisy exclaimed, panicking when she remembered the mud smeared across her face.

Raf hesitated in the doorway. "I, uh, tried the door to spare you having to open it for me. I thought you girls might be hungry."

Florence held her plastic champagne glass in front of her face and leaned toward Daisy. In a loud whisper, she said, "You didn't tell us you had a boyfriend."

Daisy shook her head frantically, praying Rafael didn't hear Florence's words. The whisper had sounded like a booming drum solo in a parade, but then again, maybe that was just Daisy's blasted heart as it flipped in her chest.

"He's not my boyfriend," she murmured. "I'll tell you about him later." She turned back to Rafael. "How thoughtful of you to bring us dinner. We haven't even started planning our next meal, so thank you for sparing us having to decide."

The other ladies added their thanks as Rafael tentatively stepped into the room.

Daisy introduced everyone. Her skin itched to be rid of the mud mask. Had she ever been more humiliated? She pretended the answer to that question wasn't so painfully obvious.

"Please excuse our monster faces. These are the things ladies have to do, you know," Edith teased.

"I've always known you women were part alien," Rafael teased back, but when he looked at Daisy, he winked and her pulse accelerated. The drums were back, blaring in her ears as they played at a volume that threatened her eardrums and should have been deemed illegal. She'd have to talk to her cardiologist after all the crazy flipping her heart had done today.

As if in slow motion, Daisy watched Florence sway her hips on her way over to Rafael. She flirted so naturally as she invited him to stay and eat the pizza, unbothered by her mud-smeared face. He accepted the invitation when all the other ladies jumped in to convince him as well. Daisy hadn't joined the chorus. She couldn't.

Her mouth had dried up and her tongue lay fallow in her mouth. Had she become mute?

Daisy could barely register the chatter of her friends as they all rushed to the bathroom together, taking turns at the sink to scrub their faces clean. Daisy followed along mindlessly, wishing she hadn't told Rafael where she'd be. Wishing the embarrassment could wash away the pain striking her in the gut. She dug in her bathroom tote for her medicine and gulped down two pills. When Alice questioned her, she lied. "Just a little headache."

Florence applied lipstick and smiled at herself in the mirror before pointing out that Daisy still had some of her clay mask near her hairline. Daisy swiped at the goop. She could never compete with a woman like Florence. Full of confidence and bold as a wild boar.

Back in the living area, the three women stumbled over themselves to set out paper plates and napkins and pour lemon seltzer water into cups as Daisy sat, dumbfounded. Florence topped off their seltzer water with a dash of gin in each cup. Daisy guzzled it down before having a piece of pizza, trying to ignore Rafael's expression of surprise.

What did his surprise mean? Was she embarrassing herself? Did she care?

This wasn't good. Daisy struggled to pretend it didn't matter to her that Florence kept touching Rafael. A casual touch on his bicep here and a gentle shoulder bump there and then what Florence probably meant to look like an accidental grasp of hand over hand as they each reached for the pizza box.

Daisy didn't dare look at Raf. She didn't want to see him react to Florence the way men always did. He wasn't hers to lose, but it didn't make the pain of him developing an attraction to Daisy's friend any lighter or easier to bear.

Daisy poured herself another cup, filling the cup more with gin than with seltzer and knowing she'd probably regret it. Too bad. She needed the relief the numbing of the alcohol would bring. She had never been a drinker, but this occasion called for something stronger than seltzer.

Daisy mumbled that she'd be right back. Thankfully, no one asked what she was doing, because her mind blanked and all she could think was that she needed space. And quiet. And to escape Rafael's penetrating gaze.

She gripped the wall on her way into the kitchen, but only for a moment when she thought she would fall. Wasn't Daisy's fault the floor moved...

"Daisy, darling, it doesn't look like you need that extra drink."

She wasn't sure if it was Edith or Alice who said it because all their voices blended together, colored only by the laughter that ensued as she stood still to gather her wits.

One foot in front of the other.

She shoved a handful of M&Ms into her mouth when she made her way into the kitchen, remembering what Kaelyn had told her about keeping a full belly when consuming alcohol to diminish some of the effects of the potent stuff. Daisy knew she had made a mistake in drinking so much, but hoped she could undo it if she guzzled down a big ole glass of plain water.

A large hand on her back had her spitting the gulp of water into the sink in alarm.

"I didn't mean to frighten you," Rafael said. "I'm worried about you. You seem... Different."

She shrugged out of his reach, branded by the touch of his hands on her back. This morning, that touch would have exhilarated her. Now it filled her with a sense of existential doom. Of time repeating itself in a loop, and of being confronted by the same mistakes over and over.

This time, she'd get it right. This time, her friendship would come before an attraction to a man she didn't need.

Daisy never wanted it to be said that she hadn't learned from her mistakes.

Florence wanted him. He probably wanted Florence. Daisy would never interfere with that.

Still, she didn't like the betrayal in his eyes that she glimpsed right before she turned away.

"Can I get you something? Are you feeling—"

"I'm fine," Daisy snapped, instantly regretting the tone and yet steeling her spine to stay strong.

"Okay, okay." He raised his hands in surrender, backing away as if afraid she'd lash out at him.

"I came in here for a minute of alone time." She hoped that though her voice was shaky, he would hear the message loud and clear.

"My apologies. I wanted to make sure you're okay, but I can see you're able to handle yourself just fine."

Daisy closed her eyes against the swell of tears that threatened as Raf walked out of the tiled room, his footsteps hammering away at her.

Had she believed she could deserve a second chance at anything? Convinced herself she deserved it? Had she told herself it was in the cards for her?

Nothing made her happier than having her friendships again. That's what she needed to focus on. And if her soul shattered, at least she'd have her girlfriends to stitch it back together.

7

───────────

KHRISTA

The town couldn't keep secrets from Clarice for long, so it was no surprise when Clarice confronted Khrista about the fundraiser. Khrista stood at the counter of the tearoom and convinced Clarice that the fundraiser was for the Kit-TEA Comfort Rescue, but Khrista hoped that knowing there would be an influx of cash reassured Clarice she'd be able to fix her leaking roof. Even if that detail needed to remain unspoken.

As Khrista shared details, Clarice expressed concern about Khrista putting herself in jeopardy. "I can't help but worry about you planning a cocktail party while still recovering from your own illness. Won't the temptation be too strong? Your sobriety is still in its infancy."

"Clarice, I'll never do anything to damage the new life I'm lucky enough to have."

"Pinky promise?"

Khrista grinned and extended a pinky. "Pinky promise."

"And if it starts to feel like too much?" Clarice pursued her caring line of questions.

"I'll reach out to my support system. I promise. Besides, we're planning it so quickly that there won't be time for me to slip."

"We need to protect that sparkle of yours, Khrista. Though I know you don't always see it, everyone else does. And sometimes people want to be warmed by it, and other times people want to consume it for themselves. Be mindful."

Sparkle? Khrista?

Clarice leaned on the counter in the most peculiar way, twisting and contorting and forcing a bright, strange smile on her face. As she straightened, a tiny little—*goat head?*—popped up from behind her. Khrista studied Clarice quizzically as Clarice pushed the—*goat?*—down and out of sight.

Was there really a goat in the tearoom?

"Um, Clarice? Did I just see a…"

"Hmm?" Clarice turned away to retrieve the tea. "Why don't you go on and sit and I'll bring your things to you?"

"Clarice, do you have a goat back there?"

"It's not a goat. Now hush. I'd never do anything to risk having the board of health in here. Now off with you. I'll be over in a minute."

Khrista had questions. So many questions. But Clarice brought the tea and took a seat across from her and clearly had no intention of explaining what Khrista had witnessed.

Clarice poured the tea and slid the clotted cream across the table for Khrista to smother her scone.

"You spoil me."

Clarice stuck her tongue out. "You're putting all these hours into planning a huge fundraiser. The least I can do is give you free tea and a scone. Besides, and don't take this the wrong way, but you've been looking a little—tired—lately. Anything going on?"

Khrista didn't believe in magic or anything, but sometimes she thought Clarice had a sixth sense.

Khrista stared at her scone as she broke off a piece, picking up the crumbs with one hand while lifting the piece she had torn off with the other. She brought it to her lips and sighed at the deliciousness of the buttery treat.

Clarice prodded. "You know you can tell me anything."

"I know." Khrista inhaled deeply and decided to go for it. Keeping secrets was hard, and she hadn't wanted to worry anybody else. Besides, Clarice could set her mind at ease and tell her she was overthinking things. "Nothing's wrong with me, but I'm worried about everyone. I'm worried that my mother isn't feeling well, and if she's not mentioning it to me, it must be really bad, right? I'm worried about Kaelyn. She always seems so tired and sad, more than typical for a new mom. I wish I knew how to help."

Clarice's face immediately crumpled into one of empathy. "Oh dear, I knew something was up. You haven't been yourself. You've got the weight of the world on your shoulders, and I guarantee you haven't been taking time for yourself."

Khrista looked away. Worry had been clawing at her, and though she told herself she was overthinking things, she hadn't been able to convince herself. And yet no one was talking about it. No one was confessing their feelings or sicknesses or stresses.

"Khrista, you need to make sure you're taking time for self-care. There's no use worrying about things until you need to worry. That only makes you worry twice."

"I know. It's just so hard. I waited so long to have the life I have now, and I can't stand the thought of anything happening to either of them."

Clarice's soft tone matched her relaxed posture. "Trust me, I know it's hard. I stand here and watch all the residents of this town as they struggle now and then, and sometimes I can help, while other times I simply need to let them know I'm here when they're ready. But you know what I've learned after all my years of caring about people?"

Khrista waited for her to answer.

"I've learned that if you want to be there to help others, you need to make sure you help yourself. You'll be no use to anyone if you run yourself into the ground."

"I know," Khrista said, staring at the scone in her hand. "I've just been so busy. And tired."

"Then let's unload some of this project from you. You need to take care of yourself. You know Elanna would be more than happy to ease some of your burden. She's always looking to add to her plate."

The thought of Khrista's long-time best friend taking over the project Khrista had been so eager to organize caused an ache deep in her chest. Elanna was known for her community service and her efficient planning. No doubt she'd do a better job than Khrista, but Khrista needed this.

"No, no. Elanna is working hard on getting the dog park built. Besides, this project has been a great distraction. And you've done so much for me. I want to give back. I feel the best I've felt in over a decade, and being able to put my energy toward this makes me feel even better. Please don't make an issue of it."

Silence hovered between them as Clarice studied Khrista, who tried to maintain her composure. Khrista sipped her tea, appreciating the comfort it brought.

"Okay. I understand needing distractions. And I know these kitties mean the world to you. But you need to agree to make a plan for self-care."

"I will. Just as soon as—"

Clarice interrupted. "Not 'just as soon as' anything. I know right now you're taking care of the world. You have a mother I know you feel responsible for. Your daughter is back in your life, and you have a new grandbaby and a new husband. You're taking care of everyone, even your new rescue cat. But if you want to continue to care for them, you need to take care of yourself as well. Make a plan you can stick with and follow through. You don't want to risk your recovery by burning yourself out."

"I swear I won't do that."

"The only way to know for sure is to take good care of yourself. Have you been meeting with your therapist and sponsor regularly?"

Khrista looked away again, humiliated at being caught. She had canceled her last couple of appointments and kept forgetting to respond to her sponsor's calls and texts. She'd been so busy...

"Khrista, you know I consider you and the other residents of this island my children. I didn't have any of my own, and I'm honored to be considered the town's mother. But I need you to listen to my words and set things in order." Clarice tilted her head. "I don't share this with many people, as I don't want to tarnish the memory of my dear mother. But she struggled with alcoholism. She was sober most of my life, but I remember well how hard it was for her when she took on too much and put everyone else's needs above her own. Women always want to care for everyone, but it's important to remember to take care of ourselves, too."

"I'm so sorry about your mom. I had no idea."

"She was a good parent. No regrets. We all have our struggles, that's all. I never want you to feel shame for the struggles you work through or the obstacles you overcome."

Clarice was right. Khrista needed to prioritize her health, and it helped to hear it from someone who cared. She lifted her cup and smiled. "I'll make appointments tomorrow."

"Today." Clarice slid Khrista's phone from the side of her plate closer to her hand. "Now seems like a good time."

"Fine. I'll call right now. But then do you agree to help me pick out the design for the centerpieces?"

"Agreed."

Khrista called her therapist's office and booked an appointment for the following week. She texted her sponsor and got a relieved text back almost immediately.

"Happy now?" Khrista asked.

Clarice sat back in her chair, more relaxed and with a satisfied smile.

"Much better. And those right there—" Clarice pointed to the picture on Khrista's laptop of the vintage teacups with the doilies and flowers filling the cups. "I like those centerpieces the best."

"By the way, you don't mind if we host the event here, right? Figured I'd ask closer to the date, but since the secret is out..."

"I'd be TEA-lighted."

A loud bleat from the back room had Khrista questioning Clarice again, but her friend simply smiled, sipped her tea, and said, "It's not a goat."

~

After leaving the tearoom, Khrista meandered down to the beach. She had to admit the tremendous relief that washed over her since she made the appointment with her therapist, and she agreed with Clarice that she'd feel even better once she worked through her mental roadblocks.

As Khrista approached a cluster of benches, she saw the unmistakable outline of her mother's shoulders and her daughter's bright hair in the distance. She increased her pace, excited for this unexpected family reunion that never would have been possible several months ago.

"Having a party and you didn't think to invite me?" Khrista teased, stopping by their bench. "Nice campfire. Did you start it yourselves?"

Kaelyn nodded. "Grandma got a chill, and someone left a small stack of firewood, so we went for it. Had to borrow a lighter from a passerby, but luckily it started up easily. There were still a few coals on the very bottom, which definitely helped."

The corner of Kaelyn's lips turned upward the tiniest bit. She didn't maintain eye contact, staring instead at her bare feet as she slipped them into the sand.

"What's going on? Where's Poppy?"

"She's with Ruby. I needed to get out for a minute. Oliver's away again."

"Aww, lovebug. How frustrating. When are they going to let him work fully remote?"

"That's what I'd like to know."

Daisy put her arm around Kaelyn as if she had already heard the story and knew Kaelyn needed reassurance. Khrista occasionally still got small bouts of jealousy at the relationship they had formed before they all ended their estrangements, but then she reminded herself how wonderful it was to have so many people love her daughter. And how wonderful it was for their circle of familial love to be complete.

"Mom, where are your friends? Did they leave early? I thought they were staying the week?" Khrista asked.

"They are. But they wanted to go into Portsmouth for antique shopping and I didn't feel up to going, so I begged off. And I wanted to see my precious granddaughter, so she agreed to meet me here on the beach."

"And still, neither of you invited me." Khrista placed a hand over her heart as if mortally wounded, then smiled and sat on the bench beside her mother. She reached over and squeezed Kaelyn's frigid hand, then let go and draped her arm on the back of the bench so she could face both of the O'Donnell women.

Kaelyn almost smiled. "You're so deliriously happy in your life and relationship, and we didn't want to bring you down."

A lightning bolt of trepidation zinged through Khrista. Last she had heard, both Kaelyn and Daisy were happy in their firmly entrenched marriage and newly budding romance.

"Besides," Kaelyn added. "Aren't you supposed to be at work?"

"Professional development day, but we're doing an online training so we can do it anytime. But anyway, don't change the subject. What's going on?"

Kaelyn released a long stream of air, and she lifted her foot from the sand and ran it along her other leg. Khrista wanted to ask if Kaelyn's bare feet were icy, but Kaelyn had always had a thing about bare feet in the sand, regardless of the time of year. Raised a New Englander, the cold rarely bothered her.

"I don't know. I'm just so mad that Oliver keeps getting called away, and he doesn't seem to do anything about it."

"Honey, I'm sure he'd rather be here."

"Yeah, that's what he says, but why doesn't he tell his boss he can't go?"

"I'm sure there's a reason." Khrista didn't know what to say. She couldn't imagine how difficult it was for Kaelyn to be away from the man she loved so much, especially with a newborn. Khrista had raised her daughter mostly by herself, but their situations were different. Though Khrista had at one point believed she loved Kaelyn's father, he never treated her with the respect and adoration Oliver bestowed upon Kaelyn, even in the early days before he showed his true colors. "I'm sure he's worried about providing for you and Poppy."

"That's what makes it worse. I know I shouldn't feel resentful. I'm the one who told him I wanted to move here, and he didn't even question my decision for a second. And I have plenty of help and everything, it's just..." Her voice clogged with tears and unshed emotion, preventing her from finishing her statement.

Khrista ached for her daughter. Kaelyn was struggling so much and not being able to make it better for her hurt worse than any physical pain Khrista had ever endured.

"Sweetie, what can I—"

"I know I'm unreasonable. I know he's trying. I know we need his income. I'm blaming him when—" Kaelyn tapped her hands on her lap. "Can we not talk about this anymore? Let's talk about Grandma and her problems."

Though Khrista didn't want to shift the attention off her daughter, who clearly needed to talk things out, she respected her wishes and turned her attention to Daisy.

"Things not going well with Rafael?"

"He has a thing for Florence."

"Florence? The one who just came here yesterday? How do you know?"

"I'm not a fool," Daisy snapped, then attempted a smile. "Well, I am, but I can tell. Florence has some kind of magical power over men. And Rafael fell under her spell. And she likes him, too."

Khrista fought to make sense of this rapid change in Rafael, the man she knew to be a stable, unifying force. "Does Florence know you liked him first? It's not cool if she's poaching your man. And are you sure Rafael likes her? That doesn't sound like him."

"He's not my man, whatever that means. I can't talk about this anymore. I came here to forget. You know, I have to face these people again soon. Last thing I need is for them to ask questions."

Khrista breathed in deep, wishing she could wave a magic wand and fix what ailed her loved ones.

They sat in silence for several minutes, each of them dragging their feet through the sand.

"Hey, Mom. I keep forgetting to ask. Did the antibiotic from the doctor clear up your UTI? I've noticed you rubbing your kidney area a lot lately and I want to make sure the infection didn't spread or anything."

Daisy's eyes widened, and then she resumed her neutral expression. "Worked like a charm. Everything's fine."

Khrista couldn't shake the feeling that something was off with her mother—something more than love troubles—but right now they needed to rid themselves of the negative vibes encasing them before they went their separate ways.

An idea struck her, and she leaped from the bench and reached her hands out for each of the women.

"Come on. Take off your coats. We need the cleansing power of the sea. Self-care is important, ya know?"

She slipped out of her shoes and removed her coat. Khrista pulled them each to a standing position, and both of them looked at her like a giant octopus had walked out of the sea to kidnap them. But they followed her, leaving their shoes and coats by the bench, and she led them to the shoreline where the cold water hit each of their toes before swallowing their feet. Daisy swayed a bit as the wave hit her ankles, so Khrista looped her arm around her mother's and then her daughter's, joining them in a loop of infinity. She'd never let them go.

Khrista walked forward, bracing herself against the cold as her feet and ankles quickly went numb. Kaelyn squealed. "How far do you think we're gonna go in? This isn't the Pacific Ocean. It's freezing!"

"My feet are already turning blue," Daisy said, but glee tinged her voice.

"Yes, it's cold. But the saltwater will purify our emotions. I read an article once about how the sea can cure depression and stuff. We don't need to dunk our heads under, but I think if we at least go waist deep, it'll wash away the blues."

"Waist deep? Are you out of your mind?" Kaelyn screeched, but she chuckled as she said it and kept walking forward.

"You've had some crazy ideas in your life," Daisy said. "But this might be the craziest."

As they trudged into the water knee-deep, a wave broke and crashed into their lower bodies, soaking them to their belly buttons. Their squeals imitated the squawks of the seagulls overhead, and the women turned together and ran back to the benches. Khrista held onto Daisy as they hobbled up the sand as fast as they could go, and then they gathered around the crackling fire and tried to warm up, all the while chortling about the adventure as their teeth chattered.

"I can't feel my feet!" Daisy exclaimed, holding them closer to the fire as Khrista bent to help her mother get her socks and shoes back on.

When their teeth-chattering and bone-rattling settled a bit, Khrista said, "Kaelyn, take the night off tonight. I'll relieve your mother-in-law of the baby and take her for the night."

Kaelyn hesitated, indecision etched into her face. "She doesn't sleep."

"Then I'll set up a rocker."

"I'm breastfeeding. You know that." Shaking, Kaelyn hugged herself.

"Weren't you telling me how much you stockpiled in the freezer? We'll do just fine."

Khrista watched as Kaelyn cowered. She had never seen her daughter practically disappear into herself like that, and the vision of it sent warning jolts down Khrista's spine.

Kaelyn stared into the fire before saying, in the tiniest voice, "Good moms don't want to take time away from their newborns."

Khrista grabbed Kaelyn's upper arms, squeezing through the puffy jacket and forcing her daughter to turn and look into her eyes. The hollowness in Kaelyn's eyes worried her.

"Great moms know that taking a break leads to being the best mom they can be."

Tears trickled down Kaelyn's cheeks, and Khrista hated the sight.

"Honey, you're exhausted. Go to my house tonight and make use of the guest room for a good night's sleep. I'll stay at your house. Poppy will be fine."

Daisy put her arm around Kaelyn and squeezed. She trembled, so

Khrista helped Daisy get closer to the fire, and then tossed another log into the flames.

Daisy assured Khrista she was quite all right and would be a hardy New Englander before the end of the winter. She then told her granddaughter, "Your mom is right. Let her have her grandmotherly time, and you get some good rest. Believe me, if I had a mother around to help me when I had your mom, I probably would've been able to do things a lot different."

The past remained an unspoken splotch on their relationship, and Khrista's mother acknowledging that she could have done things better made Khrista both uncomfortable and satisfied. The dichotomy of those emotions blending like a child's watercolor confused her. She made a mental note to mention it to her therapist.

Khrista and her mother had mostly avoided discussing the past, whereas Kaelyn had insisted on hashing out everything from her childhood and adolescence.

"Are you sure?" Kaelyn's hesitant voice sounded small. "I suppose a good night of sleep couldn't hurt."

Khrista clapped her hands together. "I'm positive. Spending the night with my grandbaby will be a dream come true for me. I don't have to get to work until nine, and if you feel like sleeping in, I'm sure Ruby would happily take the next shift."

Kaelyn agreed to let her mother play night nurse and texted her mother-in-law to let her know Khrista would relieve her of her babysitting duties.

"Well, I don't know about the two of you," Khrista said, "but these pants are feeling mighty uncomfortable."

The heavy material dripped and stiffened in the cool air. Sand trapped inside the pant legs itched. She didn't want to move because the sensation was less than desirable. But it had been worth it. The ocean hadn't solved all the problems for her loves, but it had brought much-needed laughter.

"Not just you," Daisy agreed. "They're chafing something terrible. But Florence just texted to let me know they're crossing the bridge, so I asked them to pick me up here."

Seconds later, Khrista and Kaelyn hobbled up to the sidewalk with Daisy and waved her off as her friends picked her up. Khrista smiled as the ladies in the car squealed and hooted about Daisy being soaking wet, and telling her they never imagined her to be the adventurous sort.

"People change," she heard her mother say, and Khrista didn't recognize the youthful sound of her mother's voice.

What a difference freedom made for a woman.

Together, Kaelyn and Khrista speed-walked back to Khrista's house—taking the shortcut along the street since the chill clung to their wet jeans. Once there, Khrista offered her daughter a set of comfy pajamas, changed into dry clothes, packed a small overnight bag, and sent a text to Matt letting him know she wouldn't be home and that Kaelyn would be hibernating in their guestroom. Matilda, the new rescue kitty, didn't jump off the guest bed when Kaelyn sat on the edge, so Khrista hope for both their sakes that they'd spend the night cuddling.

She then gave her daughter the run-down as to where all the good snacks were hidden, kissed her on the forehead, gave her kitties their treats, and strolled to Kaelyn's house down the street.

Khrista let herself into Kaelyn's house and knocked on the wall by the living room entrance before entering further, not wanting to alarm Ruby. Still, Ruby startled, eliciting an apology from Khrista.

"Did you get Kaelyn's text?"

In her sweet British accent, the woman said, "No, is everything all right? The baby hasn't let me put her down, and I'm afraid I left my phone in the kitchen."

"Everyone is fine. I ran into Kaelyn on the beach and noticed she's looking so tired. I asked if I could have some Grandma/Poppy time tonight so she could get some extra rest, so she sent you a text letting you know I'd be here to relieve you."

"Oh, that's lovely. You don't need to, though. I'm happy to take the baby for the night. She's already sleeping and comfortable. I'm sure we can manage."

Khrista sat on the chair opposite Ruby. She leaned forward and thought of how she could diplomatically relieve the devoted woman.

"It's really no trouble. Kaelyn is staying at my house in the guest room for the night, and I haven't been sleeping well anyway, so it's no trouble for me to get up with Poppy throughout the night. Kaelyn has been singing your praises about how much help you've been. You are an absolute treasure, and you deserve a rest, too."

The woman's lips formed a soft o, and her eyes darted around as if she didn't know what to do.

Khrista rushed to reassure her again. "Really, it's fine. I'm actually looking forward to taking her for the night."

"If you're sure…"

"Absolutely."

Ruby lifted the sleeping baby slightly, and Khrista jumped up to accept her from Ruby's arms, loving the weight of the baby as she snuggled into Khrista's shoulder. Khrista settled into the couch and shifted the baby so her ear was directly over Khrista's heart, and hoped her precious Poppy would always know how loved she was.

Ruby lingered, hesitating as if there was something she wanted to say.

"She really likes the rocking chair."

"Kaelyn always loved that, too. Did Oliver?"

"Oh yes, yes. I guess most babies do, don't they?"

Tension zinged between the two, and Khrista realized she had never been alone with Ruby. They'd always been friendly with one another and Khrista had detected nothing but kindness, but she'd sensed there was something left unsaid. Something left unexpressed.

"Ruby, I'm so glad to have this time with you alone for a minute. I never told you how grateful I am that you were there for Kaelyn when I couldn't be. And while you've been nothing but wonderful to me, I'm sure you have some feelings about me and my past and everything that went on between me and Kaelyn. I'd love to talk about it if there's anything…"

Ruby sat back down and perched on the edge of the chair, her look one of discernment.

"I've never thought badly of you. I'm delighted you're back in Kaelyn's life. Believe me, I love Kaelyn like a daughter, and I love how she lights up my son's world. Not to mention this gift she gave both of us. But I could always tell there was something missing behind her eyes. An emptiness, you know? That girl needed her mum, and as a mother myself, I know you needed her."

Tears blinded Khrista, but she didn't blink them away. She swallowed hard.

"I'll confess I've had some envy over your relationship with Kaelyn, and that you had years with her I didn't have. But I can't think of another woman I'd rather have loving my daughter, in my absence or in my presence."

This time tears sprang to Ruby's eyes, and Khrista felt their hearts connecting. Mother to mother. Spirit to spirit.

Ruby stood up and brushed her hands across her thighs, shaking her head with a smile.

"Get a couple of women together in a room and the waterworks turn on, don't they?"

Khrista swiped at her own eyes with the back of her hand and tapped Poppy's bum as the baby stirred.

"Emotions are a powerful thing, that's for sure."

"And we are fortunate to have an abundance of them," Ruby said. "I'll get the spare bed fixed up for you. I suppose I should admit that I'm looking forward to a night of binge-watching crime shows."

8

KAELYN

Kaelyn's reunion with Poppy was the most magical thing Kaelyn had experienced in ages. Poppy smiled when she saw her mommy lean over the carrier portion of the stroller, reaching out to grab the dangling ends of Kaelyn's hair. Khrista had met Kaelyn halfway, pushing Poppy in the stroller along the sidewalk that overlooked the beach.

"A night of sleep sure did wonders for you," Khrista complimented, studying her daughter with approval.

Kaelyn wasn't sure what her mother could see in her face, but she wasn't wrong. Kaelyn had passed out after slipping into her borrowed pajamas, and when she awoke in the morning, she had a drool-streaked face and a mind that struggled to figure out where she was and what happened and whether an alien life-form would deliver her breakfast. She felt as though she had slept away the week, and was startled to see it was only seven o'clock. Matt dropped a box of tantalizing doughnuts on the kitchen counter and told her not to rush, assuring her that Khrista was happy to stay with the baby longer so Kaelyn could have her shower. Kaelyn hadn't wanted to relent, but she had to admit she was a little stinky after a couple of days of not making time for basic hygiene.

"How did you get her to stay in the stroller so happily? She never lets me leave her in there."

Khrista shrugged and winked. "Grandmotherly touch, I guess."

Kaelyn leaned over again and stroked Poppy's cheek. Poppy looked away, more interested in the lapping of the waves than in continuing to engage with her mother.

Kaelyn straightened, pretending her baby's rejection didn't sting like a jellyfish to the heart. Poppy had been happy to see her at first... maybe it just took a minute for her to realize Kaelyn wasn't the one she wanted. Ever. "Mom, I can't thank you enough. And I have to say, your guest bed is delicious. I felt like I was sleeping on a cloud."

"That's Matt's doing. I moved into the house and kept it as is. Wish I could take the credit."

"And Matilda is such a sweetheart. She stayed up by my head until I fell asleep, but when I woke up, Mr. Ed had taken her place."

"They haven't quite made friends yet. She usually spends her days hiding, so I'm glad you made her feel comfortable enough to snuggle."

Kaelyn said goodbye to her mother and headed home, mentally making preparations for Sienna's visit. Kaelyn had texted Sienna earlier that morning and let her know Oliver was out of town, so if she wanted to come by for lunch instead of dinner, she was more than welcome. She told her friend they'd need the full day to catch up properly.

Kaelyn would probably need the full day to get herself to look like a mother coping well with motherhood, but the solid night of sleep would help for sure.

Kaelyn fed the baby quickly, irritated when Poppy kept pulling away. At least she wasn't fussing.

She placed Poppy in the swing, hoping she'd tolerate it for at least a few minutes so Kaelyn could get some soup heated and sandwiches made.

Shocked when she completed her kitchen tasks and Poppy hadn't interrupted even once, Kaelyn wandered back into her living room.

Fear and dread plunged her into dark, icy water, rendering her breathless.

Had something happened to Poppy?

Why hadn't Kaelyn stopped to check on her?

Rushing to the swing, Kaelyn dropped to her knees and studied her baby for a sign of breathing, not able to breathe herself until she saw evidence of Poppy's tiny chest rising and falling in a normal rhythm. Poppy was sleeping soundly. She was breathing.

Feeling returned to Kaelyn's limbs again, but her thundering pulse refused to steady.

"I'm going to have to give you to your grandmother for overnights more often." Kaelyn knew it was a far-off dream to have multiple nights of solid sleep, but the fantasy made her smile. "She wore you right out."

The rumble of a car engine alerted Kaelyn that Sienna had arrived. Joyful anticipation ran through Kaelyn's body. She couldn't believe she was about to be reunited with her best friend after all these years, and it was only at that moment that she realized how much she had missed Sienna. How much the thought of them growing apart had affected her. How much Kaelyn wished she had never pulled away.

Kaelyn ran out with open arms. Squealing, the best friends hugged each other tight.

Sienna held her friend at arm's length, exclaiming, "Look at you! Can't even tell you how amazing it is to see you! You look exactly the same as you did in high school. More womanly, but just as beautiful."

Kaelyn laughed and admitted that Sienna hadn't changed, either.

"Are you kidding? I have a good thirty extra pounds from the last time you saw me. But I wouldn't change it for the world. That little pooper in my backseat right now? She's worth every single pound. Not that I can blame her entirely for the weight gain. I really need to blame the peanut butter cups and the chocolate milk I live on."

Kaelyn chuckled. "Oh, man. I sure hope I stocked up on your favorite candies..." Her eyebrows rose suggestively. As if she could ever forget her best friend's penchant for chocolate.

"Oh my gosh, now I remember why you were always my best friend."

"Oh, I see. So it was all about the candy."

Sienna smiled, her white teeth sparkling in the sunshine. Had Kaelyn remembered to brush hers?

"I can't wait to meet Poppy. And I can't wait for you to meet my little Lila-bear."

"Poppy and I are super excited to meet Lila."

Sienna leaned down and scooped her baby out of the car seat. She gave Lila a big snuggly squish before turning her around to face Kaelyn. The baby burst into a bright smile despite her mother so cruelly waking her up. She reached her pudgy little hands out to Kaelyn, and Kaelyn leaned forward and let Lila touch her face.

"Oh my goodness, she is so precious." Kaelyn worried about what Poppy's reaction would be to Sienna. Probably not such a joyous greeting. She'd probably cry.

Sure enough, when they walked into the house, Poppy was screaming her head off.

"You're so brave, leaving her alone to come outside. I'm obsessed with having to have my eyes on Lila at all times. It's probably a sickness. I should seek help," Sienna teased, but she sounded like wanted to be complimented for this overprotectiveness.

Did that mean Kaelyn really was a bad mom? She hadn't thought twice about running outside and leaving the baby in the swing by herself, even after being terrified something had happened when she had been doing the food prep.

Sure, Poppy had been sleeping and strapped in, but what if the house burned down? What if she choked? What if...

Kaelyn forced herself to calm down and said, "I'm sorry she's so cranky. I think she's teething."

"Oh, no worries. There's nothing more beautiful than the sound of a baby crying."

Whatever Sienna was on, Kaelyn wanted a dose. Did she actually enjoy the sound of baby cries?

Was Kaelyn programmed wrong?

They went into the living room so Kaelyn could feed the baby before they attempted lunch. "Otherwise, she'll serenade us with this lovely sound the entire time. Hmm, maybe she'll be all about heavy metal when she's older."

"Imagine? Maybe our girls will form their own girl band together."

Kaelyn sighed. "I do hope we can see each other often so they can know each other."

Lila cooed at a soft giraffe rattle Sienna shook in front of her. So calm. So sweet. So low maintenance.

They spent the afternoon eating and comparing different things their babies could do, and Kaelyn shifted deeper and deeper into shame when she realized that so many of the accomplishments Sienna bragged about, Kaelyn hadn't even noticed or been aware of. Kaelyn made things up as she went, trying to change the subject to other topics. She didn't want to compare babies. She didn't want to have a contest about who was the better mother or whose baby was more brilliant. Was it too much to ask to simply enjoy her time with her friend? Maybe talk about something other than the humans they had grown in their bodies?

"You really seem to love this mom thing." What had possessed Kaelyn to say that?

"Oh my gosh, I really do. Isn't it the most wonderful thing ever?"

Kaelyn bit her tongue and nodded, hoping the pain didn't show.

"Oh yeah, best ever." Changing the subject and hopefully covering her failings, Kaelyn asked, "Hey, are you in town for the night?"

Sienna shrugged and placed a pacifier in her baby's mouth, even though Lila wasn't fussing.

Kaelyn continued. "My husband is off in LA for work for the rest of the week. Wanna have a sleepover?"

Sienna agreed without hesitation. "Um, yeah."

They spent the rest of the day as if no years had passed and as if nothing had changed, except for adding babies to their lives. No more than five minutes would pass without one of them saying, "Remember when…" and the other filling in the rest of the details of the story.

Kaelyn couldn't believe how good it felt to be close to someone who shared her history.

As much as she loved Oliver and adored spending time with him, she had forgotten what it was like to have a girlfriend. There were some roles it wasn't fair to assume Oliver would fill, and perhaps she had done them both an injustice by not seeking other female friendships.

When bedtime came, Kaelyn was exhausted and ready to collapse, but then again, Poppy had required a lot of walking around and bouncing during the day, while Sienna had the luxury of sitting with her calm, quiet baby. Lila had needed feedings and diaper changes, of course, but it was no wonder Sienna looked so much better rested than Kaelyn felt.

Kaelyn's eyes closed as they sat on the couch after dinner.

Sienna's voice startled Kaelyn back to the moment.

"I know I'm a super party pooper, but would it bum you out if I went to sleep early? Lila is such a good baby, but she wakes up so many times at night."

Relief sent euphoria coursing through Kaelyn's body. Sienna's words were a drug, hitting every pleasure center in Kaelyn's brain.

"No problem at all. I'll show you the guest room."

Together, they set up the Pack-and-Play Sienna kept in her trunk. "I don't know why I even bother bringing this thing. Mostly she ends up sleeping with me."

Kaelyn couldn't help but smile all the way back to her room, appreciating how the idyllic facade around Sienna's parenting cracked the more hours they spent together. Not that she wished for Sienna to suffer. She simply wanted to know she wasn't alone in the lack of perfection.

Later, when Poppy startled Kaelyn awake from a dead sleep and wouldn't stop crying no matter what Kaelyn tried, she ran into Sienna in the kitchen, doing the same thing Kaelyn needed to do. They paced together as their babies cried, and Kaelyn welcomed the sense of sisterhood.

Granted, she would have preferred joining Sienna in the ecstasy of happy motherhood, but if she couldn't have that, the adage *misery loves company* had certainly proven true.

Miraculously, both babies fell asleep on their mom's shoulders after forty-five grueling minutes of zombie-walking.

"Of course," Kaelyn whispered, "by this point, I'm wide awake because I just had a two-hour nap. And then by the time I'm ready to sleep, she'll be waking up again."

"Oh my goodness, same!" Sienna agreed.

"Hot cocoa?" Kaelyn offered, remembering all the nights Sienna's mother had made them Swiss Miss during sleepovers.

"You have some? That would be fantastic!"

"I don't dare put her down or we'll be back to pacing." Carefully balancing the baby in one arm, Kaelyn prepared the milk in the pan and added chocolate chips to melt them.

"Fancy hot cocoa. I see you upped your game."

Kaelyn smiled. "A lot has changed. Being away from my mother, I learned a lot of things about the finer side of life."

As soon as she said the words, she regretted them. It wasn't kind to bring up the negative aspects of her mother's past—not when they had worked so hard to move past those things.

"I shouldn't have said that. My mom has been so wonderful to me since I came back. You know how we struggled when I was younger, but she's a rare example of someone who actually puts in the work and changes."

Sienna shifted Lila to her other shoulder and untangled her wild copper hair from Lila's tight grasp. "I've always liked your mom. When I looked at her, I saw a tortured soul. I'm so glad you could make up with her. I just wish I'd known you hadn't been speaking for so many years. Maybe I could've tried to facilitate something."

Kaelyn protested. "There's no way I would've allowed that. I wasn't ready for it. To be honest, I don't think my mother was, either. I think we sort of needed to go through what we went through to get where we are now."

They sat at the kitchen table, each of them carefully balancing babies to keep them from waking up.

Kaelyn scooped mini marshmallows into her cup. "How crazy that we ended up here on the island at the same time."

Sienna sipped her cocoa and didn't respond. Her gaze drifted to the wall behind Kaelyn, and Kaelyn was dying to ask what she was thinking.

Sienna broke the silence, her voice eerie and low. "Can I confess something to you?"

Kaelyn put down her cup and nodded. "Of course. You can tell me anything."

"I don't want you to think less of me. I love being a mom so much. It's, like, the absolute best thing that's ever happened to me."

"Yeah, yeah. I can totally see that."

"I just spend a lot of time wishing I had a situation more like yours."

Kaelyn nearly choked on her shame. She never should've pretended she was adjusting so well.

"What do you mean? You have everything so well together."

Sienna stared at her cup.

"You have it all. This gorgeous house that I could only ever dream of owning. A husband who loves you and provides for you. I'm so happy for you, Kaelyn."

"Tell me what's going on with you," Kaelyn said, shifting the baby when Poppy cried out a sleepy cry. *Don't wake up now...*

"It's just, the guy I had Lila with... He was my fiancé. We didn't plan to get pregnant. I was happy when I found out and everything. I always wanted kids, you know that. And he said he did too. But a couple months before I had her, he walked away. Basically ghosted me. I mean, how do you ghost someone who's seven months pregnant with your child and has a diamond you gave her on her finger?"

"That's awful!"

"We were living together and everything, and he just packed a bag with the things he cared about the most, which did not include me, by the way, and left when I was at work."

"What a jerk!"

"He hasn't responded to any of my texts or calls since, and neither have his parents. He's not paying child support. I have no idea where he lives to even serve the papers, and we never got to the point of meeting his parents, so I don't know where they live. I had their cell phone number still in my phone from when we called them to announce our engagement, but other than that, I have no info." Sienna rubbed her eye with her full palm and then pressed down as if suppressing a headache. "It's just not the way I imagined this chapter in my life."

Guilt at the envy that had pulled at Kaelyn's gut coursed through her. She hated that her friend had such a terrible experience with a man who should have been there for her. "Honey, I'm so sorry. He doesn't deserve you or Lila. Probably better to find out early on than to get even more attached to him, or for Lila to be attached to him, you know?"

"That's what I tell myself, too. But it stinks."

"Are you working? Do you have anyone helping you with the baby?"

"Nope and nope. That's why I'm moving back to Old Castle. I'll be staying with my parents for a while, and they'll help support me while I find my way." Sienna bit her lower lip and looked up at Kaelyn through her full lashes. "I wanted to tell you sooner. I was just... embarrassed. Moving back with my parents at my age—not exactly the thing every girl dreams of."

Kaelyn didn't know what to say. She knew how strong Sienna had always been—so independent. They had talked about moving away from home and living on their own since they were fourteen, and Sienna had always gushed about all the things she would do when she was a fully independent woman. She loved her parents and got along with them, but it couldn't be easy going backward.

"I'm sorry for everything you're going through, but I'm selfishly glad you'll be back here. We can raise our kids together and see each other all the time."

"That *is* a perk," Sienna said. "I've missed you so much."

They polished off their hot cocoa, and Kaelyn warred with the urge to tell Sienna her own truth about how she'd been feeling. About how getting up every day felt like trudging through life with the full-body aches of a bad flu. How no matter how much she looked at her daughter and tried to feel the intense bond every glossy mother's magazine and ad on the internet promised, she had yet to feel truly connected to her infant. How she battled with herself over whether to pawn the baby off on one of the grandparents or Oliver at every chance so Kaelyn could go do something for herself.

Kaelyn wanted to spill about how she beat herself up for being a bad mother and for having terrible thoughts and for wanting to escape her baby and for not loving her enough and for never being enough and for caring too much and not enough all at the same time.

For having headaches from trying so hard to convince herself that reality wasn't reality and that fantasy could come true. For hoping she'd wake up one day and feel the intense bond with her baby that would keep them together for life. That everything she had learned about maternal bonds would swell in her heart and make her feel the way other mothers felt.

Kaelyn loved her baby. She wanted more for her baby.

She wanted more for herself.

But none of these thoughts were things she could share. Saying them out loud would make them real and true. She'd hate to see pity in her friend's expression. Would abhor having someone else know her weakness.

Kaelyn forced a smile and lifted a peanut butter cup from the bowl in the center of the table, unwrapping it with one hand and reveling in the newfound skill of balancing a baby and doing everything one-handed.

The richness of the chocolate and peanut butter on her tongue gave her the confidence to speak with authority. "I have to say, you're right. I'm so lucky to have everything I've ever wanted. And I'm sure you're going to find that, too."

And just like that, she sealed her fate for the night. There was no way she could sleep after turning herself into such a fraud.

THE NEXT MORNING, after helping Sienna pack up the car and saying goodbye with a tearful farewell even though they knew they'd be seeing each other later in the day because they were both living on the same island for the first time in ages and had already arranged to meet at the park near the beach, Kaelyn settled into her morning routine with Poppy. Ruby offered to help, but Kaelyn's spirit had lifted after having some quality best friend time. She wanted to put her life into perspective.

Listening to Sienna's struggles reminded Kaelyn how lucky she really was. Yes, she'd been tired, but what new mother wasn't? Obviously, it was her own immaturity impeding the bonding process with her baby. And why did she even think she wasn't bonding? She was probably misguided. Vulnerable. Insecure. Kaelyn knew well that commercials weren't slices of real-life and that promises in a magazine didn't always come to fruition. She and her baby were just fine, thank you very much, and she'd spend the next couple of days readjusting her attitude while waiting for Oliver to come home.

And Kaelyn would ask her well-meaning mother to stop dropping those stupid parenting magazines off at her house.

As Poppy settled in for her ten a.m. nursing session, the phone lit up with Oliver's handsome face.

Kaelyn answered the video call, smiling brightly and thanking the heavens she had taken the time to wash her face and put on mascara before having breakfast with Sienna. It'd be nice for her husband to see her looking like a human being instead of a zombie for once.

"You're appearing well-rested this morning, my love."

"Actually, I'm feeling well-rested. You, on the other hand, look like you haven't slept in a month. Are they making you work extra hours while you're there?"

Oliver's shoulders slumped briefly, but then he smiled. "I'd much rather talk about you."

Kaelyn filled in Oliver on everything that happened during her visit with Sienna. She told him about how cute Lila was, Sienna's plan to move back to town, and the unfortunate treatment from Lila's father.

Kaelyn loved the way fury on behalf of her friend darkened Oliver's eyes.

Oliver's voice deepened. "There's no excuse for that kind of man. I shouldn't even call him a man."

"What would you like to call him?" she teased.

"A toad. I'd like to call a man who abandons his pregnant fiancée a toad."

"You're probably right. I didn't ask her if he's covered in warts, but I bet he is." Then, in all seriousness, Kaelyn added, "Thank you for being you."

Kaelyn relaxed into the plush cushions of the sofa. Loving him always had that languorous effect on her. Poppy nursed more frantically, as if afraid Kaelyn would remove her source of food.

"Hold on to that thought while I tell you what I have to tell you."

Dread shot through her, and she knew what he was about to say before he even said it.

"Oliver, I need you home. I miss you so much."

"Believe me, it's not my choice."

"So what is it? An extra day? Two days?" Kaelyn shook as irritation bubbled within her.

"A week. There's this extensive project we have to get done before..."

"A week? You can't be gone another week, Oliver!"

"I'm sorry, love. I want to be there more than anything, but the big boss is personally insisting. They're waving my new contract over my head, and I have to tread lightly right now."

Kaelyn did everything she could to suppress the urge to rant and rave and scream and cry and to show her true colors. But she could see the struggle on his face and hear the torment in his tone. He didn't want this. And she didn't want to make it worse for Oliver.

"Okay. It's okay. We'll be fine. We can video chat when Poppy's awake so she can hear your voice. It always settles her."

As if on cue, Poppy cried out, turning her face away from Kaelyn's breast.

"I'm sorry, Oliver, I have to go. I think she needs a change."

Kaelyn got off the phone and fought the tears away, attempting to vanquish them like they were the real enemy.

It was so stupid. She had all the help in the world, a devoted husband with a good paycheck and a savings account, and none of the troubles her best friend faced. If the worst thing in the world was to take care of her own baby, Kaelyn was extra blessed.

She could do this.

"We can do this, Poppy love. We can do this."

With her mind made up to refocus her energy, Kaelyn spent the rest of the week doing everything in her power to make things better.

And over time, she believed in her own acting.

Where earlier in the week she had forced herself to spend extra time looking at her baby, now she started seeing her in a new light. Rather than thinking of her as being needy and demanding, Kaelyn reminded herself that crying was Poppy's only way to communicate and that it was her job to figure out what ailed her daughter.

Kaelyn did her best to read every article she could find on the internet about fussy babies. She begged the pediatrician's office to fit her in for a check-up to rule out any medical reasons for her fussiness. Once she got the all-clear from the doctor, she followed all the gas-relieving tips to see if that helped Poppy feel less grouchy. She learned infant massage and purchased a high-end, homemade lavender baby lotion from a local shop. She scoured YouTube for baby songs—fingerplays and lullabies—she couldn't remember from her own youth, and she bought more books to stimulate Poppy's developing mind.

It was helping. It had to be helping.

Because if she was still feeling disconnected from her baby after all that effort, then she would have to admit that maybe the problem wasn't the baby after all.

9

______

DAISY

S pending the days with her girlfriends invigorated Daisy.

Daisy loved how the days and nights blended together. How there was never a moment of silence between the four of them. How they had to force themselves to go to bed, and they were all awake at the crack of dawn, fighting over whose turn it was to cook breakfast. They had formed their own community over the few days they had been together, and Daisy loved the sisterhood. How many times had she fantasized about having a friend again? How many times had she sat in that little house with her angry husband, wishing for something like this? A group of caring people who wanted to take care of each other.

Daisy looked at her friends over the breakfast table with all the love in her heart.

"I would do anything for the three of you. You know that?"

"Oh, Daisy," Alice crooned. "You're just the sweetest. I feel the exact same."

Edith and Florence quickly agreed.

"Actually," Florence teased. "I wouldn't change your bedpans."

"Lucky for you, we don't need them." Edith smirked and poured syrup over her waffles, filling every square.

Alice lifted a forkful of eggs and pointed it at her friends. "And hopefully, we never will!"

They laughed and joked and teased and then they cleaned up the dishes together, leaving no one to do the work on their own.

Once everything was cleaned up and they all had their turn in the shower, they walked down to the beach. Alice tossed breadcrumbs to the seagulls, even though the other three told her what a terrible habit that was. Florence told them stories about a seagull attacking her when she was carrying fried dough on a walk along the beach in Provincetown. Her colorful language and explicit storytelling made them all chuckle.

Desire for a taste of the life Florence lived so freely pierced Daisy's chest. She had convinced herself that her health issues didn't need to concern her. That any time she'd been gifted had been a blessing. But now she wondered if she had made a mistake in brushing off the diagnosis and treatment.

"One of these days, I really want to take a trip with you." Daisy meant it. She craved adventure more than anything.

Florence scoffed as Alice attracted more of the pesky gulls. "Oh, you want to be pecked to death by a seagull? You don't need to travel for that. Just walk alongside Alice while she encourages the little devils."

"Not exactly what I meant..." She should have thought about her words before spewing them out. She'd get their hopes up and never be able to fulfill the wish. How could she travel if her doctor was right? "Imagine the four of us on a trip together?"

What harm could come of allowing herself to dream for a moment? Maybe if they planned a weekend getaway, some place not too far... Maybe she could live her best life in whatever time she had left before she got too sick to go anywhere.

Or maybe... just maybe...

Maybe it was time to take this illness seriously. To follow through with the doctor's request for testing. To step out of the land of denial, figure out what was going on, and come up with a treatment plan.

She'd thought she could power through, ignore her increasing symptoms, and live life to the fullest before slipping silently into the night.

But that wasn't realistic. Nor was it likely fair to those who would eventually see her deteriorate. She wasn't an animal who could crawl off to the woods to die in solitude.

Being loved and cared about was new to her. Having something to live for? A foreign concept.

She hated herself for not thinking more clearly sooner.

"Seriously. Where can we go?" Daisy urged. Suddenly, the need to run toward the next adventure fired her up. She'd be a hot air balloon and drift off toward the sun if she didn't anchor herself to reality, but she had wasted enough time in reality. Now was her time to dream. And plan. And wish.

"Oh, I see." Florence studied Daisy, raising her eyebrows and pursing her lips. "You want a fling with a hot European senior. And you know I'm just the person to help you achieve that goal."

"Don't be ludicrous. I don't want that. I've already done the marriage thing. I'm done, thank you."

"She said nothing about marriage," Edith teased, wrapping her scarf tighter around her neck as a gust of wind kicked sand up into their faces. "That fling thing is not for me. But we know how Florence likes to have her fun."

"Sure do," Florence agreed. "And I've got my eye on that hottie who keeps dropping by. You sure there's nothing going on between the two of you?"

"Of course not. Rafael and I are friends." Daisy hating the way her teeth smashed together and her heart skipped enough beats to worry her cardiologist. Her legs trembled as if they didn't want to hold her anymore.

Florence sighed dramatically. "What a waste of a good man. I'll have to rectify that."

Edith pulled the conversation away from the man drama and onto the study she had recently read about rising sea levels affecting coastal properties.

"Oh, hey, isn't that your friend, Rafael?" Alice pointed to the man in question as he strolled down the small boardwalk adjacent to the beach. It was more of a walkway or bike path than a boardwalk, but a great place to walk when you wanted the sea atmosphere without the sand.

Florence waved wildly, gesturing for Rafael to join them. He greeted them cheerfully, calling each of Daisy's friends by name before turning to say hello to her. She thought she smiled, but she lost feeling in her cheeks as he fell in line, walking alongside them. He ambled between Florence and Daisy, and Daisy shivered when his arm accidentally brushed hers. Feigning interest in a pink seashell buried in the sand, she stooped to dig it out. When she rose, Daisy moved to the other side of Alice, leaving Raf between Florence and Alice.

Daisy hadn't meant to look at him, but she did, and she didn't like the confusion on his face. She was giving him what he wanted—closer access to Florence. Daisy didn't want to make it awkward for him to make a move on Florence. It was humiliating to think he could possibly know how she had felt about him—if Khrista and Kaelyn had picked up on her misguided crush, surely he may have, too—but she hoped this would help things go back to normal. They could be friends, and he could have his fun with a woman who knew what fun was.

Each time Daisy straightened from collecting a shell, Raf was right there beside her once again, but she'd maneuver herself between her friends. When he inevitably drifted by her side again, she would repeat the pattern, dipping down to the sands to retrieve a seashell and then wandering off just enough that he wouldn't be able to get too close.

He'd better get the hint soon because her back was about to give out on her and her legs grew wobblier every time she forced them to lift her back up.

Rafael's normal jovial chatter shifted to monotonous, yet polite, answers when any of the ladies asked him anything. Florence did a great job of carrying most of the conversation, so he didn't need to say too much. Neither did Daisy, which was good because sorrow choked her and cut off all ability at communication.

Daisy could feel him drifting off. And she was the current that forced the separation.

Remaining silent gave her plenty of thinking time, and unfortunately, her thoughts drifted to the fight she'd had with Florence.

Back when they were teenagers, they'd both developed a crush on Harold. Ultimately, Harold had encouraged Daisy to run off with him. She did, leaving her family behind forever. Only later, after Harold's death, did Florence share the explosive truth—that she had been seeing Harold and had been, in fact, pregnant with his child when he had run off with Daisy. Florence didn't have the child but suffered greatly because of the whole situation, and it had led to five decades of harsh feelings toward Daisy.

Daisy had vowed to never, ever let a man come between her and a friend again.

So if preserving her friendship with Florence meant stepping away from whatever she'd imagined could bloom between Daisy and Raf, then so be it.

She straightened her chin and relished the chilly breeze that soothed her aching spirit.

The feeling of loss as Raf drifted away from her over the course of the morning was profound. Daisy had despised her husband so much that the idea of him leaving her was a fantasy.

But this loss...it was fresh. Piercing. Devastating.

A hopeful romance dying before taking its first breath.

The way Rafael had treated her...

The way he'd made her feel...

She'd never forget it.

But the joy on Florence's face as she shamelessly flirted with Rafael was worth the personal sacrifice.

No man, even one as chivalrous and kindhearted as Rafael, was worth breaking up this sisterhood.

"Anyone else ready to turn back?" Alice rubbed her left hip, pain etching her face. "I have to take pills and I desperately need a ladies' room..."

Daisy sighed with relief.

She had to get off this beach, where it was far too easy to fantasize about walking hand-in-hand with a handsome man and living the rest of her days in the warm glow of a good man's love and the bright island sun.

She'd stick to reading the romance novels Khrista and Kaelyn had gotten her addicted to. Daisy had a stack by her bedside in large print, just waiting to be consumed.

Edith rubbed her bare hands together. "I was wondering when the rest of you would get cold. I'm not a fan of temps this low. *Brrr.*"

"Aww, c'mon. It's easily forty-four degrees. Maybe forty-five. Tropical for a New England winter." Rafael sounded like his friendly self, but his voice lacked something. Joyful depth. He maintained politeness, but he sounded as though he addressed guests in his restaurant rather than the laid-back tone he typically used around Daisy.

"It's normally colder here, I assume?" Edith asked.

"Indeed. It's been a mild winter. I've seen more dandelions popping up this year than any other. Poor things are confused. We've had nearly no snow. Mostly rain. And I haven't even had to take my heavy parka out of the closet."

When they got to the house, Rafael hung back, not coming in but not heading toward his truck, either. Manners dictated she speak to him, though Daisy had avoided him for the last two hours.

"Care to join us for lunch? I'm sure Florence would be delighted to have you. We all would," she rushed to add, especially as she watched his face fall.

Daisy never wanted to see Rafael looking crestfallen, and yet why didn't he look happier that she had cleared the way for him and Florence?

"Can I talk to you for a minute, Daisy?" His deep voice sent shivers down her arms, and she clutched her coat closer around her.

"Of course. I can't stay out for long—the ladies need to be fed, and I'm sure you need to get to the restaurant, besides. What's going on?"

As if she needed to ask.

He was probably wondering why she had been so strange. Or maybe he was going to thank her for stepping back so he wouldn't have to reject her before making moves on her friend.

"You've been acting odd. Did I do something to upset you?"

"Of course not. I don't think you're capable of upsetting me." Daisy rubbed her forehead. "I think I had too much Moscato last night with the girls. Headache, you know?"

Rafael raised an eyebrow.

"Are you sure? Because you seem like you're throwing your friend at me, and I guess I'm kind of confused about that. Are you trying to unload me onto her?"

Despair landed in her gut like a million little blow darts, piercing through her flesh and wounding her enough to torture her slowly, when she would prefer a fast, fatal knockout.

Daisy avoided his gaze. She couldn't stand those soulful, dark eyes beckoning her to tell the truth. She couldn't let him see how much she knew she was losing by letting him go free.

And she couldn't tell him that she couldn't fight for him for so many reasons, with the most pressing being that she couldn't lose her girlfriends over a man ever again.

He deserved the truth, but Daisy was a coward.

"I don't understand what you're asking. You came to visit. I assumed that meant you wanted to hang out with the ladies?"

Rafael reached for her hand and she retracted it, burying her hands under her elbows, crossed over her body.

He looked stricken. She hated that she made him look stricken.

"I wanted to hang out with *you*. I suppose it would've been the gentlemanly thing to do to let you have your time alone with your friends, and you certainly could've told me you preferred that, but I missed you. And I didn't want to take up all of your time, but I couldn't imagine going the whole week without seeing you at all. I didn't actually expect to be invited on your walk or for meals or anything like that."

The urge to cry was strong, the urge to protect herself stronger. Daisy had learned long ago what tears could do to a man, and it never ended well for her.

"I'm sure I'm not understanding you right. I should let you go." Her shaky voice had her cringing, and when she turned to go inside, Rafael reached out to stop her. Daisy tensed, not trusting a man's touch during conflict.

As if Rafael sensed her sudden fright, he dropped his hand to the side. He hadn't been rough, but she couldn't undo the reaction she had developed after so many years of mistreatment.

"Daisy, if I haven't been clear, I like you. I thought you liked me, too." He ran a hand over his forehead and into his hair, gazing at the ceiling of the little porch they stood on. "That sounds so stupid. I didn't mean to declare it like I was a lovelorn grade-schooler."

It wasn't stupid.

It was romantic.

It was beautiful.

It was everything she ever wanted to hear.

Daisy would carry his words with her—those beautiful words— the rest of her life. Hopefully beyond.

But she couldn't tell him any of that.

She geared herself up to break his heart. Something Daisy never imagined herself in the position of doing, and something that made her want to tear her own out of her chest and throw it in the ocean.

Daisy forced her protective mechanisms to wrap around her words and cushion them with the strength of steel. Impenetrable. If her voice trembled, he wouldn't believe her. He would continue to press, and that would only make this all the harder.

"Rafael, I enjoy your company. Very much."

She cleared her throat, though the lump that formed there wasn't dislodgeable.

"I'm not interested in you in that way," Daisy continued, the lies burning the tip of her tongue and scalding the back of her throat.

"You must know how grateful I am for everything you've done for my daughter over the years, taking her under your wing and all. I guess that's what drew me to you and made me want to spend time with you. Not to mention, you're a delightfully nice man. I just don't see us ever being more than friends. If that's not enough for you, maybe we shouldn't even be that."

She watched all the emotions play across Rafael's face during her speech. Shock, despair, anger, disappointment.

Crushed.

Daisy hadn't been sure her own crush had been reciprocated, but there it was going full circle before her eyes.

From having a crush to being crushed. Now she understood the etymology.

Rafael buried his hands deep into his pockets. His lips drew into a straight line, and she watched as his eyes shuttered before her, not letting the slightest bit of emotion show once the shutters drew closed.

Good. It was better this way.

The sudden fear that she had gone too far, spoken too boldly, had Daisy wanting to unravel the ball of yarn she had so carefully and meticulously wound up. She shouldn't have said all of that. She wanted to be his friend. She wanted him in her life in whatever capacity she could have him.

She could sit on her emotions. She could hide them forever. But what she couldn't do was watch him from afar and never be comfortable having a conversation with him again. She could never sit and enjoy companionable silence knowing she had hurt him.

What had she done?

"I'm sorry if that was harsh. I think the ocean breeze did something to my brain. Come on in. Florence will be upset if you leave."

A muscle tightened in his jaw, and he bowed his head slightly.

"Thank you for the honesty. I'm going to take that as my cue to go."

"Rafael, wait." Her voice was shaky once again, desperation coloring the edges. "I'd love for you to stay. Really."

"No. I heard you loud and clear. I don't want to be your castoff. Your friend is nice, but I wasn't looking for companionship until I found you. My heart needs time to recover."

She watched him trudge back to his truck, the sandy gravel crunching beneath his boots. She memorized the curve of his shoulders and the width of his back, covered in the blue flannel shirt he loved so much. He glanced back at her as he got into his truck, and the sorrow in his eyes was her undoing.

His heart would need time to recover.

His heart? When had it become hers?

And why was it so darned hard to imagine Raf could care for her?

Stupid Daisy. Queen of messing things up.

As he pulled out of the small driveway, Daisy's body quivered.

What had she done?

And how would she explain it to her friends?

10

KHRISTA

The stack of mail teetered on the edge of the table where Khrista had been tossing it for the last two weeks. Matt had been excessively patient, knowing how much time Khrista had been pouring into the fundraiser and family matters, but she felt guilty as he hated clutter. Since she had some time to kill and an extreme urge to procrastinate with a giant to-do list looming over her unmotivated head, she tossed her late lunch in the microwave to reheat and gave herself the two minutes to sort through whatever she could of the mail. The rest she could finish later.

All her mother's mail had been coming to her house until Daisy could get a permanent address. Hopefully, that would be soon; Khrista hated the thought of her mother living above the tearoom, no matter how much Clarice insisted it was fine. At Daisy's age, she deserved space of her own and no obligation to work for her board. That was all Daisy's doing, of course, because Clarice said the volunteering wasn't necessary. Even so, Khrista wished Daisy would have accepted Khrista's offer to stay with her and Matt rather than above the tearoom.

As she was setting the junk mail into a pile for her mother to go through, she almost missed the envelope with the return address that made her heart pause for a beat.

A cancer center.

Why were they writing to Daisy?

She held the envelope up to the light, noting that it was a typed letter and not an invoice.

Probably nothing.

So why did her mouth suddenly dry out? Why did she pick up such a negative vibe from the letter? As if Khrista could feel the bad news pulsating out of the paper and into her fingers?

Ludicrous. And yet... she couldn't shake the suspicion.

Her brain started searching for hints. For clues. For patterns to piece together, questioning everything her mother had been doing over the past month. Something other than the feelings of dread that had been creeping over her heart and mind like overgrown ivy.

Since her mother didn't drive, Khrista took her to her healthcare appointments. Then again, there had been days where Khrista hadn't heard from Daisy for many hours and didn't pressure her to account for her time. Her mother was a grown woman and had the right to spend her days however she wanted to, but now Khrista wondered if someone could have taken her, secretly, to the cancer center.

Was Daisy withholding important information about her health?

No. They were past all the lies and the secrets.

The microwave beeped to let her know her meal was ready, but the idea of putting food into her belly made her feel nauseated.

Khrista left the mail in piles on the table and dumped her lunch into the garbage.

If she didn't want the stress of the unknown hanging over her head, she needed to come out and ask the questions she needed answered. So she shot off a text asking if her mother had cancer—might as well be blunt—and stared at her phone as she awaited her mother's response.

The immediate denial of anything being wrong and the extra emojis added to the message confirmed Khrista's fears. Her mother was hiding something.

Mr. Ed leaped onto the table and rubbed against her arm, demanding attention. He brought his head to hers as if he knew she needed comfort.

"Want to change places? I'll be the cat and you can deal with the human problems?"

Mr. Ed stalked off as if offended at the suggestion.

Khrista needed a change of scenery. Yes, a change of scenery would help her get her head back on straight and focus on what she needed to focus on. The fundraiser. The fundraiser she had worked so hard on and invested so much time and energy into. The very fundraiser that was scheduled to take place in three days.

She tore her to-do list out of the notebook, fetched a pen, and slipped her feet into her shoes. She could think better at the tearoom with the ambient noise and the caffeine infusion. Khrista grabbed her computer bag and started off, taking the car since it was pouring rain.

Though they had originally planned to hold the fundraiser in the tearoom, they'd run into a snag getting the right permit to serve alcohol in a local establishment, so they thanked Mother Nature for the unseasonably warm winter and let everyone know to bundle up for an outdoor extravaganza by the beach.

Hopefully, the rain would subside as the weather report promised it would before the fundraiser, but earlier that morning, she had arranged for outdoor tents and giant patio heaters just in case. Still, she didn't want people to have a reason not to show up. Clarice was counting on a good turnout, and Khrista wanted her first fundraiser planned entirely by herself to go off without a hitch.

Khrista had sent out a group text begging everyone to wish as hard as they could for the weather to not take a drastic turn. That certainly wouldn't be unheard of in New England.

Khrista dodged raindrops, clutching her computer bag to her side as she mounted the steps into the tearoom.

The place was packed with people all bored on the rainy day. Khrista hadn't anticipated the crowds, but hopefully she'd be able to carve out a spot for her and her computer.

Since a group of teen girls occupied her usual spot by the fireplace and smaller bookshelves, Khrista fought her way through the crowds and over to her favorite side room, the library. She spotted an available chair in the corner, sandwiched between two looming bookcases. Though she preferred to work on a table, she could manage sitting in the comfy chair. On her way to claim the seat, Khrista could have sworn she heard her name mentioned in one of the murmured conversations as she passed.

She kept going, sure she had misheard. But then Khrista had to stop as she waited for an elderly couple to navigate past a cluster of tables, carrying a tray with their food and teacups. As Khrista stood there, smiling like an idiot, she heard the discussion as clearly as if the group were broadcasting the conversation over a loudspeaker.

"It's just not good optics for our town."

"I agree. A cocktail party's all fun and everything, but I don't think an alcoholic should run the thing."

"You saw what she did at the school last year. It was a disgrace. Can you imagine if word got out?"

"Got out? It was all over Spill the Tea. The rumors just finally started dying down, and now they're ramping back up."

"It's crazy for a teacher to be..."

Khrista tuned out the rest. She didn't need to hear more than what they had already said.

Before she could make her getaway, one of the gossips, a parent Khrista recognized from the toddler classroom in her center, looked up and gasped when she spotted Khrista. The woman broke eye contact and started brushing crumbs off the table. Khrista could see her lips moving, but couldn't hear the words of her lowered tone over the gentle roar of conversation in the room. Leann, the parent Khrista had encountered at the cottage with her mother and daughter earlier in the week, glanced over her shoulder to see Khrista standing there. Khrista couldn't move—it was as if someone had poured cement into her shoes. Leann snarled and turned back toward her friends, not deigning to apologize for the hurt they had caused.

Leann was known for causing difficulties for other parents who were actively involved in volunteering, but Khrista had assumed it was guilt over not having time to commit to getting involved. But this behavior crossed a line. It was deliberately cruel.

Wanting to flee, but physically unable to do so, Khrista held her ground. Not willingly, but she couldn't have escaped if she wanted to. Too many people coming and going. Humiliation and shame rippled in waves over Khrista's stiff body.

The group rose almost in unison and left the room, two of the women casting nasty glares at Khrista on their way out.

Would she never be able to make up for the mistake she had made?

She had thought that by issuing the apology at her preschool for showing up intoxicated after a night of binge-drinking and telling everyone she knew how sorry she was for letting the town down, she could have made it past that ugly spot in her life. Khrista had thought that seeking help for her troubles and fixing the inner wounds that drove her to make bad choices would have proven her sincerity.

Running the fundraiser was supposed to be a way to give back to the community Khrista loved so much. It was supposed to be a way to make up for all the things that happened in the past. To prove she was more than her mistakes.

And yet there those women were, hurling those mistakes and her choices in her face as if she didn't beat herself up enough for all of them. As if she hadn't come painfully close to losing everything before.

Khrista took a deep breath, struggling to breathe in the toxic air the women had left behind. A cup of tea would do her wonders, and she needed to focus on the soothing steam and the caffeine rush that would soon set her at ease. Their opinions of her didn't matter to her. They shouldn't, anyway. Khrista had the forgiveness of her family and close friends. She didn't even know most of those women's names, other than the one parent she recognized as Will's mom. Clearly, that woman had a problem with her, but that was her problem, not Khrista's.

Khrista's brain kicked in and she shuffled over to the chair. She could have claimed the table the women had vacated, but they didn't leave only their mess behind. They left broken pieces of her soul that they had viciously torn out of her body, shredded into tiny pieces, and scattered on the table along with the crumbs from their cheddar scones.

Khrista plopped into the comfy seat, breathing in the scents of the tearoom which always calmed her.

She ran her finger over the spines of the shelved books, promising herself a good read once this fundraiser was behind her. Khrista hadn't been able to concentrate on a book in ages, and she missed the days when she could escape into an entertaining story. Khrista vowed to rectify that.

No matter how hard she tried, the words of those women rang in her mind. Over and over. Shame filled her belly and stung her cheeks.

The best way to prove herself was to carry on and do the deed she had set out to do. Maybe then they would see that Khrista could handle being around alcohol without making a fool of herself again. She would bring positive press coverage to the island and people's views of her would change.

Khrista opened her computer and logged in. She checked the online system Matt's daughter, Aliyah, had set up for people to purchase tickets and noticed the numbers had increased by over ten percent. Things were on track and looking great, and Clarice would have more than enough money to fix the roof.

Her phone rang and when she lifted it to answer, Khrista frowned at seeing her director's number appear.

"Khrista, I'm so sorry to bother you while you're off the clock, but this couldn't wait."

"No trouble at all. What's going on? Everything okay at the school?"

"Yes, well, um..."

Khrista hated the way Susan hesitated and that she had called right after the encounter with Leann and her friends. Susan sounded like she wanted to say something that would break

Khrista into a million pieces. Too late. Mission already accomplished.

"Here's the thing, Khrista. You *know* I know how much you've done to work on yourself and to move past the errors of the last school year."

Khrista closed her eyes and forced herself to breathe. People chattered all around her, but she couldn't make out any sounds except the trying-to-be-gentle-but-still-sharp-enough-to-shatter-her voice of the woman who was about to finish the job those other women had started.

"Just say whatever you have to say, Susan. You don't have to sugarcoat it."

"It's just that I've been fielding calls all week from people who are questioning the integrity of our school based on the fundraiser you're running. I tried to calm things down, but things have escalated. Just a moment ago, I received a call from a parent who's reaching out to the head of the parent advisory board, advising me they plan to bring this matter to the next meeting and would rally other parents to join their mission."

"Let me guess. Leann Miller." Khrista clenched her teeth so tight she could feel the sting of the nerve on the back tooth she had been neglecting—the one that had needed a root canal for the past year. She focused on the pain in her mouth, hoping to ease the ache in her heart.

"I can't say." Susan hesitated. "You know I can't, Khrista. Regardless of my personal feelings, I need to get things under control to prevent the tarnishing of the school's reputation. People trust us with their children, and we can't have anyone thinking we don't take all concerns seriously. Besides, and this is between you and me, we're in negotiations for someone to buy the center and we don't want to do anything to damage that agreement."

Khrista tightened her grip on her phone, pressing it against her cheek. She closed her eyes and imagined waves washing over her. Seaweed clinging to her hair. Salt water drying and leaving her skin itchy and fresh. Goosebumps rising on her skin. Diving back under to feel it all again.

Anything to take her out of the moment. The torturous moment of betrayal.

"Khrista, believe me when I say you're an asset to our program. One of the best teachers I've ever employed. And, of course, I've always considered you a friend. As a friend, I'd like to ask you to consider taking a leave of absence so we can get things under control. Just until things calm down."

A friend?

Rage roiled through Khrista's gut. Susan didn't have the guts to fire her. She wanted Khrista to make this easier on her. But why should she? Khrista had done nothing wrong. She didn't deserve this treatment. Planning a fundraiser shouldn't have led to this.

And yet Susan called herself a friend.

Khrista struggled to steady her ragged breathing. She rubbed her chest, hoping to alleviate the burn of the acid climbing up her throat and stifling her ability to breathe. Praying her voice wouldn't tremble, she said, "You want me to take a 'voluntary' leave of absence because some busybodies are making it their business to drag me down. Is that what I'm hearing?"

"I'm sorry, Khrista. I truly am."

"I know you're in a tough position, Susan, but if you were 'truly sorry,' you'd tell them you're not willing to lose a valued teacher over their prejudices."

Unless her value was less than she was led to believe...

Khrista couldn't voice that insecurity. She didn't want to hear the answer.

Susan's silence crackled over the phone. Before speaking again, she cleared her throat and swallowed hard enough for Khrista to hear it. Khrista could imagine Susan sitting up straighter to compensate for her cowardly stance.

"I know this is a big ask. But I have Barbara coming in to take over your class for the time being. I wish you well, Khrista, and I'm certain this will blow over soon. If there's anything I can do..."

Khrista hit the end call button and slammed her phone onto the table, unable to respond or even to wrap her mind around what had just happened. She hadn't had to ask about her value to get the answer.

Too much. This was too much.

How was she supposed to make it through her to-do list when the world kept launching cannons at her? Her entire gut ached like a giant lead ball had lodged straight through her, leaving her empty and bleeding.

Khrista jammed her laptop back into her bag and gathered her things, refusing to make eye contact with anyone as she fled the tearoom.

Khrista had trekked halfway home through the pouring rain, sidestepping puddles and ranting to herself about good deeds most definitely being punished, before she realized she never got her tea. But she wasn't about to go back for it. She didn't know if she could ever set foot in public on the island again.

If her mother and daughter hadn't just moved there, the thought of leaving Old Castle for good would have firmly entrenched itself in Khrista's mind. But her roots clung fiercely to the soil there, and she had to find a way to make this okay.

What would she tell Matt? He'd be so upset on her behalf. Would he be disappointed in her? Or worse... embarrassed by her?

Khrista trudged through the puddles on the way to her car, giving up any hope of dry feet. As she approached, she spotted Gerard and Geraldine standing by Khrista's vehicle, Geraldine gesturing wildly. The elderly siblings were known to engage in public spats when they were out and about, and though Khrista adored the two of them despite Gerard's grumpiness and Geraldine's exasperation, she didn't have it in her to put on a cheery face.

Unfortunately, Gerard's little dog decided to take shelter under Khrista's vehicle.

Come on!

Khrista hid her exasperation behind a smile as she greeted the town icons.

"Hello, Geraldine. Hi, Gerard. Lovely day we're having, huh?"

"Have you lost your mind?" Gerard spat. "This rain is ridiculous. It wasn't supposed to rain today, and it's done nothing but."

"Well!" Geraldine shouted. "If you'd quit being so stubborn, we could be in the tearoom already."

"I'm not going in there with all those cats. They won't let me bring my dog, but there's cat hair everywhere and we're expected to be okay with it?"

Khrista didn't want to hear this argument yet again. She rolled her eyes. "If you could just move your dog so I can move my car..."

"Don't be selfish," Gerard snapped. "He's taking refuge from the rain. Can't you see that? As it is, he's going to have to go back to the groomers after this storm. What a rip-off. I just had him groomed three days ago, and now this."

Patience, Khrista. Patience.

Khrista eased a calming breath into her lungs and released it before responding. "I can see he's taking refuge, Gerard. But can you see that I'm dripping wet and worried about my computer? I don't want the rain to penetrate my computer bag and wreck it." Probably too late to worry about that, but Khrista clung to whatever excuse she could conceive.

Gerard turned to his sister again, casting her the nastiest glare Khrista had ever seen on his face, which was saying a lot.

"That self-righteous Clarice won't let dogs in, but you can't tell me that creature we saw behind her counter wasn't a goat. In her so-called restaurant."

"It's a tearoom, not a restaurant," Geraldine corrected. "And it's not a goat."

"She serves food—it's a restaurant. Don't act like you're so much more cultured than me. And don't act like I don't know a blasted goat when I see one."

"You want to talk about your lack of culture? Sure, let's go!" Geraldine swiped wet hair away from her eyes. Her blue eye shadow had turned to goop and caked at the corners.

"Guys, please." Khrista couldn't take it anymore. She normally found Gerard and Geraldine a touch amusing, but lately she had an uncanny tendency to run into them when she most needed to run away.

Gerard mumbled something, but Khrista couldn't hear it over the pelting rain and the passing cars.

Geraldine called the dog to her, but the dog didn't budge. She threw her hands up in the air and then planted them on her hips.

Exasperated, Geraldine said, "That dog never listens. I don't know why you insist on bringing him everywhere. But we don't need to make Khrista stand out here in the rain just because you're a stubborn fool. We can tie Fritz up on the porch like always. You know he loves the doggy beds and the treat jars Clarice keeps out there."

Gerard yanked lightly on Fritz's leash, and the little black dog skulked out from under the car and followed Gerard up the stairs, his tail tucked under him and his typically floppy ears pressed tightly against his head.

"Thank you," Khrista muttered as Geraldine grimaced and gestured toward her brother.

"I swear, that man gets worse and worse every day. Nothing makes him happy. And accusing Clarice of keeping a goat in there? Ludicrous. We all know it's not a goat."

Khrista nodded in empathy but silently celebrated when Geraldine trudged after her brother, yelling at him about something Khrista didn't want to hear.

She hurried into her car and locked the doors.

Khrista had to drive slowly so as not to splash any pedestrians as her car sloshed through giant puddles.

As she waited to allow an SUV to pull out of the parking lot of Old Castle Gifts, she noticed her daughter walking with Poppy strapped to her body in the carrier, both of them protected under an umbrella. Kaelyn's shoulders slumped and her eyes were cast downward. Though she bounced gently and tapped the baby's back as she walked, she appeared disengaged and as if on autopilot. The intense melancholy emanating from Kaelyn threatened to break the healed parts of Khrista's heart into pieces to match the other shattered chambers.

Khrista rolled down her window—partway to limit the rain pelting her—and called to her daughter, then inched the car forward to get closer in case Kaelyn couldn't hear her over the roar of the nearby ocean waves and the splash of the rain.

When Kaelyn noticed her pulling up, her eyes looked vacant.

"Sweetie, you look exhausted."

Kaelyn smiled, but her eyes appeared sullen, tormented. Her cheeks had lost some of their fullness, and her coloring was pale. "I'm okay. I thought maybe a walk in the rain would help settle Poppy. She's been getting a little stir crazy."

"Are you walking to the tearoom? I'll give you a ride."

"I don't really have a plan. Just roaming around."

"I can give you a ride back to your place or wherever you want," Khrista offered. "One of the perks of having my own car seat installed."

Kaelyn shrugged. "We're okay."

Khrista studied Kaelyn, struggling to figure out why her words didn't match her tone.

"You sure you're okay? You don't seem yourself."

"I don't even know what 'myself' is anymore. I think I may have made a mistake moving here." The words rolled off Kaelyn's tongue as though she were commenting on the weather and not on an entire upheaval.

If Khrista had thought the cannon had wiped out her insides, she thought wrong. Because if it had, Kaelyn's sad words wouldn't claw at the raw sores.

"What do you mean? I thought you loved it here?"

"I don't know what I love anymore. I don't know what I want. Today I've been thinking a lot about going back to the West Coast. Things were good there. I love being near you and Grandma and living back in our old hometown, but—I don't know. I guess I felt more like myself out there. And maybe Poppy's been so fussy because she's meant to be an LA girl. Maybe we need sunshine and longer days."

Khrista couldn't respond. Her daughter wanting to move was the sour cherry on top of this ridiculous day, and Khrista couldn't cope with any more bad news.

Instead of making her own issues a problem for Kaelyn, Khrista struggled to sound supportive rather than narcissistic. "You have to do what's best for you and your family."

But why couldn't what was best for her and her family be what would be best for Khrista, too?

Khrista bit her tongue before saying anything else, knowing it wasn't right to burden her daughter with the weight of her angst. Kaelyn was exhausted from being a new mom and missing her husband. She didn't need her mother's guilt on top of it.

"Mom, if you don't mind, I'm just gonna walk by myself with Poppy for a while. I need some alone time. I love you."

"No problem at all. You always loved walks in the rain when you were a baby, too."

A tiny smile tugged at the side of Kaelyn's lips and then, as if she had been a phantom or a product of Khrista's imagination, Kaelyn disappeared into the fog.

She understood Kaelyn's desire to be alone because she felt the same way. Khrista couldn't handle another living, breathing soul around her while trying to bear the load of the bricks heaped on her shoulders. She needed a break, and she needed to get a hold of herself before she did something she'd regret.

Khrista dropped her keys as she tried to unlock the door to the beautiful home she shared with Matt. Groaning, she bent to retrieve them, but hit her head on the artificial plant hanging from a hook by the door.

Matt was always telling her to take care of herself. Time to listen to him. Her bathtub beckoned, and after a soothing soak, her fuzzy blankets would be the therapy she needed.

Khrista tossed her keys into the basket by the door. No matter how much she tried to dial down the spiraling in her brain, the thoughts kept coming.

Her mother might have cancer. Her daughter wanted to move across the country, so soon after Khrista got her back, and of course, she'd take Khrista's beloved granddaughter with her. The town had turned against her, and her boss didn't want her.

Khrista's bad luck was coming in spades, as torrential as the rain drumming against the porch rails.

Her gaze drifted to the table full of alcohol in her living room. Her cocktail fundraiser workshop.

With the way Khrista's luck was going, the rain would never stop and the fundraiser would be ruined. Who would want to attend an outdoor party on the beach on a cold, rainy, dreary winter night? No amount of tents or outdoor heaters or carefully built fires would lure people there. Especially if they all shared the belief that Khrista was in the wrong for putting it together. Sure, they had sold a higher volume of tickets than she had hoped for, but with the shifting tide, would they demand refunds? Splash her face on the Spill the Tea forum with a giant tattoo of the word "Shame" stamped across her forehead?

Memories of her days of turning to liquid courage nestled themselves into her head. The temptation to pour herself a glass was strong. So strong that before she knew it, Khrista had lifted a glass and reached for the Fireball, her old favorite standby. She twisted open the cap and held the bottle to her nose, nostalgia washing over her as she fought the urge and then questioned why she bothered fighting.

What did it matter if, after everything she had done to get better, things could so easily slip back to being the same?

Why reject something that brought her so much comfort when the sober world gave her so much pain?

Why deny herself this comfort when she could lose everything, even while doing the right thing?

As if in a trance, Khrista poured the liquid into her glass and watched it swirl around. She recapped the bottle and slid it away from her.

Just one drink wouldn't be bad, right?

Khrista sniffed the contents of the glass, closing her eyes and sighing at the thought of how the alcohol would feel burning down her throat. How her limbs would turn lighter and her mood would, too. After just a few drinks, the world would look happier and she could numb herself against all the torment and pain.

But when she opened her eyes, the first thing Khrista saw was a framed photo of her beach wedding proudly displayed on the side table. The joyful faces of their four smiling daughters embracing the new family dynamic.

Without another thought, Khrista crossed the room to the kitchen and poured the drink in the sink.

Almost as soon as she set the glass down and turned on the faucet to wash away the tempting stench, the front door rattled open and Matt entered. He rushed up behind her, wrapping his arms around her waist, and kissed her cheek.

Khrista's shame was as potent as the smell of the whisky in the air, and Matt scrutinized her face the way he did the crossword puzzles he enjoyed on Saturday mornings. Only this time, there was no sense of enjoyment and happy challenge. Just confusion. And disappointment.

He glanced from her to the sink, and then back to her, his face falling as if she had delivered the worst news of his life.

Khrista wanted to deny she had done anything. Her lips tried to open, and her tongue tried to work its way around the ball of fear and tension and despair.

But nothing would come.

"Khrista..."

Matt's tone said it all. He had no doubt. In his mind, she was guilty.

And with that realization, she knew she still had so much to do to earn back his trust.

Khrista forced out her explanation, knowing the silence could sever the faith he had in her. "I know you might not believe me, but I didn't drink it."

He didn't believe her. It was all over his face.

Disappointment. Sadness. Hurt.

"I poured it. I wanted to drink it. I smelled it. And then I remembered everything I had to lose." Khrista reached her hand up to Matt's cheek, appreciating the roughness of his unshaved stubble rubbing against the softness of her palm. "It will always be a struggle for me, but I love my life so much that alcohol will never truly tempt me. I had a bad day, and I almost fell into an old habit. But I didn't."

The tension between his eyebrows dissolved instantly, and his eyes resumed their familiar sparkle. He kissed her forehead, and she closed her eyes and inhaled the comforting scent of the blend of his fabric softener and of the spearmint candies he favored.

"I came home early to make you dinner. Want to cook with me? You can tell me all about your day."

Khrista nodded and kissed him, loving the way his calm presence could release her soothing endorphins.

After a quick discussion about what he wanted to make—a vegetable frittata—Matt put on the music while she gathered the ingredients. Together, they worked their way around the kitchen, as if cooking was a dance they had practiced for years rather than months. They blended together seamlessly, and if she had a hard time breathing, he picked up the effort and did it for her.

She didn't know exactly what Matt saw in her or what value she brought to his life, but Khrista was grateful that whatever it was, he could see it even through the cobwebs of her tarnished past, the fear of her potential failure, and all the issues she struggled with day-to-day.

Dancing around the kitchen with him as they whisked and chopped and sliced and poured almost helped her to forget the mayhem of the day. Yet every moment of silence, every time he turned away from her to work at the stove, her mind shifted to the accusatory words those women had uttered.

She shared a sanitized version of her day, but left out the deepest hurts.

"Whenever you're ready to talk, my ears are open."

"I know."

She loaded the dishwasher while he finished the cooking, and then squatted on the floor to pet Mr. Ed and to tell him it wasn't yet treat time.

"Voila! Dinner is ready."

Khrista's stomach lurched even as she admired the delicious scent of the onions and garlic and the way the potatoes had browned so beautifully. The cheese melted in and crisped at the edges, exactly the way she liked it. The thought of putting food in her stressed and aching belly had her wanting to toss it to the mermaids and hide in a shell.

Matt heaped generous servings onto two plates, and she poured water into two glasses. Hers with ice, his without. They nearly bumped into each other as they each placed their contributions onto the table.

As they sat across from one another, he regarded her with so much love that it made her want to both run away and climb in his lap and nestle there under his sweet and reverent protection.

And stay there forever.

Khrista reached for the pepper. Matt continued to study her, making no move to dig into his steaming food.

Uncomfortable under his perusal, Khrista sprinkled pepper on her food while her ears burned from his rapt attention. Her cheeks burned as she asked, "What is up with you?"

Khrista restrained the urge to continue studying her plate and forced her gaze to tangle with his. Matt smiled, setting Khrista's raging nerves at ease.

"Khrista, my love. I need to tell you something."

Her mind raced to analyze his tone and what it could mean. His face was relaxed, and he didn't seem anxious or nervous or angry or sad. His eyes were soft and his lips lifted slightly. If he was about to break her, he did a great job of hiding his intent.

Luckily, he continued without making her wait too long for whatever topic he planned to drop.

"Don't look so alarmed. I simply wanted to reiterate a point." Matt steepled his hands on the table. "Khrista, there is nothing in the world that would keep me from spending the rest of eternity with you. Even if you try to push me away, I'm not going anywhere. My vows meant something to me, and if you left me, I'd spend the rest of my life hoping you'd come back. Searching for you. Wishing for you. Dreaming about you. I married you knowing the struggles you face. Knowing the demons that live inside you. And I will never stop trying to help you drive them away."

Unable to eat, Khrista lowered her fork back onto the plate and slid the chair away from the table.

She couldn't handle his kindness. She couldn't handle his love.

Briefly, Khrista thought of running away. Of putting it all behind her. Of relieving Matt of the stress and the burden of caring for her and never knowing when she would go off the deep end again.

But his words meant everything. And she, too, had taken vows.

Khrista paused by his chair and tapped on his arm. Matt slid his chair away from the table. She climbed onto his lap as she'd been yearning to do and wrapped her arms around his neck. She buried her face in his neck and let the tears wash away all the pain.

Through the haze of her tears, Khrista assured him even as she assured herself, "I never want to live without you."

11

KAELYN

Kaelyn wandered around the dark cave, running her palm over every surface. Her baby's sharp cries penetrated the darkness. Where was she? Feeling blind, she clawed at the rock wall until her fingertips turned raw and bloody. The cries grew farther and farther away, then louder again, as if they were right in her ear. If only some light would glimmer through the blackness...

"Poppy. Poppy! Baby, where are you?"

All alone. All alone in a dark cave. All alone and she lost her baby. She had been right all along. She'd fail.

Hands on her shoulders startled her. Maybe she wasn't alone, after all. She tried to focus her eyes on who was there. Who touched her? The touch was both familiar and strange.

But then the voice reached her, penetrating the fog of fear and disappointment and shame.

"Kaelyn. Kaelyn, wake up. You're having a bad dream."

Kaelyn shot upright, the baby's cries dimming to gentle complaints.

"Oliver."

Kaelyn rubbed her eyes to clear away the sleepiness and to

protect them from the sharpness of the sunlight streaming into her room.

Sweat covered her entire body, and her feet were freezing cold.

"Is it Friday?"

Her eyes focused enough for her to see Oliver's smile. But something around his eyes looked different. Concerned.

"I came home a day early. Wanted to surprise you."

"That's so great. Welcome home." Her voice sounded dull, but she couldn't muster up her normal enthusiasm.

Kaelyn fell back to the pillow. Fatigue washed away any joy she should have at Oliver's unexpected presence. She should have been more excited, but mostly she felt numb. And tired. Her fingertips stung as if they had been clawing through rock for real, and yet there was no relief at Oliver having rescued their baby.

She'd feel better after some sleep. Yes, she just needed some sleep.

Oliver's weight settled next to her on the bed. She loved having him around, but couldn't he just give her a minute to sleep things off?

She grabbed the pillow and covered her head.

"Love, I got home, and the baby was crying in her bed."

Okay, so the baby cried, and he picked her up and she wasn't crying anymore. What exactly was the problem?

She kept those words to herself. She just needed to sleep.

"Kaelyn, she was on her belly and screaming. We're supposed to put her on her back, remember? The doctor made a big deal about it."

Kaelyn had put the baby on her back. She always put the baby on her back and made sure there was nothing extra in the crib. She double-checked that the monitor was working and that the baby was breathing at least ten times before leaving the room. She had been on her back.

"Kaelyn. Are you sick?" His hand slipped under the pillow to feel her head.

Maybe she was sick. Maybe Kaelyn was so sick that she should go to the hospital and maybe they would admit her for a few days and she could rest. She could sleep. She could have a reprieve from the responsibilities and the crying and the inability to live up to any of her own high expectations.

"Kaelyn, you're worrying me."

She groaned and sat upright. "I put her in the crib on her back. I know I did."

"You know what that means, then…" His voice was jubilant as he snuggled his baby. "Somebody has rolled over!"

Those words startled Kaelyn so much that she jolted upright in the bed, knocking the pillow to the floor as the reality of his words kicked in.

"She rolled over? Our baby rolled over? She hasn't done that yet!"

Oliver laughed and held the baby up in the air. Poppy's musical laughter cut through the final bits of fog that hovered around Kaelyn's head.

Kaelyn couldn't help but repeat the words. "Our baby rolled over! I can't believe she rolled over."

She felt the blood draining from her face, and Kaelyn could tell the moment Oliver noticed it, too.

"Love, this is exciting. Our baby girl reached a milestone. Early, even." He pulled Kaelyn up with his free hand, snuggling the baby so effortlessly in his other arm. "Let's celebrate."

Oliver led her out to the living room and commanded the Bluetooth smart speaker to play their wedding song.

"Who's the smartest baby?" Oliver cooed to Poppy. "It's harder to roll from back to tummy, so I suppose she's on the path to becoming a rocket scientist."

Kaelyn chuckled and rolled her eyes.

"It'll be interesting to see if she does it again or if it was a fluke."

The moment was too perfect. Fully awake from her dream, Kaelyn was caught up in a fantasy life come true, emotions flooding her and carrying her away on a cloud of happiness. The rain-filled clouds hovered in the distance, on the horizon, as if they never belonged in her world in the first place.

How could Kaelyn have doubted anything? How could she have allowed herself to take so much for granted?

Kaelyn wrapped her arms around Oliver's neck, kissing Poppy on the head as they drew close. Poppy reached up and tugged on her mother's hair, and Kaelyn showered her with more kisses in return. Kaelyn then turned her attention to Oliver, kissing him to show him how glad she was to have this moment with them.

Her family.

Would there ever be a feeling as satisfying as dancing with her husband and their baby, heart-to-heart-to-heart, around the living room in the town she had always considered her home? If she could take her eyes off of Oliver's handsome, joyful face, she could glance out her living room window and see glorious ocean waves, but even that couldn't compare to the moment they occupied.

So much love. So much to be happy about. So much to live for.

They swayed like that, together, for the rest of the song, and then for another. And then a fast song came on and they bopped around, and she didn't care that she hadn't showered and had been wearing the same spit-up stained T-shirt for at least a couple of days. Oliver didn't seem to care, either, if he noticed at all. He seemed as caught up in love's glow as she was. A love she lived for, breathed for, fought for.

Not that he would make her fight. No, he gave his love so freely.

She couldn't help but love him back with every ounce of her being.

Kaelyn's reawakened joy nearly consumed her. She clapped her hands to her mouth and had to acknowledge the big moment of the day yet again. "Our baby is rolling over. I can't believe it!"

Kaelyn kissed Oliver again, and then they put Poppy on the floor to see if she would show off for them.

Together, they urged their baby girl on, encouraging like they were her personal cheerleaders. And they were. They always would be.

Poppy kicked her feet and laughed and then cried, then laughed again after Oliver blew raspberries on her belly.

Poppy loved her daddy so much. It was the most beautiful thing Kaelyn had ever seen.

About to give up on witnessing Poppy's new skill, Kaelyn stood up and stretched her back, which was incredibly sore after spending so much time in bed.

"Where are you going?" Oliver asked.

"To grab some lemon water. Want some?"

She didn't wait for an answer, but had only made it halfway across the room when she whirled around at the sound of Oliver's delighted applause.

"That's my girl! Look at our genius daughter. Rolling over again."

Kaelyn rushed over. She had turned away too soon. She missed it again.

She sank to the floor on her knees, rubbing Poppy's back as the baby squealed in apparent frustration at having found herself on her belly again.

"She doesn't like it." Kaelyn scooped Poppy up in her arms and snuggled her tight, knowing full well she wasn't the parent Poppy preferred snuggling with, not when her daddy was nearby.

"She'll get used to it. I imagine she'll learn how to flop back over onto her back soon enough, since that's the easier skill."

Ruby entered the room, smiling brightly and asking what all the cheering was about. She cheered along with them as they filled them in on her granddaughter's new trick.

A fear struck Kaelyn. She'd been studying milestones, and this wasn't the way it was supposed to happen. "Do you think there's something wrong that she hasn't flipped from her belly yet but went straight to flipping from her back?"

Ruby grinned and draped an arm around Kaelyn's shoulders. "Babies develop like snowflakes. There are averages and statistics and predictions, but every baby is different and beautiful. They do things on their timeline, not necessarily the timelines established in the books. Besides, Oliver did the same thing. He skipped crawling, too, and went straight to walking."

Ruby's pep talk eased some of Kaelyn's concern, but she added a note to her list of things to ask the doctor.

And then it hit her. The slowness of the days, the way they dragged on, had frustrated Kaelyn. She had been so bored. So tired. So painfully aware of how her existence only meant going through the motions from sun up until she could crash for however many hours Poppy would allow her to sleep at night. And now there she was with a baby who was already flipping over and was one step closer to getting up and walking out of her life.

Kaelyn carried Poppy to the couch and sat with her, not caring when Poppy fussed and tried to squirm her way out of her arms. Kaelyn tightened her hold, determined to make this baby want to be with her.

Eventually, Poppy settled down. She stared up at her mom's face, and tears prickled Kaelyn's eyes.

Poppy had so rarely made eye contact with Kaelyn. She normally stared blankly ahead when she was at the breast and scrunched up her face when fussing. She made eye contact freely with Oliver and with each of her grandmothers, but rarely with Kaelyn.

Kaelyn greedily drank in the beautiful blue depths of her infant's eyes. She marveled at the reflection of herself she saw there.

She ran a hand over Poppy's chubby arms, her squishy thighs, and her little toes.

She needed to memorize everything. Every dimple in her skin. Each tiny breath she took. All the ways she moved.

Though the days would blur together, and sometimes they'd seem to move like molasses, all those people who shared unsolicited advice and opinions had been right. Time would go too fast and rob Kaelyn of these moments. She needed to remember them. Memorize them. Make sure they remained firmly entrenched in her brain.

She needed her daughter to know Mommy would always be there for her.

She stroked a finger over Poppy's wrinkly feet, watching as the baby's toes flexed and then curled. When Poppy started rooting around at the breast, Kaelyn helped her attach and watched as her little mouth took all the milk she needed. At least Kaelyn had been able to do that for her.

"I love the whispery way she breathes when she falls asleep at the breast," Kaelyn said as Oliver paused in the doorway, leaning against the wall and watching them with so much love in his eyes.

Kaelyn brushed a finger over her daughter's soft, coppery hair and traced the curvature of her ear. Heat rose in her neck and flooded her cheeks. She loved this precious human with everything she had, but was love enough? Was she enough?

"Oliver, am I a bad mother?"

She couldn't look at his face and risk seeing whatever truth played across his features. He had never lied to her well—not even when trying to keep a gift a secret.

"No," he rushed to say, springing to her side in two seconds flat. "You're a lovely mother. A tired one. And that's my fault. But I can't stop watching you and the way you mother her so beautifully. Poppy is lucky to have you. I'm lucky to have you."

Tears fell from Kaelyn's face onto her baby's cheeks, but Poppy didn't stir.

"I thought it would be easier. I feel like all I do is mess up. I didn't even know she was crying, and you came home and had to save her. She could've suffocated. She could've…"

Oliver pulled Kaelyn's head over to his shoulder and wrapped both arms around her. He rubbed her back and kissed her hair.

"Kaelyn, love. She was completely fine. You would have woken up. She lifted her head with no problem and there was nothing in there for her to suffocate on. Babies roll over. That's what they do. Even if I had been here, we could've been sleeping in the middle of the night and she might've rolled over. There's never a guarantee that we'll be there for every single thing she does. But don't beat yourself up. You're so tired. My mother told me you've been exhausted, and I know I need to be here more."

"The only reason you're not around as much is because of me." Kaelyn wiped her nose on the back of her hand. "All of this is my fault. You've always done what I wanted."

He chuckled, his warm breath soothing her scalp and her soul.

"You make me sound quite complacent. I assure you, if I thought this was the wrong move, I would have put up a fight. I went along with you because I sensed this was where we needed to be. And I don't regret it."

She crooked her neck to see his face. "You don't? Because we could move back."

"No. This is our home now. We're staying. And if I need to get a different job, that's what we'll do."

She hadn't wanted to move, but she'd been desperate to fix whatever ailed her, even if it meant grasping at imaginary problems.

He held her while she cried, though Kaelyn hadn't realized she needed this kind of cleansing. When she was done and knew she wouldn't ever be able to cry again because she had spent all her tears, Kaelyn still had questions.

She inhaled deeply and exhaled, trying to calm her hammering heart. "Being a mother has taught me so much. And I feel so bad that I was so horrible to my mother."

"Your mother doesn't seem to hold a grudge over it. And from the way she talks, you were far from horrible as a child."

"Magical rewriting of history?" Since letting down her guard, Kaelyn had allowed herself to remember many of the beautiful aspects of her youth and her life with her mother, yet the guilt of all the lost years weighed heavily.

Before having a child of her own, Kaelyn had so much faith in her ability to be everything to her daughter. And yet there she was, not measuring up to her own expectations at every turn.

Oliver kissed her again and then stood up.

"Enough guilt and second-guessing for one day. Let's go do something fun to get your mind off these crazy thoughts of yours."

Though she didn't have the energy, she allowed him to lead her through the motions. He took charge of getting Poppy dressed and changed and loaded into the car, all while calling into the local sub shop to have sandwiches made up for a picnic.

"I've been wanting to explore more of the island. Let's go to a beach somewhere else other than our backyard."

"Tired of our beach already?" she teased.

"I'll never tire of anything about this life of ours. But you're in a rut and that calls for making new memories and trying something different. I want you to take me to all the places you hung out as a kid. And then I want you to take me to all the places you thought would be naughty to sneak away to with your husband."

"Well, don't threaten me with a good time," she said, the smile on her face feeling more genuine than it had in ages even as her brain warred with her swinging moods. "Guess that means we're going to the lighthouse."

12

DAISY

Daisy wanted to curse Edith for being so insightful, but she had felt too sick over the last couple of days to put up a fight or hide it. The progressing illness was taking its toll with the burning, the weakness, her swollen feet... but worst of all was the fatigue.

"Living with my husband taught me a lot about seeing past someone's words and reading how they're truly feeling. And I could be completely off here," Edith said, handing Daisy a buttered piece of toast, "but I think there's something you haven't been telling me."

Daisy hedged. This was her secret to keep. She didn't want pity, and she didn't want people fussing.

But Edith saw straight through her, and the look on her face had Daisy squirming.

Maybe the promise of new love had kept Daisy feeling lighter and less sick. She certainly felt her health deteriorating ever since that last encounter with Rafael. And though she kept trying to convince herself she didn't care, he crossed her mind every other minute.

Rafael hadn't reached out to her since her outburst. He hadn't stopped by for a surprise food drop-off or an encounter on the beach. He hadn't called or texted to see if she needed anything. He hadn't reached out about the fundraiser. It was as if he had vanished from her life.

That's what Daisy had wanted. But she thought he would've at least shown up to discuss the menu planning duties they'd agreed to share.

Instead, Daisy had been stuck fielding questions from Florence about when the handsome man would be back and why he hadn't been around.

Edith prodded her back to the present. "Daisy, I haven't seen you eat anything in over a day. Please take a bite of the toast."

Her stomach threatened to unload at the thought of eating. She had developed new pains in her lower back and abdomen, and no longer experienced the vibrancy she had embraced since moving to the island.

"Daisy, please. Tell me what's going on."

Daisy couldn't keep the information to herself any longer. Surprising herself with her lack of hesitation, she poured out all the facts as she knew them.

"I haven't wanted to tell anyone, but I went to the doctor for what I thought was a urinary tract infection. There was some blood and pain and, based on a preliminary scan... well, the doctor's concerns aren't so good."

"Cancer?" Edith asked frankly.

Daisy nodded. "I haven't said the word aloud. But yes, he suspects cancer."

Edith sat back in her seat, her eyebrows drawing together as she took a deep breath. "Oh, my dear friend."

Daisy smiled. Life was too good and too short to feel sorry for things not under her control. She had enough to feel sorry for.

"It started in the bladder, but he thinks it's likely that it has spread. Of course he didn't say it like that, but I could read between the lines."

"Have you started treatments?"

Daisy cast her gaze downward. "I haven't even gone for the testing to get the diagnosis. I planned to, but... I don't know. Thinking about it is just..."

"I know it's hard, my friend, but you have to get that diagnosis. The treatments will work best if you catch it before it gets worse."

"The doctor warned the treatments would make me feel sick and probably worse than I do now, and may not be as effective as we'd hope. I haven't wanted to take time away from my family. Not when I just got them back."

"But you have to do the treatments, Daisy. Otherwise..."

"I know. I know where this diagnosis leads. And while I'd like more time, I don't want the time I have to be marred by the treatments."

As Edith sat in stunned but composed silence, Daisy made a request. "Please keep this between the two of us. I don't want Kaelyn and Khrista worrying about me. I don't want them knowing and having this color any remaining time we have together."

Edith wrapped her arms around Daisy, and it surprised Daisy how comforting it was to be touched by a friend. Still, she couldn't relax into the embrace. After years of being mistreated, touch didn't feel natural. That was something she had tried to work on. Clearly, she still had work to do.

As they sat in comfortable and compassionate silence, Florence burst into the cottage. The screen door slammed behind her. Fury marked each step as she stomped her way into the kitchen.

"Daisy O'Donnell. We need to have some words."

Nausea gathered in Daisy's throat, and she was grateful she hadn't taken a bite of the food. What could Florence be so angry about? Had she somehow heard her confessing to Edith?

"Guess who I ran into in town?" Florence didn't wait for Daisy to respond. "That's right. Rafael. The man I've been going on and on about having a thing for. I casually asked him why he hadn't been around. He told me you didn't want him around."

Daisy stiffened. Florence would think she sent Rafael away so Florence couldn't have him!

Oh dear, what had she done?

Voice shaking, Daisy tried to explain without over-explaining.

Florence held a hand up to stop her.

"I don't want to hear anything from you quite yet. It came out in our conversation that you pushed him away, even though the two of you had a little thing going and he had thought you were growing closer. He can't understand what went wrong."

"I can explain," Daisy started, her mouth making smacking noises as she searched for words to form.

"Oh, you better believe you're gonna do some explaining."

Florence slammed her purse onto the table, shaking the plate that held the toast.

Softening her voice, Florence said, "Daisy, I'm not mad that you had a thing with him. I'm mad you didn't tell me! Are you really going to do this again? Didn't we talk about this?"

Florence scraped the chair out and sat, scooting it closer to Daisy. "I told you we would never let something like this come between us again. I'm never going to lose a friend over a man. Not again. They are a dime a dozen. Our friendship is gold. He's a good-looking guy, but I was only looking for an island fling. He wants you. All of you. In every sense of the word. Not a fling. I'm pretty sure he wants forever. Poor man is heartbroken, and obviously, you are, too."

Florence rolled her eyes.

"I don't do men who want forever. I am not into that kind of commitment." Florence brushed each shoulder, one at a time, as if dislodging the idea of something sticking to her. "He's the kind of guy who's built for forever."

And with those words, Daisy's desire to keep her potential diagnosis private fell out of the sky.

"I probably don't have forever. It's not confirmed, but so far everything is progressing just as my doctor warned it would."

"What?" Florence fell back in her seat, realization at what Daisy was telling her reflected in her eyes.

"I wasn't planning on telling anyone. But you might as well know. I was just telling Edith."

Her friends each laid their hands on her as if they couldn't resist trying to transfer their strength into her. She wished it would work. How she would love to have a bit of their strength and confidence.

"Does Rafael know?" Florence asked softly. Daisy had never seen her looking so serious.

"He doesn't need to know. Rafael already lost a wife too young. He doesn't need to experience that kind of loss again."

Florence straightened her shoulders and pursed her lips. "Well, I, for one, will not be leaving your side. And you will get through this. Heaven isn't ready for you yet."

Florence and Edith held the silence for Daisy. She couldn't bring herself to feel sad. She was too full of love, too grateful for all fate had given her over the last year.

The day Harold died, Heaven granted her a new lease on life. She wanted a longer-term rental, but she had made good use of the allotted time and no matter what happened, she was fully satisfied.

That's what she tried to tell herself.

Her mood shifted as her mind finally opened to all that was happening. Though it was easy enough to avoid thinking of the realities of her situation, it was harder to gloss over the truth when spoken aloud.

"I thought I'd be okay with dying. That I'd been so blessed with my new life after gaining my freedom." She wiped her running nose with the cuff of her sweater. "But all of a sudden, all I can think about is how I want more time. I want to see my great-granddaughter go to her first day of school. I want to feel a man's gentle touch. I want to travel with my friends and explore the world." She broke into a sob. "I want to make up for all the time I lo-lost with Kaelyn and Khrista."

"Oh, sweetie." Edith rubbed her back while Florence gripped her hand tight.

Daisy hiccuped on a sob. "I've been so dumb. I've put off going to the doctor because I didn't want to deal with it. Who does that? And now it could be too late."

"It's not too late," Florence assured. "We'll get you to the doctor this week. Figure out what we're working with. We're not giving up."

Daisy closed her eyes and let their reassurances wash away her anguish. "Please don't tell anyone outside of our little circle. I'll tell Alice when she gets back, but it's really important to me we keep this between us."

Edith shook her head, her brow furrowing and her expression long. "I think it would really hurt Khrista and Kaelyn to not know. They would want to help you through this. They'd want to spend all their time with you."

Daisy paused before speaking. "That's why I don't want them to know. They've already given so much to this old woman. I want to watch them living their lives, not waiting for me to die. I want to see the happiness in their eyes as they flourish. I don't want to see sorrow as they watch me struggle. Eventually, I won't be able to hide it. But while I can, please allow me to have this gift of their happiness."

It took several moments for them to agree, but when they finally nodded, Daisy broke into a wide grin.

"And I am counting on the Quad to help me live my life in style."

13

KHRISTA

Khrista replaced her fleeting urge to drink with a new habit of sitting on the couch with a giant box of cookies dipped in a melting pint of ice cream, with the fireplace blazing and Christmas movies—recorded and saved from the Christmas season—blaring on the television. Corny and clichéd, but incredibly comforting.

Her to-do list loomed over her, but with people in town questioning whether she should be the one running the fundraiser, she didn't know how to progress. Ensnared between not wanting to let anyone down and not wanting to cause difficulties for anyone's business, she did nothing, her next step a mystery.

Khrista shoved another cookie in her mouth and crunched.

Messages mounted on her phone, piling up and pointing to the disaster her life had become once again. People wanted answers and direction from her. How could she face them knowing she had brought the worst kind of attention to something that should have been pure?

Khrista continued to ignore the phone, promising herself one more movie before facing reality. One more pleasant stroll down a picture-perfect Main Street with townspeople who didn't turn on one another. A beautiful Christmas tree lighting followed by a gingerbread building station and perhaps a Christmas cookie bake-off. Khrista paused the movie to make herself a cup of cocoa, immersing herself in the full experience. A true escape.

Three-quarters of the way through the film, when the small-town guy was about to lose his big-city girlfriend who had come home to manage her widowed father's estate before returning to her regular life in the city, Kaelyn called. Though Khrista could ignore most people, she couldn't ignore her daughter.

"Hey, baby girl. What's going on?" Khrista invoked her happiest voice. She didn't want anyone worrying, especially Kaelyn.

"Mom, Clarice said she's been trying to reach you. She said people are being mean? What's going on? And why didn't you call me?"

"Oh, honey. You don't need to worry about this. You've got enough on your own plate."

"Mom. Did you think I wouldn't hear anything? Rumors fly through this island faster than a runaway kite on a hurricane day."

"I guess I just hoped you'd be so busy with that beautiful grandbaby of mine that you wouldn't be paying attention to silly island gossip."

"I'm never too busy to care about you. You're not letting those women get in your head, are you?"

Khrista bit into another cookie.

"Of course not," Khrista said around the dissolving cookie crumbs. "Everything is fine."

"Mom. You're eating cookies. Let me guess. Dipping them in ice cream?"

Khrista glared at the pint of ice cream in her hands as if it had betrayed her.

"I don't know what you're talking about," she lied. "But honestly, I'll be fine. I won't flake on my responsibilities. I just have to move past the idea of little things, you know, like having a job."

"What does this have to do with your job?"

Khrista filled Kaelyn in on all the details. Her director asking her to step down, the protests from the woman they had run into on the beach that night, and everything Khrista had heard while she was in the tearoom.

She could practically hear her daughter's redheaded temper igniting through the phone.

"This is why I didn't want to tell you. I don't want you getting mad on my behalf. They're probably right. I had no business jumping into a cocktail party fundraiser after everything I put this town through. They're right. It's not good optics. I could've done something else. A cupcake fundraiser or a cookie walk or a gingerbread building event or something."

"Oh, Mom. You're watching Christmas movies, aren't you?"

"So judgmental today."

Kaelyn's melodic laughter had Khrista smiling and putting down the cookie she was about to shove into her mouth.

"Listen, Mom. You chose a cocktail fundraiser because you knew it would raise the most money. Everyone loves a good cocktail. And whether you can handle your alcohol is none of their business. They're not in charge of you. Nobody tells Harvey he can't roam around the beach collecting aluminum cans after the tourists leave. No one tells Gerard he can't throw a fit everywhere he goes. No one tells anybody else what they can and can't do."

Khrista's ravenous sweet tooth vanished, and her stomach ached. She hated feeling so judged. If only she had done a better job at hiding her secret life. If only she hadn't messed up to the point of going to work while skimming along rock bottom.

"Mom, seriously. We have plenty of quirky personalities on this island, and they're allowed to just be. You're allowed, too. Those of us who know and love you understand how hard you've worked to overcome your problems. But even if you were getting drunk every night, as long as you're not hurting anyone, it's none of their business."

Immediately after her pep talk, Kaelyn got off the phone to tend to a crying Poppy.

Kaelyn had given Khrista a lot to think about. When had her daughter turned into such a wise woman?

The people flinging accusations surely had secrets and flaws of their own. And the only one who would be hurt by Khrista checking out would be Clarice.

Warding away the self-pity, Khrista tidied her station on the couch and checked all her voicemails. So many people loved and cared about her, as evidenced by the number of calls asking what they could do to help. Friends from the Knot-TEA Knitters club took turns leaving messages and threatening to beat down her door if she didn't respond. Bess, a previously homebound senior Khrista had developed a friendship with after helping her clean up her life, left a message saying she had selected her winter cocktail gown and expected to be picked up as planned, no matter how those self-serving nasty gossips attempted to derail the event. Her co-teacher, Danielle, freshly off maternity leave, begged to know why she wouldn't be teaching with Khrista upon Danielle's return to the class-room. There was even a message from Sienna, Kaelyn's childhood bestie, saying she'd heard rumors and wanted to reassure Khrista that not everyone subscribed to the stories certain people told.

Khrista would have to reach out to her caring friends, but for now, she had a to-do list to tackle and only a few scant hours to accomplish her goals. Part of her was dying to hear what everyone else had heard, but she understood small town politics well enough to know not to trudge into that muddy hole of gossip.

Hiding from the truth and reality drove her into self-medicating and destroying her life before. Shame couldn't win. She wouldn't allow it.

Kaelyn was right. The women speaking out against her repre-sented a small, vocal group of busybodies who were making an issue of things that weren't any of their business.

A few hours later, Khrista had made a big dent on her to-do list.

She confirmed with the vendors that all the tables, chairs, tents, and buffet tables would be set up before the caterers arrived. She contacted

Rafael at the restaurant to confirm he didn't need anything and to let him know what time he and his staff could deliver the food. Khrista took inventory of all the cocktail supplies and made sure everything she hadn't yet dropped off at the tearoom was packed and ready to go. She contacted the local Scout troop, who had volunteered to collect driftwood and rocks to build temporary firepits around the perimeter of the entertainment area, to check that everything was on schedule.

And then Khrista dragged herself into the shower, satisfied that, although she had lost half a day to indulging her self-pity, things would run as intended.

The weather even seemed to prepare to cooperate. According to her weather app, the temperature would hover around forty-two degrees most of the day and would drop to the upper thirties, but with the patio heaters, firepits, warm clothing, and hot cocktails on the menu, not to mention the option to dance, the islanders would be just fine. Residents of Old Castle knew how to cope with less-than-ideal weather.

The next day, when Kaelyn asked if she wanted to meet up for lunch, Khrista jumped at the opportunity. Sitting around in her house with alcohol surrounding her wasn't the wisest idea, although her ability to surmount the hurdles of the previous day reassured her she would remain on the right path.

They decided to eat at the tearoom since Khrista had supplies to drop off.

In the morning, Khrista would arrive early to complete the last-minute tasks, but for now, she just needed to drive everything over there.

Once she had stored her boxes and bags in the kitchen, Khrista ordered a digestive tea, grateful for Clarice's blend. Her gut hadn't forgiven her for the previous day's junk food binge. If only Clarice had a blend for undoing all the mistakes Khrista had ever made.

"Everything okay with you, dear one?" Behind the counter, Clarice's tilted head and narrowed eyebrows exposed her concern.

Khrista chuckled, slipping her credit card back into her wallet.

"Why are you looking at me like that? I'm fine. Kaelyn's meeting me here momentarily."

Clarice tapped her chin. "I haven't liked the things I've been hearing around here."

"Can't say I've liked them, either," Khrista replied with an eye roll. "But I promise I'm not letting the judgments get to me. And nothing from my past will affect how I run this fundraiser. You have my word."

"That's not what I'm concerned about."

Khrista glanced around to see if anyone was lingering nearby. Only a few tables were occupied, and everyone seemed tuned into their own conversations.

She waited for Clarice to share her thoughts.

"Something tells me you're not forgiving yourself the way you're supposed to. Remember what we talked about? The past is the past, and you've made amends. It's not enough for everyone else to forgive you. The most important thing is for you to forgive yourself. And sparkle. Always, always sparkle."

Khrista smiled warmly.

"I'm trying. I promise I'm trying."

Clarice grinned. "That's all I ask for. Let me get you your ginger peppermint chamomile tea."

"You're a goddess." A moment later, Khrista accepted the cup of tea Clarice handed her, bringing it to her nose so she could breathe in the steam and the scent.

Clarice handed her a napkin. "You know I prefer to be referred to as 'royal-tea.'"

Khrista groaned at her friend's tea pun, though in all honesty, the silliness was exactly what she needed.

Khrista staked her claim on her favorite corner seat, putting her purse on the extra chair as she awaited Kaelyn's arrival. She sat so she could more easily reach down to pet the two kitties who rubbed against her legs.

As Khrista sipped her tea, Clarice joined her at the table to review some of the last-minute fundraiser details. Clarice had insisted on not only providing the tea for the cocktails but also creating special goodies to complement Khrista's creations.

Once Khrista had answered the questions, Clarice leaned back in her chair. "I can't tell you how much this means to me. I was able to tell a rescue in Texas that we could take some more animals."

"That's fantastic. You make such a difference in the world, Clarice."

"*We* make such a difference," Clarice emphasized.

When Kaelyn arrived, Clarice bent down to the stroller and kissed the baby on the top of her head before she excused herself.

Kaelyn said hello, but her eyes were wide and seemed distant. Her voice sounded hollow.

Khrista studied her. What was going on with her daughter? She'd sounded fine on the phone, but she looked like she just learned that mermaids weren't real.

She hadn't been herself, but Khrista had wondered if after the five years of estrangement she just didn't know exactly what Kaelyn's grown-up personality had become. Khrista had tried to dismiss the strangeness, but something wasn't right.

Alarm bells went off as vibrantly as the Christmas bells had in the movies Khrista watched yesterday, and she knew she needed to probe, even at the risk of driving Kaelyn away. Khrista had never trusted her mommy instincts—had often wondered if she had any—but fear that she'd miss the opportunity to support Kaelyn in a way she hadn't earlier in her life beat out the worry that she'd overstep her bounds.

"Kaelyn, sweetie. Are you..."

Kaelyn interrupted, but the bright smile on her face looked pained.

"I'm so surprised you wanted to come here after what happened last time. Very brave. We could've eaten at my house."

Khrista leaned forward, placing her elbows on the table.

"That's the thing. I have no reason to hide. Shame is what drove me off the deep end last time, and I never want anything like that to happen again. I refuse to hide. I can own my mistakes, but what I won't do is accept other people's perceptions of me as proof that I'm doing something wrong. If I'm doing something wrong, it will be up to me and those close to me to figure it out and reveal it and work on it. As you pointed out, it's not up to those people who don't even know me."

Tears welled in Kaelyn's eyes, but she frantically blinked them away. Poppy woke up screaming, and Kaelyn's hands shook as she unstrapped her from the stroller. She held Poppy close to her, but the baby stiffened and arched her back. Kaelyn thrust her daughter into Khrista's arms and excused herself, then rushed to the bathroom.

"Someone's not having a good day," Khrista whispered to the baby and hummed a few bars of a lullaby. Poppy immediately settled down as Khrista rocked her back and forth, swaying to the soft music playing over the speakers.

Moments passed, and Kaelyn didn't come back. Khrista picked up her phone to type out a text with her free hand but noticed Kaelyn's phone on the table. Odd. She never went five feet without her phone.

The baby sucked on her fist happily, her eyes searching the lights around the room. When Clarice came over to see if she could take Kaelyn's order, she immediately noticed Khrista's concern.

"I'd be happy to hold that baby," Clarice said, extending her hands to receive the gift.

"But what if someone needs you?"

"Someone *does* need me. Now give me that baby and go see your girl. You think it would be my first time working while caring for an infant?"

Khrista nodded her thanks, grateful for Clarice's perception. She rushed to the bathroom, afraid of what she'd find. Would she be equipped to handle her daughter's emotions? Was she the one who should be entrusted with this level of care?

Yes. Of course. She was the mother. And though she hadn't mothered her daughter properly when she was young, this was her chance. This was the do-over she'd been waiting for. And while she never wanted her daughter to suffer, if Kaelyn was going to have a moment of suffering, at least her mother would be there this time.

Khrista pushed open the bathroom door and knocked on the stall where she could see Kaelyn's feet underneath.

"Baby girl, I'm here. Talk to me."

To her surprise, Kaelyn opened the door and threw herself into her mother's arms. Khrista faltered on her footing a bit, unprepared for that reaction. Her arms hurried to cocoon her baby girl, wanting to sob alongside her as her daughter's emotions poured out onto her mother's shoulder.

Though she didn't know what was going on, Khrista gripped her daughter, speaking soothing reassurances as she encouraged Kaelyn to let it all out.

"Sweetheart, you have an enormous burden on your shoulders. What is it? Is it because Oliver has been gone?"

Kaelyn sniffled and wiped the tears away from her eyes, stepping back slightly to take some space.

"He's back. I thought that would make me feel more normal again, and it did for a bit, but something's wrong with me, Mom."

"Nothing's wrong with you. You're exhausted. That's normal in a new mom."

Kaelyn's bright red face warned Khrista to tread lightly. She had never seen her daughter this fragile. Not since moving her off the island way back in Kaelyn's teen years.

And not since the miscarriage.

"I've been thinking my strangeness was because I've been so tired. But I think it's something worse. I don't feel like a mother. I feel like a babysitter. Like someone left me in charge of their kid and then forgot to pick them up again, and I'm tired. I'm so tired, Mama. Not just for sleep, but I'm tired of this life." Kaelyn buried her face in her hands. "That sounds horrible, and I know I'm a terrible person."

Khrista pulled Kaelyn's hands away from her face. There would be no hiding in shame. "No, you're not, Kaelyn. You're so brave to talk about the despair you've been feeling."

"I was happy as anything when I left the house, and then walking here with Poppy I started feeling emptier and emptier." Kaelyn swiped tears away. "I've been so terrified that I'll mess everything up. That—"

"That you'll make the mistakes I made?"

Kaelyn covered her face again and burst into a fresh wave of tears.

"That's the thing, Kaelyn. I didn't know how much I was messing up while I was messing up. You're able to identify the negative feelings you're having. That puts you *leagues* ahead of where I was. It took me way too long to realize the mistakes I was making. Maybe I could've got help way back then and things would've been different for you and your childhood." Khrista gently pried Kaelyn's hands away from her face once again. She cupped her hands on her daughter's cheeks, swiping away her tears with her thumbs.

"Listen to me, Kaelyn. Poppy is so lucky to have a mom who's so tuned into her own feelings. My guess is you're experiencing postpartum depression. I thought things were a little off with you, but I wasn't sure and I didn't want to push you away by saying anything that sounded like an accusation. But whatever it is, it's not your fault."

A light went on behind Kaelyn's eyes, as if she hadn't thought about the fact that it could be postpartum depression.

"Oh, honey. I'm sorry. I should have spoken to you about my concerns."

"You know I wouldn't have listened to you. I've been trying, I really have. I love Poppy. Please don't think I don't love my baby."

"Of course I don't think that. You're such a loving, sweet mama."

"I've felt so strange. Poppy likes everyone else but me."

"No, she's probably picking up on the anxiety you're feeling. But now that you're realizing there's a problem, you can do something about it."

"I don't know what to do. Oliver will be so disappointed in me, if he's not already. No matter how hard I try, I don't seem to get better at this parenting thing."

"You couldn't disappoint that man if you tried. You can't help it if you have depression. It's obvious you love Poppy, and you meet her needs." Khrista rubbed Kaelyn's arms. If she could absorb some of her baby girl's pain, she'd do so without hesitation. Nothing Khrista had ever endured in her life burned as deeply as watching her daughter fall apart and not being able to glue her back together. "Will you let me help you get an appointment with your doctor?"

Kaelyn nodded, and relief rippled through Khrista.

"Where's Poppy?" Kaelyn looked around the room as if the baby would materialize.

Khrista laughed uncomfortably. "Clarice is holding her."

"Mom, she's working."

"Have you ever tried to deny Clarice anything when she had her mind set on something? Yes, Clarice is a busy working woman. But she revels in taking care of babies. She can do all of her work one-handed while holding a baby, so no worries there. I've seen her in action."

"I'm gonna splash water on my face and then I need an extra-large cup of tea. And Poppy."

Khrista rubbed Kaelyn's back as she splashed her face, then put an arm around her shoulders while they walked out of the bathroom. When they turned the corner to enter the main part of the tearoom, Khrista dropped her arm so as not to draw attention to Kaelyn's sadness.

Her bright, flushed face and swollen, red-rimmed eyes would give away that she had been crying, but Khrista didn't need to make it even more obvious.

They were both surprised to see Daisy standing by Clarice, playing with the baby's toes as Clarice sang along to the song in the background.

"Oh, my two other favorite girls," Daisy exclaimed. "I love all these family reunions we keep having. What a joy to live on a small island."

They invited Daisy to join them, and Khrista pulled over another chair. Clarice told Kaelyn the baby seemed hungry, so Kaelyn took the baby back and helped Poppy get latched on. The tension drained from Khrista's body as she observed the way Kaelyn relaxed, relieved to nourish her baby.

Daisy studied Kaelyn's face, and before Khrista could think of something to distract her, her mother leaned forward. "Sweetie, I don't want to probe, but I can't help but notice that you look like you've had a rough day."

Tears brimmed in Kaelyn's eyes once again, but she gave a weak laugh.

"Yeah. It's been a doozy. But in a good way. Kind of." Kaelyn pressed her hand to her temple.

Kaelyn always developed headaches after crying, so Khrista dug in her bag for a lavender peppermint headache stick she always carried with her. She had developed a friendship with the woman who ran the alchemy booth at the farmer's market on the town square, but she lived off-island during the winter, so Khrista had to buy in bulk while the markets were in season.

Khrista offered the stick to Kaelyn, who uncapped it and started rubbing. "Can you fill her in? I can't talk."

Khrista nodded and then turned to her mother.

"We suspect Kaelyn may suffer from postpartum depression. She's been having a tough time with her emotions since the baby was born. Probably all hormonal and easy to fix with some medication and therapy."

Daisy's face wrinkled in concern. "I remember having similar feelings after having your mother." She placed a reassuring hand on Kaelyn's arm.

"You did?" Khrista had missed out on so much by not having a relationship with her mother. So many things they never talked about. So many things they could have fixed if they had known how to communicate.

Daisy grimaced. "After the emergency hysterectomy. They didn't have explanations for those feelings back in the day nor easy access to diagnosis or medication that could actually help. Things were so different back then. So many women I knew in my neighborhood were still stuck in the 1950s routine of taking uppers to be the perfect housewives during the day and then sedatives to bring them back down so they could sleep at night. But mental health? Depression after something as natural as having a baby? Ludicrous."

"Thank goodness things have changed," Khrista said.

"Absolutely," Daisy agreed.

Khrista watched the pain etching her mother's face. A tide of sorrow washed over Khrista. Even with therapy, Khrista struggled to overcome the pain of all she had learned of her mother's tough childhood and what Daisy had endured with first her parents, and then her husband. Khrista had spent so much time hating her mother for not protecting her from abuse that she had never viewed the full situation clearly.

"I'm sorry you went through that, Mom." Khrista fought the tears that threatened. After years of numbing herself so she couldn't cry, her tear ducts sure were catching up for lost time. She fervently prayed that her mother had been honest about her health status, and though she wanted to delve deeper and ask more questions, now wasn't the time.

"Grandma, I'm sorry you had to feel this way with no hope of having anything to help you feel better." Kaelyn brushed the hair off Poppy's forehead, her expression so loving that it made Khrista breathless.

Kaelyn's eyes no longer looked so distant. "I feel so much better even now, just knowing it's possible there's something I can do to feel better. I felt so hopeless for so long now and so afraid of messing things up. Thank you for listening to me, Mom. And thank you, Grandma, for sharing your truth, so I don't feel so alone."

Daisy grabbed one of Kaelyn's hands and one of Khrista's hands and squeezed them tight. "This world hasn't been kind to the three of us, has it? But we all have wonderful lives now. And this may sound crazy, but I think we should hold our heads high. We need to claim the lives we want. We won't let anyone shove us back into the shadows. Our lives are ours to live and we will do whatever it takes to live them to the fullest."

They all agreed, and Khrista noticed each of them sitting a little taller—even Poppy once she withdrew from the breast and burped. Poppy sat on her mother's lap, her back to Kaelyn's chest, and seemed to have a little twinkle in her eye as if she knew it was her generation that would fully break all the curses. She would grow up loved and protected by the flawed women who came before her.

Once they finished their tea, the four O'Donnell women walked to the beach together to check the progress of the scouts as they set up the fire pits. Kaelyn left the stroller on the paved area before the beach and carried Poppy facing outward. Her little legs kicked in excitement as they walked toward the water.

Pausing, Kaelyn squatted down to pick up a seashell. She held it to her heart and said, "I think this occasion calls for something ceremonial."

"Ceremonial?" Khrista asked, amused by her daughter's dramatic flair. Kaelyn's beautiful red hair whipped into a fierce frenzy when the wind blew, and she lifted her face to the wind as if inviting it to cleanse her.

"Yeah. Ceremonial. Doesn't it feel like that kind of a day? Grandma said we need to claim our lives. Doesn't this seem like the perfect time and place to do that?"

Khrista crouched to retrieve a seashell of her own, following Kaelyn's lead and pressing it to her chest. She held out a hand in case she needed to steady Daisy, but Daisy hunched over and got back up with no trouble. Daisy's smile engulfed her face as she emulated the seashell-over-the-heart routine.

"I think we should all close our eyes and imagine how we want our lives to be." Kaelyn closed her eyes, wishing as fiercely as she had as a child. Always whimsical and a bit wild-hearted.

Khrista didn't have to close her eyes to make her wish, because everything she had ever wanted was right in front of her.

"Did you make your wishes, Mom and Grandma?"

Khrista nodded, biting the inside of her cheek to keep from crying. Daisy let out a whoop and held her seashell up in the air.

"I will love all of you as deep as the sea," Daisy offered solemnly.

Kaelyn lifted her shell, touching the edge to Daisy's. "I will love all of you—and myself—with the strength of the sharks and the whales."

They waited expectantly for Khrista to add her vow, so she

brought her shell to join theirs and said, "I have more love for you than there are grains of sand on all the beaches of the island."

Each of the O'Donnell women rested their shells over Poppy's heart, channeling their love and strength into her. Khrista hoped their lessons would stick with Poppy so she'd never have to learn them the hard way.

14

KAELYN

Oliver held Kaelyn tightly as if loosening his grip would force her to let go and she'd float off into a universe far, far away. She had tried to explain to him that knowing she could reach out for help and that there could be a biological reason for her feelings helped her feet remain grounded to the floor.

"I knew something was off with you, but I thought you were just tired and moody. Hormonal." He attempted a smile and teased, "Don't hit me."

Kaelyn didn't like the dim light in his eyes. "Stop looking so guilty. You did nothing wrong, and I didn't even know there was fully something wrong with me. But the important thing is that now I can get it fixed."

"You sure you don't want me to go with you to the doctor? I want to be there to help you every step of the way."

"My mom really wants to take care of me today. And if you could just keep Poppy here with you, I think that would be helpful."

Oliver squeezed her hand and kissed her.

"Whatever you need. And I mean that."

Kaelyn finished getting dressed, taking a luxurious shower while

Oliver watched the baby. She nursed Poppy before leaving, holding her tight and telling her precious love that she would be a better mommy soon. When Oliver heard, his eyes filled with tears, which only made her hurt even more.

"We can't both be emotional wrecks," Kaelyn said, swiping tears away.

"Everything about you is so beautiful, Kaelyn. I'm glad you're getting help. Thank goodness the doctor could squeeze you in today." He brought her hand to his lips and kissed her knuckles.

Kaelyn wrapped her arms around him and squeezed tight.

"I've gotta run. Mom will pull up any second, and my nerves are going a little crazy. I'll wait outside and get some fresh air before she gets here."

"You sure you're okay?"

"I am. I love you."

Kaelyn hoped that once she had answers from the doctor, along with a treatment plan, Oliver's face could relax again and he could look at her with only love and not worry. More than anything, she wanted him to ease back into their relationship and not think he needed to take care of her. She could take care of herself, and she hoped she proved that to him by taking this important step.

Her mom acted too gentle with her as well. It was an uncomfortable thing to have everybody walking on tiptoes around her, but Kaelyn reminded herself that she would feel the same way if one of her loved ones was having a crisis. As her mother kept reminding her, Kaelyn had to learn to forgive herself the way she forgave others.

It was something they were each working on. Something she wanted for her mother, so it made sense to want it for herself.

The ride off-island and to the medical facility was quiet, but the companionable sort of quiet that helped set her at ease. Her mother had checked in with her for a minute, then respected her need for silence.

When they pulled up in front of the building, Khrista let out a playful whistle. "Look at that, a parking space right out front."

"You don't have to come in with me. I'll be okay."

"I won't go into the office with you unless you want me there, but I'd really like to walk you into the building and wait in the waiting room. I feel better knowing I'm there if you need me. I'll give you all the privacy in the world. Look, I brought a book." Khrista held up a ratty paperback she probably picked up from the library's annual book sale. She and Kaelyn had always loved second-hand, well-loved books. They used to talk about giving books eternal life.

Kaelyn accepted her mother's offer of compromise and had to admit that she welcomed Khrista's presence even if walls would separate them.

It didn't take the doctor long to agree with Kaelyn's theory.

"I want to run some tests to rule out a medical cause, but I'm going to prescribe you an antidepressant so we don't waste time getting you started. Postpartum depression affects so many women. You're lucky you noticed it this early on." The doctor handed Kaelyn pamphlets on the subject. "It is in no way a reflection of your parenting or your love for your child. In fact, that you're here seeking help tells me how much you love your baby. The meds can take a while to kick in, but you should start feeling better within a few weeks. We might have to play around with the dosage for some time before we get the right amount for your particular body chemistry, but many people experience the placebo effect after their first dose just knowing they're taking a step toward feeling better."

Kaelyn thanked the woman profusely and promised to schedule an appointment with her therapist. The doctor took a few moments to caution her about warning signs to watch for, and the prospect of having thoughts of harm toward herself or her baby terrified Kaelyn, but knowing she had a card with a phone number she could carry in her wallet set her at ease a bit.

"You have a support system?"

Kaelyn nodded, her throat closing around her sobs again. She did. She had the best support system. A support system a year ago she wouldn't have thought she'd have. A support system she hadn't even thought she would ever want or need and that she now never wanted to live without.

Her mother hugged her when Kaelyn walked out of the room, probably because she could tell she'd been crying yet again. Though Kaelyn had learned to accept her red hair, she hated the paleness of her skin and how it gave away her emotions so readily.

"How are you feeling about everything, baby girl?"

Kaelyn assured her that everything was great. And then they walked out of the building in silence. Kaelyn turned down her mother's invitation for a boba tea at the little shop down the street, just wanting to get home to her baby.

"It's so strange. I've been so desperately wanting a break from parenting, and now that I'm away for a couple of hours, all I can think about is getting back to Poppy. I miss her so much now that I'm not with her."

Khrista chuckled low. "The curse of the mother. You can never not miss your child."

Her mother's mood turned darker, and Kaelyn knew that was her fault when Khrista said, "But that's not to say I don't support your decision to move, if you decide it's right for you."

"Mom, I'm not moving away."

"What?" Khrista looked like she was trying to hide the fact that she was wiping tears away, but it was too late. Kaelyn could see them.

"I know I said that I was considering leaving the island, but that was when I was upset. And it had nothing to do with you, I promise. I realize now that changing location won't make everything better. And I know I'm where I belong. Oliver and I both love living in Old Castle, and you and me and Grandma have so much lost time to make up for. I'm sorry if I made you feel bad when I said I wanted to move back to the West Coast."

Khrista stopped descending the cement staircase leading to the sidewalk and turned to her daughter.

"That does make me happy. But I'll always support any decision you make. There's no distance that could keep us apart. Not like before."

"I'm so thankful for you, Mom."

"Oh, honey. You have no idea how thankful I am for you."

The buzzing of Khrista's phone interrupted their tearful declarations. Khrista fished the phone out of her purse and apologized. "I'm so sorry, but with the fundraiser happening today, I told everyone I'd be reachable."

"Go for it," Kaelyn encouraged.

From what Kaelyn could piece together by hearing her mom's side of the conversation, something not great was going on in Old Castle. And from the sounds of it, it had to do with that group of nosy pains in the butt who had been making trouble for her mother.

Khrista was somber when she ended her call. Kaelyn almost didn't want to ask, and yet she needed to know.

"Is someone causing trouble?"

Khrista nodded and unlocked the car doors. They entered the car and buckled up, and Khrista turned the radio on softly.

"There are threats of picketing and protesting the fundraiser. And in true soap-opera-on-the-island fashion, rumor has it someone plans to notify the journalist who's coming to do a feature story that the event is immoral and not worthy of our town. Bet I can guess who that 'someone' might be."

"You've got to be kidding me." Kaelyn bunched her hands into a fist and grimaced. She loved most of the people she knew on the island, but she didn't remember there being so many self-righteous, interfering jerks. "They realize this is a fundraiser for innocent kittens, right? Like, how immoral could it be?"

"Don't let that temper flare, baby girl," Khrista teased. "Everything will be just fine. I'm not letting anyone get in the way of our successful event."

Though Kaelyn was grateful her mom sounded so relaxed about all the drama, she couldn't stop worrying that if the women followed through on their threats, maybe her mother would slide back into her old, self-protective, damaging habits.

The thought of losing this version of her mother bothered her more than her own depression. Kaelyn slouched in her seat and spent the entire drive home hoping whoever had called her mom had blown things out of proportion.

Because Kaelyn wasn't sure what she'd do if anyone messed with her mom.

15

DAISY

Of all the things Daisy should feel leading up to the fundraising event, trepidation shouldn't have been one of them.

Daisy stared at her reflection in the bedroom mirror. Though she hadn't worn makeup in years, she had allowed Alice to talk her into a makeover. Florence had insisted they drive off-island to pick out fancy dresses for the fundraiser, and Daisy now wished she hadn't allowed Florence to talk her into such a flashy, sequined affair.

Her friends had stuck around Old Castle longer, and they had been lucky enough to secure an extra week at the cottage. They wanted to be there to support her through her treatments, which she should have more information about in the next week. They had also declared the importance of being there during the fundraiser, especially when they noticed how troubled Daisy was at the treatment Khrista had been enduring. Daisy wanted to punch the lights out of the people who were so cruel to her daughter. It wasn't right.

But Khrista had assured Daisy she was handling it all just fine, and that she didn't want Daisy to hold the actions of a small group against the whole town. Khrista echoed Clarice's assurances that every town had some misguided souls, and it wouldn't be right to judge them all too harshly.

But oh boy, did she want to sock it to them. And she would, too, if they tried anything.

Then again, Daisy's mood had been horrendous ever since she had ended things with Raf.

Daisy couldn't bring herself to call him, though she thought about it all the time. Imagine. Seventy-two years old and as immature as a young girl. She had thought it strange when Kaelyn told her most people her age didn't like making phone calls anymore, but now Daisy understood the underlying anxiety.

"Everyone ready to go?" Edith rattled the keys, swinging her hips back and forth to make her floral dress tangle around her legs.

Daisy ran her hand over her hips. "This is too much. Too sparkly. I'll be ready in a minute—I need to change."

Florence shot out of nowhere and stopped Daisy from returning to her room.

"You most certainly will not change. You look stunning. Rafael will wish he pursued you when he sees all the men on the island going goo-goo over you. That red is outstanding."

Daisy pressed her cold fingers to her heated cheeks. "I know you're exaggerating, but I do feel as though people will be staring. But not in a good way."

Alice entered from the kitchen, slipping a fistful of granola bars into her purse.

"I'm bringing some for all of us, just in case we need a little pick-me-up before the food is served." She looked up and caught sight of Daisy. Her jaw dropped. "Daisy O'Donnell. You are stunning."

"You're just saying that to be nice."

"No, I swear it. I'm jealous you still have such a lovely figure."

Daisy blushed more ferociously. "You're sure it's not too much?"

All her friends rushed to assure her that her dress was just right. She smiled and accepted their word. Life was too short for a lot of things, but especially for insecurity. She'd been given this beautiful day, and she refused to squander it... even if that meant stepping out of her comfort zone. Heck, if she grew uncomfortable, she'd simply take advantage of all the cocktails available. She already knew how potent Khrista's concoctions were.

"Okay, girls," Daisy said, gesturing for her friends to gather around. "We need a selfie while we're all dolled up."

The series of photos Daisy took would be some of her most cherished possessions. She flipped through them on her phone, loving every laugh they had shared while trying to fit in the photos together.

Edith drove the Quad to the other side of the island. As they pulled into the parking lot near the beach, Daisy could see how festive her daughter had made the setting. Lovely tents peppered the beachfront, adorned with twinkling lights that flickered like fairies. Stone fireplaces encased the warm glow of fires, all strategically placed to keep the partygoers warm. The ocean cooperated, too, rolling in the gentle tide as the full moon lit the path. A band played, and Daisy remembered that Matt's daughter was the one singing. Her voice was angelic as it greeted the guests piling onto the beach.

Even though it was chilly, Daisy couldn't stop sweating. The brisk night air on her legs helped to cool her. Normally, she was freezing. But normally she wasn't filled with terror at the idea of running into Raf.

As soon as Daisy and her friends crossed onto the beach, they exchanged their tickets for goblets brimming with sparkly red liquid. Daisy couldn't remember all the cocktails her daughter had designed, but as she sipped, she knew this one was the best thing she had ever tasted.

"This sure is something," Alice said.

"Very elegant," Edith agreed. "Khrista outdid herself."

Daisy's face lit with pride. Her daughter sure was something. And though she could take no credit for it, the pride was strong just the same.

Florence gripped Daisy's arm and tried to steer her toward the ocean. "Here, let's go over this way."

"I want to go over there. I see Khrista and I want to let her know how beautiful we think this is," Daisy said, tugging her arm away from Florence, who was being quite forceful in her redirection attempts.

Florence's grip and tone tightened. "We can go to that station in a few minutes. Let's get an appetizer from the booth over there. I'm starving."

"Oh, dear. Did you hear what those women just said about our hostess?" Alice asked.

"Really, Alice? You didn't notice I was trying to keep her from hearing it?" Florence glared at poor Alice, and Daisy glanced back and forth, trying to decipher what the problem could be.

Sure enough, gathered on the edge over by where Khrista greeted her guests, just outside of the sandy area, was a small group of those little bullies. Daisy's hands turned into fists as she started hobbling her way across the sand, wishing her legs were stronger and her back didn't ache.

"What in heavens are they doing? Are they holding signs?" Daisy stopped and observed. Her stomach clenched and her pulse pattered. Oh, how she wanted to lash out!

Florence lightly gripped Daisy's arm again. "Breathe, Daisy. Don't let them get you worked up. They're not worth you hurting yourself."

Daisy couldn't respond. Her throat was too darned tight.

Edith responded. "I noticed on the way in that they had put up a banner calling it an alternative way to support the Kit-TEA Comfort Rescue. Seems as though they're running their own fundraiser. Something about morals."

"Morals!" Daisy's voice shrieked. She had never been more livid. "What is of higher moral value than supporting your fellow townsperson? How dare they put a moral value on someone else's healing!"

"Doesn't look like they're getting the support they hoped for," Alice offered. "Seems like it's just the three women over there. And an embarrassed-looking teenager, from the looks."

"I'm going over there to give them a piece of my mind," Daisy said.

Florence dropped her hand but walked alongside. "Daisy, let's think this through. They have the right to peacefully protest."

"Nonsense. Protest what? This isn't political. This is just a bunch of bored housewives being nasty."

"How do you know they're housewives?" Alice asked, looking confused.

"I don't think that's what we're supposed to call them anymore," Edith said.

Daisy pointed her glare at Alice. "I don't. But that's how things were back in our day."

Alice cleared her throat. "Not in my world. My mother worked full time, and so did all of my aunts."

Daisy snapped. "Is my word choice really the most important issue right now?"

Edith intervened with her typical clearheaded caution. "We mustn't embarrass Khrista. She's a grown woman who can handle herself."

"She sure is," Daisy agreed. "And her mother is here, so she doesn't have to."

What she didn't say—what she couldn't say—was that Daisy hadn't defended Khrista when it had mattered most. Daisy hadn't saved Khrista from the violent abuse of Khrista's father, and Daisy would have to live with that painful truth for the rest of her life.

But she could do something now. And she would. Daisy would never let anyone hurt her girl again.

As Daisy got closer to Khrista, she could see that though her daughter wore a bright smile on her beautifully made-up face, her eyes told a different story. Khrista was feeling the abuse. But like the survivor she was, she ignored it and pretended those women had no power over her. Daisy recognized the look from Khrista's defiant childhood face. Khrista rarely let anyone see her in a moment of weakness, especially her abuser.

Everyone in the area looked uncomfortable as the small group of women chastised Khrista from their cowardly distance and held signs declaring this as bad for the children of their town.

When the word "corruption" reached Daisy's ears, she couldn't hold back any longer.

The rest of the world blurred as Daisy's raging eyes zeroed in on the ringleader of the so-called protest. Daisy got a tiny thrill at the fear in the women's eyes as Daisy approached.

"Not one of you little snots is worth the time to speak out right now, but I guarantee no matter what you have to say, you will never amount to nearly as much as Khrista. That woman has a heart of gold, and to flaunt her mistakes like this is absolutely abysmal. Shame on you for your pitiful attempts at detracting from an event all these people are attending to support Clarice and her endeavors. I don't know how you live with yourselves."

Daisy was so heated she didn't even know if anyone was still around her. All her attention was on the women who stared at her. Daisy had never been one to make a scene, but this was her flesh and blood they were after, and she'd give them a piece of her mind.

Leann, the horrid ringleader, raised her face and looked down her nose at Daisy. "We're simply offering an alternative to those who would like to support the cause without enabling an alcoholic."

"I'm certain if I asked around here I could uncover some dirty deeds of yours. Shall I start asking? I haven't lived in this town long, but I'm sure there are people among us who have secrets they'd be happy to share."

Daisy paused, anger filling every pore as she sweated despite the chill in the air—for different reasons than moments before. The busybodies had the good graces to look taken aback, and maybe a touch humiliated at the little woman coming at them waving her finger. Even so, Daisy refused to back down.

She didn't know what to do next. Daisy's bones ached and the pain in her back nearly crippled her. She couldn't drop in front of them. No, she wouldn't give them the satisfaction of seeing Daisy back down.

So Daisy pushed the pain aside and stood as strong and proud as she could.

Because she was proud.

Proud of Khrista.

Proud of the community Khrista belonged to.

Proud of all Khrista had overcome to reach this point where she was doing what she believed in, helping someone who had taken her under her wing long ago when Daisy couldn't, and standing strong in the face of the shame these other people flung at her.

Daisy continued to hold her ground, loving the way the women around the ringleader shriveled and practically dropped their hand-made signs.

And then the most miraculous thing happened. The kind of thing Daisy thought would only happen in a movie.

One by one, people she recognized from the tearoom stepped forward to back her up. Daisy's friends circled around her, and one woman, the sister of the grumpy Gerard, Geraldine, spoke with strength and compassion.

"She's right. You all should be ashamed of yourselves for turning somebody's mistakes into island fodder. Khrista does a great job helping to raise all those children at the preschool, and your need to run your mouths cost her a job, but even worse, cost those children an outstanding role model and teacher. You know very well it's hard to get good quality early childhood education here with the cost of living on the island making it impossible to live on a preschool teacher's salary, and yet you didn't think twice before running your mouths and putting the school in an impossible position. I don't know why you even showed up here. I don't know why any of you even live on this island if this is how you feel about our community."

Leann found a spine and started pleading her case. "I've lived here my whole life. And we need to maintain some level of integrity on this island. She showed up drunk at the school. What if parents didn't smell the alcohol on her? What if no one intervened? Kids could have been hurt!"

Her stubborn retort only drew the attention of more people who stepped forward in defense of Khrista.

A very tall, very round man took a place next to Daisy. He smiled at her sympathetically. "I was born and raised on this island, and my kids have been lucky enough to have Ms. Khrista as a teacher. I guess you misunderstood the spirit of the island. Sure, people talk trash to one another or about one another now and then. But we don't turn on them like this. What Khrista went through was her own personal issue, and I've seen no evidence to suggest she hasn't turned herself around the way we hope someone we love and care about would. If anything, the young people on this island can look up to her for being able to make amends and to fix what's broken."

"She drove *drunk* when they kicked her out of the school. You're fine with that? She was transported to her house in the back of a police car. And now you want her to be the star?"

"The one who is the most not okay with that whole situation is Khrista. You think she has ever made an excuse for her behavior?" Bess, an older woman Khrista had provided transportation and emotional support to, hobbled forward, using a cane to balance herself on the sand. "You all should be ashamed of yourselves. If you had half the heart Khrista had, you'd be on this side enjoying a cocktail instead of making fools of yourselves. Do yourselves a favor and look to Khrista to see how you can better yourselves so your children grow to have someone decent to look up to."

Calming down now that everyone came to Khrista's defense, Daisy scanned the crowd behind her in search for her daughter. Was she hearing all of this?

Khrista remained busy with Clarice by her side, pouring drinks under one tent and then shifting gears and wiping down a table under another. The only hint that she was bothered was the stiffness of her shoulders. She was close enough to hear at least some of what was said—hopefully the good parts.

Leann doubled down, though her cohorts were putting physical distance between themselves and their fearless leader. "Yeah, sure. Great role model for the kids. Have you all lost your minds?"

Amanda Martin, the hospice nurse who adopted senior cats from Clarice's rescue so she could spoil them for the remainder of their lives, stepped forward. Her waist-length, auburn curls cascaded over her shoulders as she addressed the protesters. "Have you ever spent time with Khrista? Have you seen the way she loves the animals in the tearoom? Listen, I'm not one to get dressed up for anything—I had to borrow this dress. But Khrista is pouring her soul into doing a good deed. What you're doing is the opposite of that. Anyone who cares so deeply about animals is a good, moral person in my book. Put your signs down and come over and try the crab cakes. They're to die for."

Daisy watched in awe and through a gathering storm of unshed tears as person after person stepped forward and gave their testimonial in support of Khrista and the hard work she had put into planning the event.

Always the voice of reason, Clarice entered the squabble. Dressed in a sparkly blue wool pantsuit with small hoop and feather earrings, Clarice looked both elegant and authoritative. She held up her hands to stem the flow of words being exchanged between the larger group and the small, misguided one.

"Leann, dear," Clarice began. "I appreciate that you're standing up for what you believe, and I especially appreciate your efforts to help raise money for our rescue. But sweetie, this isn't the way."

Leann's face crumbled, the pressure finally doing her in. "You've always told me I should stand up for what I believe in! This is important. Our kids—"

"Our kids deserve to see people correct their mistakes. To grow stronger because of them. And to forgive others for the mistakes they've made, especially when those mistakes didn't affect us..."

Leann opened her mouth as though she intended to continue arguing, but as she raked her gaze over the crowd gathered to support Khrista, she must have lost her nerve.

Clarice extended a hand. "Leann, honey. Come on over and have a drink with us. We'd love to have you."

Khrista joined the crowd, looking radiant and royal with her chin lifted and her posture perfect. Flanked by Matt on one side and Aliyah on the other, she stopped only a few feet from where Leann stood. Everyone hushed to hear what Khrista would say—it seemed as though even the waves ceased their roar—though the last thing Daisy expected to see was the warm smile on her daughter's face.

"I understand your worries, Leann, and I think you're brave to stand up for what you think is right. Believe me when I tell you how much I regret my past. What I won't do, however, is stand here in shame when I know, and everyone close to me knows, what I've done to rectify my mistakes. I can't undo them. But I can move forward, and I hope you can put this behind you, too. I agree with Clarice, Leann. Join us. We have a lot of off-islanders here tonight. Let's show them what our community is made of."

Leann scoffed and turned away. She gestured to her co-conspirators, who interestingly enough hadn't said a word in support of their leader, and stormed off, leaving her friends to trail pathetically after her.

The crowd on the beachside cheered, but Clarice turned to the gathered group and waved a finger at the group. "If you didn't approve of what they were doing, don't do the same. Remember to treat others with grace and allow them the dignity of making a mistake."

Daisy wouldn't have had it in her to be so diplomatic, but she admired Clarice for staying level-headed and not choosing one child over the other, so to speak.

Daisy hadn't expected Leann and her crew to leave, but she could see the relief on Khrista's face as she watched them go.

She sidled up to her daughter and rubbed Khrista's lower back.

Khrista inhaled deeply. "Thank you for fighting for me, Mom. I never expected—"

"I'm sorry, dear. You shouldn't have had to go through that."

"I'm just glad Kaelyn is running late. I would have hated for her to witness any of that."

"She'd be proud of the dignity her mom possessed in the face of adversity."

Too choked up to respond, Khrista tried to smile at her mom, then nodded to the people gathered around. Daisy wanted to hug everyone who stood up for her daughter, but knew they needed to get the attention off of Khrista.

"This sounds like a dancing song if I ever heard one!" Daisy declared. "Who's with me?"

Her friends joined in with hoots and hollers and acted completely inappropriate for their age, but loved every minute.

Dozens of others joined them on the makeshift linoleum dance floor in front of the hobbled-together stage, singing along as Matt's daughter lit up the night air with her melodies. Daisy helped herself to the myriad of cocktails offered, amazed that Khrista had such a talent for concocting magical drinks. The world tilted in the most pleasant and fun way possible, and her smile molded itself into a permanent crevice on her face.

At the end of the song, the crowd cleared and revealed the one person she had both dreaded and eagerly anticipated seeing.

Rafael.

"Am I seeing things?" Daisy whispered the question to Florence but based on how high Rafael's eyebrows rose, she assumed he had heard her.

The crowd made way for him to walk toward her, and though the world spun as if it might fling her off, Daisy suddenly felt as sober as a teetotaler as he held his hands out in invitation.

He looked too handsome. Too kind. Too familiar.

Too much like a man ready to sweep her off her feet.

And though she still had her wits about her, she certainly didn't have the strength to turn him away when he was everything she needed and wanted.

"Dance with me?"

Daisy looked away, bashful.

"Please?"

"Mom, dance with him." Where had Khrista come from? Daisy had thought for a moment that she and Rafael were alone. The presence of all the other people made little sense. No, it was her and him in the future that couldn't quite be and yet seemed inevitable all at the same time.

She thought she said yes. Daisy could've sworn her throat helped to push the words out. And slipping her hand into his was the most natural thing. As soon as they touched, everything fell away. The air warmed. The waves hushed. The moon pulled.

Was she in a fantasy fairytale or did the music switch up to a waltz? And did Rafael actually start leading her in the dance? Did her feet remember how to move, seamlessly following his lead, recalling the moves from dance classes she had taken way back in her high school years? And did the crowd of people really gather around in a circle and clap along to the rhythm as she and Rafael soared over the dance floor, bits of sand that had made their way onto the tile crunching under their feet?

And then, *and then*, was it really her face turning up toward his as he lowered his mouth to hers?

There was no way to deny it. He was about to kiss her. In front of everyone. Rafael was going to give her everything she had been dreaming of since meeting him. He was about to set all her worries at ease and give her the happily-ever-after she had never known to dream of. The happily-ever-after she could never have believed she'd have.

"Did you mean it when you sent me away?" His voice, gruff and emotional, cut straight through every fear she'd ever harbored.

"No. I've missed you, and I wish I never said any of that."

His lips were warm and sobering, and he tasted like the smoothest whiskey punch. He was far more intoxicating than any of the cocktails served that night. And she felt...

She felt...

Sick.

Even as his lips hovered over hers, waiting for her reaction from the kiss, the threat of a fainting spell loomed over her.

"I need to sit down."

He went from nonchalant amusement, probably thinking it was his kiss that made her weak in the knees, which wasn't far from the truth, to concern when he recognized how sick she was feeling.

Khrista must've noticed too, and then Kaelyn and Oliver, whom Daisy hadn't realized had arrived, were suddenly by her side.

They helped Daisy get to a seat. Oliver fetched her a bottle of water. After a few sips, she continued to feel sick but her head returned to Earth.

Daisy exchanged a glance with Edith, who calmly nodded as if telling her what she knew she needed to do.

"I've been keeping a secret," Daisy began. "I promise I did it for you, so you wouldn't worry about me, but I realize now it's worse to see the look of concern on your faces and to keep you guessing."

"Mom, what's going on?" Khrista knelt in front of Daisy, lifting her hands into hers.

Rafael stood guard over her, his powerful presence comforting her and helping her to believe she could actually fight this thing. That anything was possible according to the energy there on the beach. Raf kept a hand firmly planted on her shoulder. She hoped he'd never let go.

Daisy told them everything she knew and how she'd been in denial but that she'd made an appointment because she realized how much she had to live for and how valuable time was. She searched each face as they absorbed the news and wished she could tell them how beautiful it was to live every day as if it could be the last.

The music continued to play in the background in a soothing lullaby. Daisy appreciated how the world kept spinning even while she was breaking the news that she may be leaving it sooner than anticipated.

The circle of love surrounding her pulsated through her, setting her nausea at ease and helping her regain her strength.

"How could you not tell us as soon as you knew?" Khrista knelt in front of Daisy, her eyes pleading for answers. "We swore we'd be open and honest. And I want to be there for you through anything."

"Khrista, darling. I didn't tell you because I wasn't ready to acknowledge it myself. And I didn't want you to worry about me. You have so much to be happy about."

"Yes, and you're a big part of that happiness."

"Grandma, you let me rant on and on about my stupid, shallow problems while you were dealing with this? All by yourself?"

"Nothing you've shared with me has been stupid or shallow. I never want my health to be the focus. I want to hear every rant and every concern. Always."

"But—"

"I didn't tell any of you because I didn't want these looks of pity. Don't pity me." Her voice sounded weak to her own ears, so she focused on the healing power of their love and found her strength. "I've finally lived the life I didn't even know to dream of, and even if it was for a short time, I know how lucky I am. Some people don't even get that. I didn't think *I* would even get that. I still have some time left to enjoy each and every one of you in each and every beautiful moment this world offers, but even if I were to drop dead at this very moment, I'd have no regrets. And that's because of all of you."

Khrista looked like she wanted to say more, but a rush of activity interrupted the tender moment as a group of goats burst into the party area, ransacking everything they could reach. Daisy covered her mouth as one goat, wearing a hand-knit sweater, climbed onto the table with the scones and pastries and eagerly gobbled up all he could reach while others clamored to get their fair share.

"What am I seeing?" Daisy asked.

Khrista gaped. "A repeat of my wedding, apparently."

The group roared and talked over one another as they remembered the scene where Khrista and Matt were about to serve the wedding scones and a group of frenzied goats burst in out of nowhere. No one had figured out where the feral creatures came from, but none of them were wearing hand-knit items at that point.

"Seems as though someone has taken a liking to the creatures," Daisy commented.

All eyes turned to Clarice as she ushered the goats away from the table. The whole thing was comical with the way some people tried to help, while others tried to pet the troublemaking goats, and still others fled the area to avoid the chaos.

Kaelyn wondered aloud, "Should we help?"

"She'll just tell us we're not seeing goats. Remember how strange she got at my wedding?" Khrista reminded her.

"Okay, I'm new here," Florence said. "But I swear she had a goat in the tearoom the other day. Am I crazy?"

Almost in unison, they all said, "It's not a goat."

And then they dissolved into laughter.

"Who would have thought Clarice would gaslight an entire island?" Kaelyn pondered, crossing her arms and shaking her head.

Khrista chuckled and said, "Who would have thought we'd let her?"

16

KHRISTA

As Khrista looked at every face joining her at her impromptu tea party, she realized she had never possessed so much love. From her knitting group pals to her old coworkers to her best friend Elanna and her beautiful children to Khrista's own blood relatives. To the man who delighted her with the marriage of a lifetime and the daughters he brought into her life. Each one held the space in her heart that was carved out specifically for them. And just when she thought she wouldn't have any more space, she was proven wrong.

She held her grandbaby close, smelling the top of her head and marveling at how intoxicating the scent was. Khrista tried to remember what it had been like to smell Kaelyn's head way back when, but some memories faded, especially when they snowballed together in the traumatic past.

But now was all about the future. Khrista forgot she had started to make an announcement until the intent gazes centered her way reminded her.

"Thank you all for joining me. I'm so pleased to announce the fundraiser was a success. Feedback from attendees was overwhelmingly positive. We got high marks for decor, food, cocktails, and overall ambiance. Many people wrote in the comment section of the follow-up survey that they'd like to see this event become a recurring event on the island. We had a great deal of people come from off-island, too. We were asked to assemble a cocktail recipe book and tea kits to sell as a continuation of the fundraiser, so we're looking into options for organizing that."

Their cheers threatened to raise the tearoom's roof, and it made her want to float into the clouds. After so many years of hating herself, it felt marvelous to find value in her existence.

"Amazingly, the vast majority of respondents to our followup poll were unaware of the, um, drama that occurred. All of them, however, were aware of the goats."

Clarice cleared her throat as Khrista sent her a meaningful look. Would she spill what she knew of the goats? Nope. Clarice darted out of the room.

Daisy pushed back her chair and stood with Rafael steadying her. "I have an announcement as well, and I hope you don't mind me crashing your tea party to share it."

Dread turned Khrista's veins icy cold, fearing the worst. But one look at her mother's bright, happy, madly in love face and she convinced herself the fear was unwarranted. Though she looked weak in the body, her spirit was anything but.

"I asked her to marry me," Rafael announced, his voice booming and proud.

They held a collective gasp until Daisy burst out with, "I said yes!"

"Mom! You kept this a secret from me!" Khrista wasn't angry. It delighted her that her mother found love and that Rafael was getting a second chance at love as well.

"There's more," Daisy teased. "We're getting married tonight. By the lighthouse. You're all invited, of course. Life's too short to wait. I have faith that I'm going to go into remission, but even if I don't, I'm so thankful for every single minute of every single day I've had with my beautiful family and this lovely community."

Daisy had, in fact, been diagnosed with the cancer her doctor suspected, and she had started treatments. Though it had spread, her treatment team remained positive that they could help her through it.

Khrista and Kaelyn agreed to not let their hope waver. With the positive energy of their island community collectively rooting for Daisy, there was no doubt this would be one unpleasant blip in their story.

"And no matter what the future holds," Rafael added, "I want to spend it with Daisy."

"Well then," Khrista said, rubbing her hands together. "Let's get going. We have a wedding to plan!"

Edith took the lead on assigning jobs while Daisy insisted they didn't need to make a fuss.

"Are you kidding?" Florence gestured to each member of what Khrista's mother affectionately referred to as the Quad. "This is the best way to spend our last night on the island. We're going to help you give us the time of our lives. Raf, baby. You have some handsome single friends you want to invite?"

Khrista loved the way Rafael grinned and shrugged, and the way Daisy glowed. After a lifetime of never knowing her mother to have friends, watching her with her own circle of supportive women and a man who wanted to marry her connected certain dots in Khrista's emotional roadmap that she hadn't even realized were disconnected.

For a wedding planned in only a few hours, things came together perfectly. Rafael had already arranged for a Justice of the Peace to meet them there to marry them, and anyone who had other plans rescheduled. Though Rafael and Daisy insisted they didn't want a big shebang, Rafael's employees put together a buffet of pastas and pizzas, and Clarice volunteered a tray of pastries. And the tea, of course.

The beach overlooking the lighthouse needed no extra decor. Especially with the cotton-candy sky and the brilliant colors as the sun guided them to the end of another day-well-lived.

And guided Daisy into a new life. Full of happiness.

As Khrista grabbed Matt's hand tightly, appreciating his warmth and the way his calmness flowed from his hand to hers, she rested her head on his shoulder and tried not to sob as her mom and Rafael recited their vows.

"I promise to love, cherish, and dance with you anytime you want," Daisy vowed.

"And I promise to love, honor, protect, and cook with you. I'll never take you for granted." Rafael wiped the tears trickling down Daisy's cheeks.

Khrista's gut tightened. The beauty of this second chance for Rafael and Daisy... she had no words for it.

Daisy sobbed through her next words, but Khrista understood.

"Rafael, you've been my lighthouse since I came to this island looking for another chance. And though I wasn't looking for you, you guided me forward and filled me with hope. You shined brightly while I struggled, and you helped ease me into this new world."

"And you, my love, my pure Daisy, showed me I could love again. That I could yearn again. That I could make a new life again."

The crowd applauded and sniffed and oohed and ahhed, and then they cheered when Rafael pulled Daisy into his arms and kissed her soundly as the Justice of the Peace declared them legally married.

Khrista could see the weakness growing in her mother, and apparently, Rafael could, too, because he practically carried her to a picnic bench and helped her sit while Clarice poured hot tea from a giant thermos. Khrista rushed over to hug her mom and her new stepdad, and she scrutinized her to make sure it was safe to proceed with the celebration.

As much as Daisy appeared tired, she didn't look like they needed to stop. In fact, Khrista knew if she tried to rob her mother of this moment, she'd never live it down. They'd proceed with caution, but Khrista also knew Rafael would make sure she rested after the ceremony. Though the lovebirds talked about taking a honeymoon, Daisy had treatments several times per week, and tomorrow was an "on" day, so they aimed to use their international honeymoon as a reward to celebrate when she was better.

Aliyah pulled out a Bluetooth speaker she had brought along and connected her phone. "Sorry for your sore throat, Gabby, but I guess I get to play DJ this time around."

Gabby rolled her eyes and moaned, but since she barely had a voice for speaking, there was no way they could expect her to sing, even though they had adored having her perform at the fundraiser.

Khrista sat next to her mom and watched her daughter, whose eyes had become bright again, dancing around with her husband and baby on the beach. All smiles, all joy. The medication had been working, and Kaelyn had said she felt more like herself. Her bond with the baby was obvious, and Khrista could breathe easier again.

As a group, they all started dancing to a party song, and everybody hooted and hollered when Rafael retrieved the garter Daisy's friends had insisted she wear.

Khrista couldn't help but ask Kaelyn what she was thinking as Kaelyn stared up at her husband's handsome square jaw. Oliver stood over them, swaying with Poppy in his arms and pointing to the birds that flew overhead, waiting for their opportunity to sweep in and collect any crumbs they could get.

"I probably shouldn't tell you this," Kaelyn said. "But I was thinking about how I want to have more kids."

The idea of more little Poppys running around the island kicked Khrista into full joy mode, and she jumped up and dragged Kaelyn to dance with her. When the music died as Aliyah searched for a requested song to add to the queue, Kaelyn's mood turned serious. Khrista followed her gaze to where Rafael had brought Daisy back to her seat. He retrieved pills from her purse and handed them to her with a bottle of water. Even from afar, Khrista could see the weakness in her mother's limbs as she struggled to raise the bottle to her lips.

"Mama, do you think Grandma is going to be okay?" Kaelyn bit the side of her fingernail and looked as vulnerable as she had when she was eight and her favorite cat was sick.

"Oh, sweetie. It's impossible to know. What I do know is she's getting the medical care she needs. The doctor said that if for some reason this treatment doesn't put her into remission, she may be a candidate for an experimental treatment in Boston. Her attitude is great, which I've always heard is one of the key indicators for healing." Khrista put her arm around her daughter and squeezed. "And no matter what happens, she's happy. And we'll do everything we can to keep her that way. No matter what."

"I hate the idea of losing her so soon after getting her."

Khrista swallowed past the lump in her throat. She had the same feelings, but this moment was about helping Kaelyn to cope.

"I know, baby girl. It's impossible to imagine. But I have a feeling we'll be watching her and Rafael dancing together for a long time. Look at them now!"

Kaelyn turned as Rafael guided Daisy into a slow dance. He held her upright, and she rested her head on his chest.

No matter what, Khrista would always cherish this day. Her mom and her new stepfather swaying in the cold winter night air with the backdrop of the lighthouse guiding them toward their happily-ever-after.

Now was no time for sadness. Or regret. Or wishing to regain lost time.

Tonight was a night to dance the negativity away and to revel in the joy of community and forgiveness and resiliency.

And hope.

And, most importantly, love.

FOR GIVEAWAYS, behind-the-scenes info, and to stay up-to-date on Old Castle happenings, please sign up for my newsletter and/or follow me on social media. (Be part of my "chosen family!")

If you enjoyed this book, I'd love for you to leave me a review on Goodreads or wherever ebooks are sold! This helps me find new readers and to access advertising opportunities so I can continue to write. :) Thank you!

For book 3 of the Happil-TEA Ever After Tea Room series (featuring Khrista and Elanna as they go on a road trip to help grumpy Gerard reunite with a lost love), please check out Old Castle Road Trip.

ACKNOWLEDGMENTS

This book came as a bit of a surprise to me. In fact, I had already written what I thought would be books 2 and 3 in the series when the O'Donnell women spoke up and let me know their stories were not complete. So those other books got shuffled around and this next step in their journey was born.

Thank you to all the professionals who helped me bring this book into the world—Jaycee DeLorenzo of Sweet 'N Spicy Designs for a cover I adore, Stacy Juba for her insightful developmental edits, and Stephanie Richardson for the outstanding audiobook narration.

Thank you, also, to the wonderful readers who have made my Facebook page more fun! Thank you for letting me know your thoughts on the first book and for sticking with me as the rest of the series is born. I appreciate you tremendously!

Thank you to Amanda Martin Ray for letting me write a version of you into the book. :) I hope you enjoy reading your name! I loved getting to know so many wonderful things about you. <3

Thank you to Kimberley Arnett Hardwick for naming Gerard's dog. Fritz will feature heavily in book 3, so stay tuned for more Fritz adventures. :) I'm glad your beloved dog is living a second life in Old Castle.

Thank you, once again, to my friends and family who enrich my life in so many ways. I love all of you. So very much. <3

AFTERWORD

If you or anyone you know struggles with postpartum depression, please reach out for help.

One good resource is https://www.postpartum.net/.

Always know you're not the only one to experience this darkness, and healing is possible.

ABOUT THE AUTHOR

Amanda Daire loves spending time with her adult children and her real-life hero. If she had to pick a few of her favorite things, they'd be trees, elephants, castles, tea, and traveling.

Amanda loves to write about complicated family dynamics, flawed characters who could be your friends, and healing hearts. But no matter how emotional the story may be, she prides herself on ending in the most uplifting way possible and maintaining hope through any hardship.

Know what else she loves? Connecting with readers! So please sign up for her newsletter and find her on social media to stay in touch!

facebook.com/amandadairebooks

instagram.com/amandadairebooks

tiktok.com/@amandadaire

goodreads.com/amandadaire

bookbub.com/authors/amanda-daire

ALSO BY AMANDA DAIRE

Old Castle Secrets

Old Castle Sparkle

Old Castle Road Trip

Old Castle Rumors

Old Castle Courage

www.ingramcontent.com/pod-product-compliance
Lightning Source LLC
Chambersburg PA
CBHW031012190726
48286CB00003BA/809